# Undercover Alien

The Hat, The Alien, and the Quantum War

Nathan Gregory

Nathan Gregory Author dot Com

**Publisher:** Nathan Gregory  https://www.NathanGregoryAuthor.com

**Kindle ASIN:** B09YNG2JD3

**Paperback Edition:** September 26, 2022

**Amazon ISBN-13:** 979-8843314705  **Lulu Press ISBN-13:** 978-1-387-63508-5

# Contents

# Introduction

Beyond entertaining the reader with an exciting story, we have two crucial missions. First, raising awareness of the fragility of our technological society and the worldwide cyber war. Professional cyber warriors inhabit countless air chairs, defending critical infrastructure while the world remains largely unaware. Nevertheless, the threat is genuine. Because the language may be confusing, I include the **R**ed **T**eam **F**ield **M**anual appendix to aid the less-technical reader.

Second, calling attention to the crucial role of the neurodivergent. So much we take for granted has sprung from the hyperconnected brains of people like Elon Musk, Thomas Jefferson, Woody Allen, Dan Aykroyd, Anthony Hopkins, Sir Isaac Newton, Steve Jobs, Tim Burton, Albert Einstein, Beethoven, Michelangelo, Nikola Tesla, and many more. Without these beautiful minds, we would be deeply deficient in every area of science, technology, and the arts. We would not even have the music we love.

Autistic minds see the world differently and thus bring different perspectives and insights on wide-ranging issues, making valuable contributions to our daily lives.

Autism isn't a bad thing, abnormal, or a condition to be cured. On the contrary, it is a crucial part of being human.

# Foreword

While our technological advances have been, and continue to be, genuinely mind-blowing, a growing number in our communities are excluded in many physical, mental, financial, or sociological ways. Through my work with **TheGivingMachine** over many years, I have come into contact with thousands of amazing non-profits, many of them focused on creating opportunities for those excluded people to experience "belonging" and with support to grow in confidence to become part of, and contribute to, their communities.

Diversity in all its forms is an opportunity to celebrate the differences that make our communities and societies stronger. As we continue to learn more about how our brains work individually and collectively, we now look back in horror at how our forebears dealt with differences.

A brief conversation a few years ago led me to discover I have aphantasia—an inability to visualize imagery. This was a revolutionary finding at the age of 45 as it explained why I thought the way I did and had difficulties in some areas but excelled in others. I figured I had a bad memory which is clearly not the case as I can recall plots and characters from books I read decades ago even if I cannot recall images of my family.

Storytelling is such a vital part of all cultural histories. It can give us experiences, emotions, and understanding of other points of view.

Thank you, Nathan, for your contribution to this endeavor by blending your insight into the fast-paced technological world we live in and our diverse human engagement with it.

**Richard Morris**, Entrepreneur, Author,
Co-founder *TheGivingMachine*

# Chapter One

# Not Some Skinny Kid in a Hoodie

*Some neurodiverse are exceptionally good at focusing on abstract problems and possess an astoundingly high IQ. The paradox is their near-superhuman abilities arise from an intense focus on one field, often supplanting social and other challenges with fantasy. When the focus is Cyber Warfare, we award them Hats.*

C HOLESTEROL SIZZLES ON THE grill, and an aromatic fusion of burgers, pizza, and beer seasoned with weed's acrid stench fills the cafe. It is mid-week, 3:18 a.m. @*The HashTag Cyber Cafe and Gaming Emporium*, perfect for anonymity—the time of Vigilantes and Superheroes. Wee-hour habitues concentrate in the arena, focused on the FPS {First Person Shooter} or MOBA {Multiplayer Online Battle Arena} competition du jour, leaving the cafe quiet and dark. Our hero is not here for big-screen competition or questionable food. He plays a more dangerous game: Vigilante Justice.

Tonight's tournaments include a pair of engagements NOT playing on the arena's giant screens. One opens in *HashTag* booth #9 and closes in a heavily encrypted clandestine Dark Web enclave of cyberspace. The other begins in outer space's vast and cold universal vacuum. A small rock, drifting along at the leisurely pace of *pfft*, shifts trajectory as though acquiring a target.

Ph3DoRA {Fedora} is not some skinny kid in a hoodie! His chest swells, and his imaginary cape flutters.

The *Milk Road* Dark Web bazaar—the hidden darknet market which provides illicit goods and services ranging from illegal narcotics to assassinations to hundreds of thousands of eager, if immoral, buyers, is poised to fall.

The Agency targeted the online bazaar for months without success until the Ph3DoRA decided to join the chase—as a result, the online store closes forever tonight, and its proprietor goes to jail.

Sleeping trojans planted throughout the illicit network spanning a dozen nations; a globe-spanning row of dominoes aligned with care, ready to tip at the most delicate touch—a global cascade primed to launch, taking down the dark-web criminal the vigilante hero has stalked for these many months.

The vigilante's digital munitions are armed, ready for detonation. Ph3DoRA reaches for the metaphorical grenade pin! The Milk Road's encryption is an open door to the cryptographic skills of the Hat, through which he is about to tilt the first domino.

A clamshell's faint glow illuminates Booth #9, accented by the WiFi Pineapple's lone blinking multi-color LED. Between the Pineapple and the discarded Hak-X logo mask stands a carefully stacked, OCD-aligned double-column of spent cans: equal quantities of Amp, Jolt, and Red Bull. Hat fuel with a double side-order of the caffeine jitters.

Without warning, as he reaches to trigger the cascade, caffeine and adrenaline overload—**Crypt-O-nite!** He freezes. His cape droops.

Eyes closed, he begins rocking. Frozen, nearly catatonic, unable to act. Anxiety-driven rumbling heralds the crescendo of events awaiting his touch.

Momentarily overwhelmed by synesthesia, the superhero is down, hands covering his face, fingers quivering rhythmically.

He mutters a robotic monotone. "Beauty in the rules," he intones recursively, "Rules in the beauty, chaos' invisible code hides the face of order," he repeats.

A skinny kid in a hoodie, a Paladin unknown to the Hat, sits three seats behind. Observing without the Hat's knowledge, the kid has drafted off his work, monitoring, and learning, pursuing the shared goal of the Milk Road's destruction. Now, the Hat's imminent loss of control endangers months of work. The Paladin's clamshell is a window into a dark-themed cyber world. His hands hover mid-keystroke, alarmed, unseen in the darkness; disaster beckons.

Moments pass. Struggling for control, the Hat places his hands over his ears, rocking, whispering. "Would you like to play a game? Destruction is always the answer."

Quiet as a mouse's fart, the Paladin sits close, poised to act, fingers deep into the Hat's bits for this purpose; to intervene if the Hat fails. Hoodie screen mirrors Hat's. The Paladin can tip the domino in the Hat's stead, but at what cost? Dare the Paladin show his hand? Dare the Hoodie act?

Then, as it began, echolalia abates. The hero's cape unfurls.

The freeze passes, and the superhero is again in control and ready to pounce. Perfectly timed, almost as though the big-screens are monitoring the Hat's battle, cheers erupt from the arena, though the Hat does not hear them, nor does the increase in the dead skunk odor infiltrate his consciousness. He is hyper-focused, and nothing IRL {**I**n **R**eal **L**ife} distracts him.

Unable to acknowledge the social challenges, mild face-blindness, and the rare freeze-up, the Hat dismisses the momentary anxiety-driven freeze as mere butterflies—a paralyzing wave of stage fright induced by the sheer magnitude of the chaos he is about to unleash. Everyone experiences moments of self-doubt, he insists.

And in the cold and dark of outer space, an inert piece of rock again tweaks its course ever so slightly.

A superhero naturally develops a network of operatives, people, and resources ready to act. Homo Sapiens are infinitely exploitable. Any script kiddie can SWAT a target; the Ph3DoRA cultivates allies, the law's minions. Finally, after months of effort, his purloined minions stand by, primed to act.

It's opening night; time to be a cop-tease.

His fingers dance. Emails and texts blast to the inner circle, anonymous tips to others, well-placed robocalls to dispatchers in multiple jurisdictions, and, of course, SWAT calls too. The superhero utility belt carries many tools, each with a purpose, and the Hat uses them all. This is Vigilante Justice; it's not a game.

Countdown, careful minutes spent gearing up. Tick. Tick. Tick. The first domino tilts.

Forced encryption key renegotiation; restart the channel with stolen keys. Key exchange equals vulnerability. The exploits are legion: Athena/Hera, Archimedes, BEAST, Scribbles, Grasshopper, Marble, Dark Matter, Weeping Angel, Heartbleed, Poodle, Drown, CRIME, and Breach, to name a few. Others lack comic-book names but instead bear the unique signature of Ph3DoRA. Digital munitions are his forte.

Encryption is transparent to the Hat with an exploit—security is an illusion. Hoarded zero-day exploits, undisclosed vulnerabilities, fragile tools, easily blunted.

A revealed exploit is a patched exploit, a dull and useless tool; the Hat keeps his tools sharp.

A White Hat must follow the rules; the White Hat is accountable. Constrained by law, policy, and procedure, the White Hat serves justice retail.

The vigilante dispenses justice wholesale. Though the Hat is battered and dingy, it is no less a Hat.

As the dominoes accelerate, the skinny kid in the hoodie, satisfied, closes his clamshell and softly pads away.

The tilting dominoes have ceased falling when the minions reach the citadel, as his undetected man-in-the-middle splices the encrypted data stream. The ensuing session-key cloning goes unnoticed. Key-renegotiation ceases, and one more exploit disables fail-safe encryption. Another and the Smoking Pirate's panic key becomes impotent.

Meanwhile, a small meteor glows from friction with the upper atmosphere.

The Pirate's bits take a detour. Credentials, watermarks, and bitcoin wallet take a side journey—with fingerprints of the servers and client computers alike, all carefully stored for the law.

An exquisite joke—using his target's own bitcoin to purchase his personal assassin. Of course, law enforcement will doubtless preempt the deal. If not, well, a laugh.

Pirates live on the razor's edge, a sharp edge it can be: one dark web crime lord, gift-wrapped.

Couch-Potato 3.7 controls webcams. Real-time video streams as Kevlar-clad invaders assume control of open, unlocked systems. He will savor the replay, a souvenir of this night's victory.

Years to build, months to pwn, moments to fall. One less evil abides. Ph3DoRA douses the Pineapple, slams the clamshell, closes his eyes, and sighs.

His lungs inflate with the surge of awareness; he takes in his surroundings. The unmuted noise from the arena assaults his ears; the dead skunk wafts past his nostrils, covering the food odors from the grill. Games and drugs do not interest him. Taking down an international villain is a greater high than any herb. His cravings have matured since he donned the superhero cape.

Rising, he stretches. Chin high, standing tall, feet apart, and hands-on-hips with bent elbows: his superhero stance projects power and confidence; his cape ripples in the breeze, though no one sees.

A moment's celebratory pose. Then, the vigilante stuffs his tools into a backpack and vacates the scene. Swapping his Hak-X logo face-covering and Dark Web identity for a generic white covering and innocent visage, he hails his rideshare.

It's 4:20 a.m. as he Ubers away, blissfully unaware as a baseball-sized meteorite smashes into The Hashtag's roof above Booth #9 mere moments after his departure.

# Chapter Two

# Lil' Friday

*Many respond to their challenges by working harder
and are driven to succeed. However, that they cope does
not mean their challenges are minor.*

A COMPULSIVE, ATONAL WHISTLER—C-VERY-FLAT
accompanies his stroll, his mask askew to give free flight to
his misshapen notes. Traffic noise, clogged intersections, shuffling
crowds, and near collisions with the less joyful do not quaver his
tuneless trill. Pedestrians dodge his ebony form by arcane reflex;
most decline to notice him. An occasional sneer; unmasked cheer
on the city streets? Horrors! He ignores decorum, unaware of the
turbulence in his wake.

His bare face projects merriment, a deliberate lie—his glee is
a mask; his ready, lopsided smile cloaks despair, masking the
irascibility of missed sleep. The emotional high from last night's
Dark Web victory and the caffeine overload had prohibited rest.
Near dawn, endorphins waning, the Morning News delivered an
ice-cold shot of adrenalin.

Unnerved, staring in slack-jawed shock and horror at the news-babe, pondering the unthinkable as his wonted smile froze into a pout of paranoia. Meteors do strike buildings and even cars; rare but not unknown. His imagination plays with scenarios catering to his natural neurosis until he forces himself to dismiss the incident as a coincidence. Meteors do not target people, much less dark-web vigilantes.

Girding for the work day, he hopes Lil' Friday is anticlimactic, permitting a mid-day power nap.

Candy fuels Hats, White, Gray, and Black, from innocuous Modafinil to dangerous and illicit Hard Candy, not ignoring the nearly intravenous caffeine. He has sometimes toed the thin line between necessity and the abyss but avoided falling in. Few are so agile.

The Agency tolerates and often encourages the more benign nootropics. However, Uncle Spook officially proscribes Hard Candy; nonetheless, illicit brain ticklers are not wholly unknown in the hallowed halls of Hats.

The Hat eschews chemical aids, mostly, though he occasionally liaises with Modafinil. Instead, strong coffee is his choice as a study buddy; quite addicting enough. Coffee! At the mere thought, the monkey stirs.

The sound effects falter, fade, and mute, and the faux cheeriness dissipates as his destination looms. A dark, gray, featureless monolith sits almost unnoticed in the city's heart. The darkest and most iconic of skyscrapers, a grim, seething fortress nestled among countless innocent buildings. A brutalist structure, not on any map, not in any guidebook. With neither windows nor illumination, the building glowers at the city, a massive shadow at night, melding into the city's dull gray duskiness.

He steels himself to confront the sally-port. A wan grumble leaks through tight lips, his face turns pale, and his heartbeat quickens with stifled dread. He loves his work and exalted White

Hat status but despises the authoritarian environment fostered by the Agency. Oppressive security measures imitating needless harassment are a necessity he accepts, albeit with a coarse internal dialog.

Approaching the entry, he recognizes a familiar form. Raising his right hand with fingers spread in the classic Vulcan salute, he falls into line next to a coworker. "May the Source be with you, Sprocket," he says with a lopsided grin as he joins the queue. His nerd humor often includes cross-pollination of familiar movie tropes searching for amusement.

Today, he fails to find it.

Stuck for an answer, she scowls. Dour and crotchety, Sprocket lacks Ritz's sense of humor; she lacks anyone's sense of humor. Moreover, a repertoire of polite chitchat is not among her prominent attributes.

No matter; She has others.

Sprocket is a toolmaker; although not a Hat, she is a skilled wizard, a highly specialized programmer who takes rough toolscraps forged in the heat of battle and crafts them into polished munitions. The Hat is a hunter who uses her tools. Their professional yin-yang benefits the Agency, much to the detriment of many villains.

Despite shared expertise and professional relationship, their rapport falls flat. Predictable, as programmers and Hats operate on opposite ends of the cyber supply chain. The toolmaker creates what the Hat breaks. Exposing inadequacies in a programmer's code can be like telling a mother her baby is ugly. The gut response can be visceral.

"Good morning, Ritz," she replies, face rigid as though studiously ignoring something unpleasant on her shoe. After a moment's hesitation, "Crikey, it's chilly this morning," she muses, as much to the aether as to the Hat. Drawing her heavy bomber jacket tighter, she clutches a cup of Bux, her mask dangling from one ear.

He smiles at her propensity for pseudo-cursing. He understands Sprocket well; she is someone who rejects 'no' for an answer; she often struggles with 'yes' as well.

She is a gentle soul, unwilling to give full vent to the frustrations of life. He seldom embraces profanity, although when life demands expressiveness, he prefers his unexpurgated. Thus, when warranted, he does not eschew colorful language, a minor annoyance among many far greater on her list of his flaws. At the end of their brief dalliance, she enumerated the entire accounting quite loudly and publicly.

His ego still bears the bruises, but harboring a grudge is against his nature. He imagines himself as an extrovert, notwithstanding his continual struggles with social intercourse. A grievance is a burden too weighty. Forgiveness? Perhaps a reach too far; he is grateful their encounters are limited to the sally-port.

He takes a deep breath, inhaling her blend's aroma, savoring its richness, and his caffeine addiction pings. "Ah, what a wonderful aroma."

As though uninterested in further conversation, she turns away. Given the environment, Ritz tries to ignore the snub but quickly settles his mask into place, lest his naked features fail to hide his torment.

The captivating aroma wafts his way once again; his craving chafes. An aromatic blend is dear to his heart; even so, he does not have the fatuity to carry a brew into the Access Control Vestibule.

The mantrap! Some say portal. No one uses the formal nomenclature. Ritz prefers sally-port; it's romantic, perhaps a tad swashbuckling. He pushes the term in hopes of viral acceptance, but his nerdy humor fails to resonate. His quixotic whimsies often fly by without so much as a grimace. So, he contents himself with private amusement.

Security Theater requires props. Before entering, Sprocket must discard her cup; The powers above decree no open food or beverages in the sally-port. Of course, they will also ask her to remove the jacket for inspection. These guys make the TSA look like amateurs, although perhaps not as challenging as it sounds. The TSA practices security theater; these guys don't need to practice and aren't acting. The sidearms on their hips are not props.

He would cache the coat in a convenient locker—not that policy forbids a jacket inside the secure area, particularly in cold weather. Still, heavy clothing with many pockets invites extra attention. He dislikes attention.

He neither wears nor carries anything unnecessary for his immediate duty within. No jacket despite the chill, Madison-fit trousers, pockets empty save for his ID and security token, belt thin and light. He wears no smartwatch and carries no mobile. His custom-fit Milano shirt—he's upgraded his attire of late—is without pockets; his shoes are penny-loafers, minus the pennies to not alarm the metal detector. No necktie, though the top button is tightly secured; his neurotic OCD perfectionism demands it.

The Agency proscribes a litany of contraband. The list explicitly includes most digital toys. Security forbids anything which might smuggle sensitive information, from thumb-drive to paper and pen. InfoSec, as practiced by the Agency, is a brutal, tyrannical matter, especially post-Snowden.

Exempt from the harsher prohibitions; rank and security clearance hath its privilege; he keeps a lower profile than necessary, the better to slide under Uncle Spook's radar. Extraordinarily wary of trackable and hackable toys, he prefers privacy and keeps his secrets under his Hat.

The challenge of the mantrap, the x-ray, and the metal detectors all waste time. The sally-port demands a precise yet nimble choreography. Carrot and stick; merits accrue to the punctual.

Predictably, Sprocket bogs the line. Discarding her beverage's remains, she manages to complicate the simple. Determined to waste as little as possible, she glugs the hot liquid, provoking sputters and coughing before tossing the still half-full cup. Unfortunately, her sloshing cup misses the bin, making a mess and further confounding the process. The leather coat triggers extra screening; she should have cached it in a convenient locker. No great hardship—nonetheless, scanning the garment adds delay.

Noticing two more entrants behind him, he nods a greeting with a pleasant smile without speaking, forgetting his smile is invisible behind his mask.

The charade of anonymity remains intact. Uncle encourages anonymity; the oppressive shroud of secrecy smothers the gray monolith.

Ritz and Sprocket work in different, though related groups. Still, of the hundreds of souls who work inside the fortress, he remembers the names of few; he is not so facile with handles and finds faces yet more challenging. Computers? He remembers each one by hostname and IP address. Exploits? He memorizes every detail. Humans? Well, let's merely say he often struggles. His immediate coworkers top the list of those he remembers. A smaller list enumerates those outside this group with whom he interacts. It is no coincidence those whose names he remembers tend toward attractive women. A superhero is incomplete without his Lois.

Moments later, despite Sprocket's fumbles, he gains the portal and pantomimes the ritual. Knowing and avoiding the triggers, his screening is swift and perfunctory. His cape sways with pride.

# Chapter Three

---

# Red Team
# Eyes-Only

*The neurodivergent often experience crippling anxiety and paralyzing sensory overload that renders them incapacitated at inconvenient times. Even when stress and anxiety do not manifest as a partial freeze or a complete meltdown, they can result in self-recrimination and suppressed anger, wasting time and energy on angst and unfounded worries.*

H E SETTLES INTO A cubicle on the 29th floor, but not before taking a turn past the corner office. The Executive Assistant's desk is vacant, and the executive office door is closed. Yet the lights are on inside. He wonders if Director is present for an early day or taking Director's privilege. "Early, I bet," he silently whispers. Director is #1 on his list of those remembered. He has been observing Director for months, meticulous notes stored under his Hat.

Inserting his YetiKey, his imposing, triple-screen workstation blinks awake. Tossing his mask on the desk, he leans into the camera. The on-screen avatar spins as facial recognition matches stored biometrics. He leans forward for the retinal scan at the prompt, muttering, "Like I couldn't remember a damn password!" into the microphone. His choice of spoken passphrase betrays his scorn for the Agency's extreme, triple-layered cybersecurity profile.

Awaiting his workspace materialization, he idly ponders the day ahead. Although he cannot admit awareness yet, the Milk Road case is closed; he must await official notification. His other assignments, too, are complete, or nearly so.

He is at a standstill; no new assignments litter his inbox, an unusual circumstance. Normally, as undoubtedly the most capable Hat in the Agency, his skills are in high demand. "Perhaps," he thinks, "today is the optimum time to ask for a vacation, right after Boss announces the Smoking Pirate's arrest."

After an annoying moment of uncertainty, the screen clears, and his secure, encrypted desktop appears. This digital world is his arena; this is the battle station where, as a Cyber Warrior, he mounts a potent offense in what some call World War Three.

"I wonder what war crimes I must commit today," he muses. "Or what international acts of war the Red Hats downstairs will face. At least cyberwar doesn't involve bombs and missiles. Or airplanes."

In the mysterious realm of cyber-warriors, he is a White Hat. The title means something! The appellation White Hat denotes extreme cyber skills and responsible professionalism. Scant few earn the title, and he is at the pinnacle. Anyone working cyber on the side of law enforcement wears a white hat in a generic sense, but the title holds significance in the covert forces. Any Hat title bespeaks elite skills. A White Hat bespeaks talents skirting the supernatural, a savant-like focus fueled by patriotism, caffeine, and occasionally, more potent stimulants.

The Agency practices a brutalist 'clean desk' policy. His desk holds no spent caffeine-laced sugar cans, perhaps due to his compulsive need for neatness as much as Agency policy.

Expressly, no work files or data may sit unlocked on any untended desktop, including the secure virtual desktop of a Hat's workstation. Physical or virtual, all work-related materials must remain under secure lock and key except while in active use. Files are never left unattended for a moment. Merely stepping away to refill a coffee mug while leaving sensitive case files open is unthinkable.

The Agency's top White Hat does not think the unthinkable, but his curiosity is aflame. His otherwise policy-compliant virtual desktop holds one item; an evidence board bearing a Top-Secret shield labeled '**Red Team Eyes-Only**.' He sighs as he mutters, "WTF is Red Team?"

This folder, unencrypted, although on his secure desktop, is a protocol breach! His angst is palpable.

His cape droops and curls.

He hesitates, but curiosity wins. On opening the suspicious folder, he finds a singular item. An eyebrow tilts in mild surprise; his mask of cheerfulness falls, exposing sleep-deprived grumpiness.

"Dubya Tee Eff!" He almost spoke aloud. "Couldn't the Skiddies downstairs at least do the Effing research? Why send this upstairs without basic processing?"

He leans back, eyes closed, inhales a slow, deep breath, and holds fast a few seconds before releasing his stress with a forceful bilabial horse snort. Wrestling forth a recalcitrant calm, he mouths a silent apology for the slur.

Scarcely above muggles, Skiddies are mudbloods. No one in the Agency is a Skiddie, a Script Kiddie. Cyber-warriors earn their Hats, the Cyber Warrior equivalent of an advanced degree, by demonstrating world-class Cyber skills. The Hat Training Center

(HTC) is an academy from which few graduate. Even a lowly Green Hat is far above a Script Kiddie.

So, why break policy? Why this strange delivery? What is Red Team? Routine vetting and background research is the job of the Green Hats on the floor below. So, did this mysterious document come via Boss? Or Director? Someone else? If so, who? Yielding grumpiness to curiosity, he examines the anonymous enclosure.

The folder before him is not a traditional assignment; an assignment should contain much more. There should be an active incident report, including Threat Status assessments, a general background, a high-level overview, and mission-specific instructions and warnings. The Hat expects additional sub-folders containing related or referenced documents, perhaps unstructured material depending on the assignment's nature. He expects at least an hour of reading the research before touching the target.

Instead, a solitary text containing a single 128-bit global address. A pointer to one in $3.5 \times 10^{38}$ possible locations in the digital realm.

Could this be a Phish? A phish inside the covert citadel? Impossible! No spoofing attack can penetrate the Agency's air gap. The AI guard-dog would catch whaling in a heartbeat, with dire consequences.

Or a test from OpSec, testing whether he might fall to temptation?

Pondering the unorthodox document, he notes the telltale underscore of a hyperlink. Hovering the link, a yellow tooltip with bold red lettering flies up.

**"RED TEAM EYES ONLY! Treat as hostile and highly dangerous! Memorize and destroy. Speak to no one, take no action until briefed."**

Astonished, he sputters, "Grody!"

Again, he wonders who or what is 'Red Team?' Why him? Why is this here? Does this unknown entity want him to work on an assignment without Boss's knowledge? This assignment didn't come from Boss! Not thru regular channels! But who? Who is to brief him? Director? Sidestep procedure? Decidedly odd! WTF?

Warning notwithstanding, his instinct is to vet this before bypassing his chain of command. His nature demands it. When you're incredibly proficient at something, it is excruciating not to act.

What makes this assignment so significant?

Flying up a toolbar, he ponders the collection of sophisticated, proprietary, official tools at his disposal. Passing over a host of beautifully-crafted, game-like GUI munitions unknown outside these hallowed halls, he opens the console and reaches through the firewall. He hovers over ZoneCruncher, a popular threat-hunting tool used by Corporate Hats. Corporations need Hats the same as governments do, only they're not called Hats; they're called security consultants, cyber warriors in suits.

He hesitates. He prefers simple tools. Curl? Nslookup? Nikto? ZAP? Wpscan? Nah, he decides, Nmap will suffice to start.

In the Warrior's armamentarium of advanced tools, Nmap is simple, almost ugly, and also the most under-appreciated. As he opens an encrypted RDP portal to the external global network and prepares a port scan, he whispers, "Mess with the best, die like the rest."

Something tugs his cape. He pauses, hand hovering mid-keystroke. He contemplates the odd set of circumstances and still odder warning.

"Bizarre!" he espouses in a soft burst of imprecation. Through clenched teeth, he mutters, "Not! Right! Now!" Though burning with curiosity, aching to dive in, he backtracks, opting to heed the warning, treat the address as dangerous, and await briefing—but from whom?

Slamming the backspace, he erases the command he had begun and types 'whoami' instead, entering an innocuous test command, and closes the gateway. Fortunately, routine surveillance does not include a keystroke logger, and regular history logs will reveal only the innocent test. Not that he expects scrutiny, but a Hat can't be too careful.

The document sits open on his desktop. His brow furrows in thought. Hovering the link, he right-clicks and selects edit. He starts by removing the tooltip. He double-checks the destination, memorizes, and clears the hyperlink. Next, he changes the displayed address to one belonging to a previous case. Finally, he places the document into the earlier project's top folder.

Obfuscation instead of deletion, misdirect but never hide. No one is innocent; pretending to innocence only invites deeper scrutiny. If you don't want scrutiny, it's often safer to aspire to incompetence, laziness, or even stupidity than innocence. A reprimand for being lazy is insignificant. Working under the oversight of an AI watchdog teaches one humility. Deleting the document might draw attention, possibly forensic review. This way, his action should pass as innocuous.

Even the most obsessive Hat leaves tracks, and tracks can get one burned. One can't hide every trace but can guide the path away from apparent incendiaries.

Having moved and obfuscated the evidence, he reopens the Milk Road project. Feigning intense concentration, he bends one eye to the hallway as he sham-works. Director might venture to the break room. Not likely, he tells himself. Director seldom leaves the corner office and need not pass his cubicle. Need not, yet sometimes does so, occasionally registering eye-contact en passant; a form of stimulation without caffeine.

Fortune smiles. Within mere minutes, the corner office bustles with activity. Director emerges, mug in hand, and sallies past his open cubicle en route to the break room. He thinks Director catches his eye. Is this an invitation? Or his imagination? He can't decide, yet either way, it appears, opportunity raps its seductive tap upon his door.

Caffeine. Yes! He has squelched a growing hunger for an Arabian Mocha-Java since breakfast. Desire turned into lust the moment he inhaled Sprocket's aromatic waft. Now, any excuse to visit the break room on his mind, the hunger gnaws. He secures his workstation and waits a brief moment lest he might appear to be following too closely. Seconds later, his empty mug hugged tightly against his body lest his hand give way to trembles, he saunters along the hallway, imagining he appears nonchalant. Intrigue pushes aside, for the moment, the vestiges of a busy night.

As he enters the caffeine cubicle, his eye lands on Director, back toward the door, wrestling the Kafe-Krescendo. He admires the cut of her crisp double-breasted business dress—Brooks Brothers, of course—always sharp and professional. She cycles through a collection of near-identical dresses, each distinguished by subtle variations in wear and cut, suggesting individual purchases over many years.

He notes the slightly askew top button as though the worn thread is near breaking. She is wearing number six today, he decides.

He imagines a crouching puma beneath the heavy, deep black Italian wool. No matter how button-down, clothing cannot mute her innate animal magnetism.

For months, he felt her irresistible pull. Each time he encounters her, he mentally catalogs her wardrobe. He notes subtle differences in trim and stitching. He studies how she never repeats the same outfit but instead wears each one in a consistently repeating pattern. Scrutinizing each one, identical yet subtly distinct, he imagines a closet bulging with near-identical, costly, high quality, and gently worn professional outfits, numbered hangers dictating the order and wear frequency.

He inventories the numerous identical yet subtly distinct dresses in her wardrobe. But, of course, an executive at her level must dress the part.

She does so like an ardent thespian.

Another is also present, back facing the entrance, though lacking Director's trim cut. He does not track the other's wardrobe; indeed, he would scant notice had the other appeared stark naked.

The more substantive form impedes the view; a faint grimace of annoyance flits across his face too quickly for the others to see.

Gentle laughter echoes as the pair argues with friendly geniality. Each expounds on the relative merits of a preferred tweak to the formula. The rotund one alleges one cocoa packet as satisfactory; Director insists on two. Boss turns and greets him with a slight wave and a toothy grin as he drifts closer.

"You see the news this morning? Meteor impacted some cyber joint; wiped out half the bar and grill. Fortunately, no one was present at such an early hour; no one hurt. Say, isn't that your hangout?"

At the mention of the morning news, he puts on his best blank face; slightly shaking his head, he addresses the second question.

"Nah," Ritz responds with a shrug. "Eh yeah, long time before I became a Hat."

"Don't I recall you won a couple of championships?"

"Yeah, but a White Hat plays a bigger game," Ritz answers with a shrug. "Haven't played in years."

This is not—quite—a lie. He visits The Hashtag for cyber hut anonymity and fast Wi-Fi, not competition. He is too busy to play.

Boss nods in understanding. Boss well understands real-world cyber warfare is more engaging than any MMORPG.

Boss asks, "Heard anything more from your smoking pirate?"

An eyebrow askew, a humorless silence descends as he transfixes Boss with an icy scowl. A soft Director-like cough skids around Boss's suddenly inert form. Mentioning casework in such an insecure setting as a break-room is an egregious breach, a career-ending mistake for mere mortals. However, Boss is no mortal; he is a legend, albeit one somewhat faded. He will survive this round of foot-in-mouth disease.

Some claim the man is past his peter-pinnacle, although his field career had been exceptional. As an Analyst, he was capable, well-liked, and respected—but, promoted to a management desk job, his currency is fading. He has grown inept, unfocused, and bumbling. Now desk-bound, he appears in danger of losing his grip on the slippery edge of obesity. An office pool books wagers on the date he will open his golden parachute.

"Sorry, I was only making polite noises," Boss mumbles with eyes down. He yields a wan smile while awkwardly extracting Florsheim. "Better make it 'How's the weather?' instead. Let's hold the shoptalk for a formal briefing, and I do need to brief you. Big things." His eyes again dip and grimace as Boss realizes he is still gnawing shoe leather.

"The weather's hot," the Hat responds with a crooked smile and a wink. "Let's hoist the Jolly Roger; SCIF {*RTFM*: **S**ensitive **C**ompartmented **I**nformation **F**acility} conference later?"

As though granting Boss a dispensation, Director turns back to the machinery. With a quick nod, Boss bolts for the doorway without waiting for his coffee, nearly waddling in haste. An ignominious retreat appears preferable to risking another indecorous solecism.

As the rotund one retreats, a sensual contralto asks, "Do you like cocoa, chicory, and cinnamon in your coffee?" Turning toward Director, he suppresses a start of surprise. Despite working in her orbit for months, she has ever barely acknowledged his existence.

He can count the number of times she directly spoke to him on his thumbs, with leftovers.

Awkward pose, empty mug outstretched; Director gives him an odd, fixed stare. Something is strange. He puzzles, unable to interpret her expression and posture. He finds interpreting body language arduous.

His mouth opens and closes as he swallows a squeak. He reaches deep for his voice, not quite finding it but willing his quivering vocal cords into submission. "I ... I've n-never tried it, al-though it sounds interesting. I've been trying out Bulletproof Coffee recipes and experimenting with alternative blends. Y-you ne-ver quite predict the result. Is that what you're brewing?"

Glancing at the mug in her hand, she nods, tapping the side with a manicured nail. She holds a uniquely distinctive coffee mug, almost stein rather than a cup. As she draws attention with her eye and finger, he spots the logo of an Irish pub. The empty vessel echoes a faint click as she pinky-taps the emblem.

Perhaps as they are alone, he might broach the subject of the strange evidence board. "Something odd…"

He jumps when she slams her cup on the counter with a slight shake of her head.

"…is always worth a try," he finishes with a squeak as he realizes his own near mistake.

Recognition dawns and his eyes widen. Director smiles, head tilting in an almost imperceptible half-nod. Anxiety elevated, senses overloaded, he teeters near a freeze; his hands begin to convulse in unpredictable arcs. As he struggles for control, his Hak-X-logo caffeine conveyor leaps from his hand as though it too were desperate to hide.

Director deftly plucks the flying mug from the air and holds it out to him. Shocked by his clumsiness and awed by her reflexes, his cape curls and shrivels.

Turning the mug, she reveals a napkin bearing the same Irish Pub logo as her mug. A practically illegible scrawl on the corner reads '10:30 PM.' She rotates the napkin several times to emphasize the handwriting and ensure he spots the text.

As he accepts his mug, she wads up the napkin and palms it, making it disappear like a practiced stage magician, making an elaborate show of tapping it twice before it vanishes. The question as to why she didn't discard the tissue in the trash momentarily pricks his curiosity.

The question gurgles in his brain; the Jura gurgles too. Unfazed by his nervousness, Director lifts the carafe and waves it toward his mug. "Try it; you'll like it, I promise."

Recovering from his near freeze, still puzzled amid growing comprehension, he accepts the fill while muttering an apology. With visible effort, he steadies his hand to receive the brew. As Director pours, he whiffs the bouquet. His face lights up. He samples a cautious sip.

The Hat is back! His cape unfurls, and his quirky smile spreads, underscoring the twinkle in his eyes. "Ah, heavenly concoction. You are a wizard! Thanks for the suggestion."

As his eyes gleam, Director flies up a small fluffy smile. Her pheromones insist he must immediately fall in love. He insists he never lacks feminine company. His dimpled chin, slightly-pudgy mesomorphic physique, and lustrous onyx, pomade-polished mane carry movie star appeal. Ladies encircle, though his chin somehow fails him.

Love is a fragile butterfly who never lingers and soon tires of his social stumbling and feigned empathy. Although he frequently enjoys brief romances, he'd rather have a friend. So, is Director to be either? Or just another warrior with a smile for armor?

"See you ... later," she intones with an odd cadence, inserting a sensuous pause after the second word. Her pheromone sucker punch as she turns to exit the break room leaves him barely able to stand. Moving with Cougar-like grace and speed, she heads toward the corner office; suddenly, the fact she is much older than he is unimportant.

His face reflects dreamy mystification as she glides away. She magnetically pulls him, drawing him, unwilling, into strange and dangerous environs. "My failure lies not in my passions but my lack of control over them," he quietly misquotes; a soft, tuneless whistle echoes along the corridor as he drifts toward his workstation.

In his cubicle, his smile fades as he ponders what just happened. Unless imagination buried reason, Director correctly anticipated his nascent query, preemptively cutting him off. Did she send him the cryptic folder?

She made such a dramatic point of cutting him off before he could speak! She must have been the originator of the mysterious folder. He instinctively dubs it the "Director's Special" in this instant, despite lacking any provable connection to her.

Her sleight-of-hand with the cup and napkin and the stilted departure salutation feel significant. Admittedly, his interactions with Director are few. Common enough expression, though; it may all be his imagination.

He ruminates with mounting angst. Is he summoned to a clandestine rendezvous at an Irish pub? Odd, as indeed, Director is not Irish, except perhaps on St. Patrick's Day. Well, neither is he; he is aware of the term Black Irish; Perhaps that's the point. In any case, it appears he has a surprise date this evening, but why the secrecy?

If she merely wants to brief him in a private conference, why not use a SCIF? Most odd. Is something so sensitive the most secretive spy organization on the planet's paranoid secrecy is insufficient? Improbable!

His next step; scouting *The Irish Counting-House*. He can do so from his desk; innocent web inquiries seldom draw ire from above. Management rarely chastises valued employees, especially Hats of his rank, for minor personal web usage.

Given his evening's sub-Rosa plans, he wishes no unnecessary attention. No, he shall check out the pub later from a private and secure portal. Online security is his wheelhouse. He is not paranoid; he well understands many things Snowden only suspected.

Please follow me on Twitter.
I rarely tweet, but when I do, it's a keeper. You won't want to miss a single one.

https://twitter.com/nathan_gregory

# Chapter Four

## Hat Nap

H E JERKS UPRIGHT WITH a start, sits up in his chair, and scans the office with apprehension. Routine office noises signal unawareness of his micro-sleep, and he relaxes. He arranged documents on his screen to impart the illusion of engaged thought to any passerby. As long as he doesn't snore and no one spots his closed eyes, he might snatch a wink or two with none the wiser.

Regretfully, power-napping is not a résumé-enhancing skill, though perhaps it should be. In any case, as with the technical elements, his mastery of this talent, too, is exceptional.

As a cyber-warrior turned vigilante, he keeps irregular hours far beyond the nine-to-five office environment. His odd hours favor the extracurricular, though his employer might feel unsympathetic.

Nonetheless, his off-book activities impact his sleep cycle. Though still well on the deficit side of the sleep ledger, the brief doze helped. He wishes to forgo candy. Another Arabian Mocha-Java, perhaps. "Never drink coffee at lunch; it will keep you awake all afternoon," he thinks. "Yeah. Right."

A head peeks into his cubicle. "Got time for our briefing now?"

He shrugs. "Of course, Boss. Got a SCIF?"

With a nod, Boss leads him to the opposite corner of the building, away from the executive offices. Moments later, they are ensconced in a secure briefing room.

"Boss, you said something about my *smoking pirate*, I believe. So, what gives? Been movement on the case?"

"Big news, young fella, big news. Months of hard teamwork finally paid off; we arrested the whole gang and took down their entire operation last night. Coordinated teams under my direction and raided offices in five countries. Arrested over forty people, including the Smoking Pirate himself. Caught them with their drives unlocked, too." Assuming a thin, raspy voice, echoing some long-forgotten 'B' movie character, Boss adds, "Hehe. For a lazy man, I work awfully hard. Hehe." As usual, Boss's odd cinephilic humor sallies past Ritz unmolested.

His cape flutters—he smiles at Boss's readiness to take credit, unintentionally encouraging the older man's strange humor. Of course, he would not dispute the elder's claims; Boss is one of the resources the Ph3DoRA tapped in taking down the pirate.

His lopsided grin on high beam, he asks, "Wow! You were there when they grabbed the smoking pirate?"

"Unfortunately, no. I ran the operation from home. The cops on site said the expression on his face was priceless."

"Well, congrats. That's amazing! I hope my small intelligence efforts helped."

"Nonsense, I didn't do it alone." This is true enough. "I had support from many quarters. Not the least being your outstanding efforts." Again, quite true. "I shall see you are justly credited. I wanted to tell you the case is closed and handed over to legal now. So, you can file your final report and close up the files."

"Terrific, I'll knock it right out."

He tidies the investigation files for an hour before deciding to ditch. He briefly ponders Boss's odd movie quote but, at the moment, doesn't care enough to look it up. The older man is always quoting old movies, and the temptation he once felt to reframe jokes from a bygone era is long faded. Hasn't the man seen anything from this century? That's Boss, he muses.

With no new work, ignoring the mysterious Director's Special, it's either candy, another Arabian Mocha-Java, ditch, or another power nap. Boss already vacated; else, he found an invisibility cloak under which to power-nap himself. Unlikely, as the legendary invisibility cloak does little for sound. Boss is reputed to dream he is diesel-powered.

Besides, there is another project he would prefer the Agency remain unaware of.

He hits the street, aggressively walking head-down, drool catcher firmly in place, pounding the pavement like any urban dweller. The sky is leaden; rain is imminent. He charges as any urbanite hoping to beat the storm.

Please visit the Undercover Alien Reviews Page and leave a nice review.

https://amazon.com/review/create-review? &asin= B09YNG2JD3

*If you're enjoying the story so far, why don't you help an author out by leaving a nice review on Amazon?*

# Chapter Five

# Vigilante

*"What would happen if the autism gene was eliminated from the gene pool? You would have a bunch of people standing around in a cave, chatting and socializing and not getting anything done. — Dr. Temple Grandin"*

H IS CURIOSITY PIQUED BY Director's legerdemain; he intends to scout *The Irish Counting-House* online. Opening his clamshell, he is about to do so from his home Internet service's presumed anonymity.

Remembering the Hashtag, he reconsiders. Paranoia? Not if they're genuinely after you.

Is the naked web safe? Silly question! It is decidedly unsafe. Is concern warranted? Obvious questions with self-evident answers. He opts for stealth.

Reaching behind his dresser, he withdraws an odd contraption, a product of his own ham-handed handiwork, crafted from a snack container, wire, and aluminum foil, plus a small tripod meant for a camera. The unwieldy apparatus is part of the prepared vigilante toolbox—or should be. He sets the ungainly device in his apartment window and aims it across the cityscape.

From a drawer, he extracts a WiFi Pineapple. The scuffed and scratched exterior belies its potential in expert hands. This Pineapple is not a Wi-Fi hotspot. It is something more, a whatsit enabling him to connect to a remote access point and act as a proxy and firewall, protecting whatever is behind it. The homemade microwave antenna allows connection to distant hotspots blocks away. His custom-designed VPN software moves his apparent browsing origination to somewhere else—almost any random data den on Earth he cares to choose. Safe, anonymous, secure.

Reaching inside a desk drawer, he pulls out a key, opens a tiny, locked wooden box sitting on the dresser, and removes a compact storage device. He connects the drive and boots his clamshell with the eclectic conglomeration active and blinking. He interrupts normal startup to force the loading of an operating system from the storage device. After a brief boot period, the distinctive Kali dragon logo appears. He has transformed his mundane clamshell into a Cyber Warrior's armamentarium.

Flying fingers stroke the keyboard, invoking programs with odd, cartoon-sounding names such as aircrack, hashcat, cowpatty, reaver, pixiewps, and wifite. Each tool flies up and does its thing, only to quickly vanish. Within moments, the Wi-Fi connects to the Wi-Fi signal of an unsuspecting neighbor. Previously-Shared Keys? Encryption? Ha! What's encryption?

His cape flutters.

The anxieties and distractions—the pressure cooker of human engagement—fade away as his hyper-focus engages. The *Ph3DoRA* is online.

Securely anonymous, he scopes the web presence of *The Irish Counting-House*. Finding nothing exceptional, he notes the address and studies the map. Minutes away by rideshare, walking distance if one is an enthusiastic walker.

Initial mission accomplished, he considers his next step, the real reason he is online—the cause of such extraordinary precautions.

He is burning to explore the mysterious Director's Special. Intrigue demands investigation. He pauses to consider the risk. Engaging a second inner firewall, he flies up a VPN—magically relocating his apparent web presence to a small Scandinavian country. Next, he flies up a honeypot to deflect anyone's attention, random Skiddie or minion of evil, away from his firewall.

Confident of his safety behind multiple firewalls and anonymous via an unsuspecting neighbor's Internet connection and protected by his VPN, he dives into the Dark Web. He has hours before he must head out for his date—time enough.

Flying up a suite of cyber tools, he probes the mysterious Director's Fancy. He port-knocks, looking for hidden services. Searching for related sites, he checks for a legal owner of the address and finds it is non-existent in the global Domain Name registry. Further, he also discovers a series of encrypted tunnels, cyber rabbit-holes leading down and down into an unmapped underground realm.

The dark web beckons.

Momentarily powerless to crack the encryption, he traces the tunnels from link to link, from portal to clandestine server, all tightly locked, unregistered, and secure against his best weaponry.

He recognizes such encrypted structures often mask the illicit movement of stolen media, crypto of various forms, NFTs, and other digital merchandise. Still, he can see these tunnels do not carry stolen videos. Traffic patterns betray the character, if not the specifics of encrypted traffic. Vast volumes of data flow through these pipelines, but not video.

Stumped beyond this solitary deduction, he traces links between the original site and many others, all connected via a far-flung web of encrypted tunnels. He maps a dozen affiliated sites and realizes he is sniffing around the topmost portal into a deep, hidden cavern without penetrating the outermost layer.

Sometime later, he mutters, "Tempus Aviates." Unprepared for the complexity he found here, the Vigilante resolves to revisit with more time and a couple of new tools inspired by the experience. Hat tools not yet created. For now, he must put away his Hat and cape. He has a date!

Pausing, he eyes the Pineapple's LED as it blinks furiously, signaling intense activity.

Any network presence attracts tentative pokes from the cyber-curious. Pings, root login attempts, random bots and script kiddies attempting to guess passwords, virus bots looking for open ports, and advertising bots looking to fake a few page views are the typical hazards of a global web address.

The honeypot reflects the expected number of random hits and an average number of malicious payload deposits. These are generally not a cause for concern; such is the purpose of a honeypot.

Such frenetic blinky-blink implies something far more significant, an uncommon fusillade from a well-organized and funded entity, doubtless a state-sponsored Advanced Persistent Threat (APT) organization. Unfortunately, the unrelenting firehose ignores the honeypot. Worse, it also bypasses his VPN, instead directly targeting his firewall. His mouth falls open in dumbfounded surprise.

Web anonymity! Now, who's the fool?

Numerous nation-states field such massive cyber weaponry, but why should one take such an interest in him? Is this a response to his investigations? Why? What threat did they imagine he posed?

He tables his research and investigates the attack. His firewall confirms the unrelenting onslaught. A gigantic and utterly dark entity resides behind those multiple layers of encryption, and it plays hardball!

Probes, originating from the addresses cataloged and at least one-hundred-thousand untouched network regions, are slamming his firewall. Nearly a million discrete attacks in the time he has been online. No coincidence there! No random script-kiddie has targeted his presence. He shudders at the implications as he kills the Wi-Fi.

Attack abated, he relaxes and examines the logs. His probe of the mysterious address provoked a massive counterattack, far more aggressive than anything he had seen as an Agency White Hat. His paranoia was justified; it appears his firewall held. Nothing penetrated his hardened outer barrier, insofar as he can tell, much less his DMZ or inner firewall.

The honeypot shows no significant hits from this assault, only the expected pokes and scans. Still, the blast against the firewall came like a firehose, a massive torrent of attempted exploits. Ritz counted thousands of CVE cracks, many of which he discovered and hundreds more he didn't recognize. He smiles as the logs show his firewall holding where most would fail—his cape ripples.

His probing indeed plucked a tripwire, which, of course, he had no reason to expect. A casual probe should not elicit such a reaction. So, note to self—*purloin a different neighborhood Wi-Fi before the next attempt—one much further away!*

He wipes the leet operating system and reboots the clamshell. The storage drive joins the homemade antenna and Pineapple, tucked away in their respective secluded station. No casual visitor to his tiny apartment would suspect him of cyber vigilantism.

This evening's off-book adventure isn't his first risky foray into the web's dark, dangerous underbelly. It is, however, one of the more memorable, even a bit frightening. He ponders whether his precautions are sufficient and contemplates ways he might improve his security.

He often imagines establishing an anonymous Cyber-Dojo for off-book activities. Remiss to draw attention to where he sleeps, he considers this idea anew.

He spends several moments compulsively arranging the window slats before focusing on his evening plans.

Glancing at his mobile, he notes with surprise how much time has flown since he fell through the rabbit hole into the dark web—in his best, quavering white rabbit voice, he mutters, "Oh dear! Oh dear! I shall be too late!" He had intended to nap before meeting Director, but time is much too short.

Sleep must wait; a caffeine pill, a quick shower—quick despite the extra time spent meticulously folding and hanging his used towels—and he must summon his rideshare. Moments more spent choosing a stylish chin holster for his evening wear, and he dashes out the door.

Sleep is overrated!

# Chapter Six

# Assignation

*The neurodiverse are not inherently asocial, of course, despite challenges negotiating the social landscape. Our superhero is one such individual, socially awkward with OCD behavior elements but possessing a stratospheric IQ and, of course, extraordinarily gifted in the ways of the cyber.*

T HE WEATHER WORSENS WITH wind and misty rain. Upon attempting to summon a ride, Ritz finds surge pricing is applied. Worse, snarled traffic, jammed, and unmoving. His planned fifteen-minute journey projects an ETA well beyond his assignation.

One of his many flaws, which list Sprocket had enumerated so loudly, is his deep fear of tardiness. As a result, he is early to a fault. All the more so when he wishes to scout the terrain ahead of a clandestine meeting. Thus, he is visibly distressed when, instead of early, he is late. Not only tardy, but having run the entire distance, he arrives at the pub disheveled, mask askew, drenched, and out of breath—not the proper way to greet a date!

Fingering his hair in a vain attempt to mitigate the storm's damage, he scans the establishment for Director. He spots an Asian woman with long black hair in a business suit and, for a moment, mistakes her for his date. When the woman turns his way, he realizes his error. Although similar in build and hairstyle, she otherwise bears no resemblance. Her attire is professional but not Brooks Brothers. He continues searching.

Failing to spot his quarry, his confidence wanes, and his resolve weakens. He debates whether he misinterpreted the invitation. Had he imagined it, in truth? His anxiety rises. Or perhaps she merely encountered similar transportation difficulties, or worse, has given up on him and left. Paranoia creeps in. Is she nerd sniping him?

Overwhelmed and near abandoning the quest, he closes his eyes to filter the noise and light and quell his rising anxiety. "Beauty in the rules," he mutters silently. Seconds pass; long, deep breath; he opens his eyes and bites his lip. He opts to wait. And wait some more. Snipe victim or not, he resolves to stay.

Settling himself on a vacant barstool in a position to eye the door, he signals the bartender. Although not usually inclined to drink alcohol, he considers a virgin something-or-other but decides one cannot visit an Irish Pub and ignore the aqua vitae. He orders a Jameson. "Besides," he tells himself, "Non-alcoholic spirits are like hiring a hooker for a hug."

Continuing to scan, he spots a stranger eying him from a table across the room—lean with pale, ashen gray skin, small-boned, pristine suit, blue shirt, bow tie, thick plastic-rimmed glasses. The man is hardly an international assassin. Who wears a bow tie these days? Editors, he guesses. Or accountants, perhaps? Yes, an accountant. He searches his memory, wondering if he might have met the man somewhere. After some thought, he decides not.

Studying the man's appearance and mien, he decides the man is looking for a date and debating whether to proposition him. Not the first time he's been approached with such a misapprehension. He supposes it might double the chances on a slow Saturday night. Still, he is not interested and has other plans anyway. Besides, this is only Thursday.

He needs something to focus on to quell rising anxiety. His drink appears, his bristle bag lands on the counter, and the stranger is forgotten.

Nose deep into the glass, the first whiff clears his nostrils with a blast of pure alcohol. The second and third begin to uncork the bouquet. He can smell the oak from the barrel and a hint of vanilla. As he continues sniffing, the more profound and subtle flavors emerge. He takes a tiny sip and lets it roll around his tongue as he tries to match the flavors and the aroma. Absorbed, hyper-focused on his drink to exclude his surroundings, he continues, alternately sniffing and tasting. Savoring the flavor and aroma instead of downing the whiskey, he makes love to the drink.

With a start, he remembers why he is here. Reclaiming his focus, he forcibly sets the glass on the counter. With cautious sipping, waiting, and watching, he nurses the remainder of his drink and waits for Director to appear.

# Chapter Seven

# The Brass Nail

*The neurodivergent often find crowds and social situations stressful and react by narrowly focusing on something immediately at hand. It's not that they cannot handle such situations, but the effort required to stay engaged and aware of their surroundings can be exhausting.*

H E WAITS A LONG time with neither sign nor portent of the meeting he expects. He fights the temptation to use anything as a diversion, as with the drink. He resists and forces himself to focus on the crowd despite the noise and confusion. Slowly, time passes. His anxiety is elevated, and he is nigh to abandoning the quest. He downs the last sip of his drink, sets the empty glass on the counter, and turns for one last scan of the crowd as he prepares to bolt for the exit. Someone sidles up to him, takes his arm, and a seductive voice coos in his ear, "Buy a lady a drink?" Irritated, he turns to extract his arm and dismiss the speaker. He does not wish to be hustled.

"Play along," she whispers.

With a double-take, he changes his mind. Mouth open in stark disbelief, moronically staring until she smiles and touches his cheek, breaking the spell.

"W-What'll you have?" he asks, voice quavering. She nods at his glass and coos, "I'll have what you're having." He raises a finger to the barman.

He leans in and studies her appearance. It is unsurprising he hadn't spotted her sooner, or hadn't recognized her—the button-down persona appears to have stayed at the office—along with the buttons!

He wonders, which is the real woman? The staid, stiff, professional Brooks Brothers sporting Director inhabiting the corner office? Or the stunning, attention-grabbing décolletage brandishing exhibitionist on the stool beside him?

Her face is bare, and the rest of her is not substantially otherwise. She has traded demur office attire for something hard to classify as attire. Attire conceals; this displays and emphasizes. Everything is different; her soft Amerasian features are more Amer and less Asian. Her hair is brownish ginger instead of the classic deep glossy black he knew and much shorter. How did she do that?

Her heavy makeup trills stripper, or rather prostitute, he decides. Her tissue-thin micro-dress echoes the chorus. Not only short but thin, almost translucent, rouged aureole tantalizing. More slip than a dress; it appears Victoria has mislaid one of her secrets. The short skirt emphasizes her legs; she appears much taller, no doubt, due to the extreme heels. He imagines she is wearing nothing underneath the wispy costume. The result is hypnotic. Face-challenged enough in ordinary circumstances, he would never have recognized her had she not forced herself into his personal space. Even now, he is almost uncertain who sits before him.

He realizes it is a cunning disguise. Though every eye might be on her, no one would remember her face. No one knowing Director as he does would possibly recognize her.

He whispers to her, "Nice disguise, Dir--."

Placing her finger on his lips, she whispers back, "Shush. I am Trixie. No talk." She raises her voice, "Want some company?"

He stares at her for half a second, blank stare on full dunce. Then, grasping this is role-playing, and she expects him to join in, he recovers. He leans forward, his face a wolfish leer, voice low and sensual, giving his best Hollywood leading-man imitation. "How many shares are you selling?"

She leers back. Her leer is better; she has practiced. Ritz decides his nerdy pun has fallen flat until she responds, "I doubt you can afford more than one."

He smiles; he likes it when people acknowledge his puns. He recognizes they are nerdy and lame yet enjoys eliciting a laugh or even a groan. Her drink arrives. She lifts it to take a sip, eyes on the crowd.

He scoops her up and sits her on his knee without spilling a drop. "Come closer; let's negotiate."

Not content with the position on his knee, she laughs raucously as she slides into his lap and places her arm around his neck. Despite the apparently focused intimacy, her attention is on the crowd rather than him. The accountant looks on without expression.

She laughs again, louder and more boisterously, and squirms suggestively against him. "Umm," she moans as she moves sensually in his lap. Eyes closed, she fingers his tightly buttoned collar. Slowly, sensually, she unbuttons the top three buttons on his shirt, slips her hands inside, and slides them around to the back of his neck.

The predictable develops; she reacts with an animalistic moan as she grinds against him. Eyes closed, head tilted back, voice soft and husky, she coos, "Ooh, perhaps a small discount for a refined gentleman with cash."

"How about Dogecoin?"

Another button falls open, and his shirt gapes as she pauses mid-squirm and stares at the crowd. Abruptly she slams her drink in one gulp as though surprised.

"Let's go," she says, peering about the room, "upstairs ..." She tilts her head and motions with her eyes toward the stairway; his eyebrow arches. She hops from his lap, takes his hand, and pulls him to the stairs, fast. Drawing him up several flights and along a dingy hallway, he follows, practically dragged while awkwardly attempting a pocketeer tuck and fingering his unsecured shirt buttons. Neither effort succeeds, and his engorgement rages almost painfully as his shirt gapes.

The building reeks of bis, booze, and body odor. And worse things better not to contemplate. The rain is pounding the windows—the misty shower he braved on the way here is now somewhat less than misty. The promised storm has arrived.

The upper floor appears empty. Believing they are alone, he starts to speak, "What the..." he begins. Before he can utter the third syllable, her soft hiss shushes him. She squeezes his hand and shushes again. "Turn off your phone," she whispers.

He expects her to lead him to a room; she does not. Instead, she leads him down a long hallway to a dirty, rain-streaked window; by a substantial effort, she forces it open and drags him outside onto the fire escape, slamming the window closed behind them. He is still fumbling with his phone, shutting it off. She snatches the phone from his hand and hurls it far down the alley.

"Hey!" he exclaims.

"I'll buy you a new one if we survive." Her seductive tone has vanished—her voice crackles with a high-voltage snap.

The storm is slamming with firehose force now, rain driving hard, cold, and wet, the steel fire escape is dangerous and slippery. Her tissue-thin costume is soaked, sticking to her skin like a gossamer sheet of cellophane, though less opaque. The flimsy fabric appears ready to disintegrate from the storm's force alone. His initial imagination of what might, or rather, what might not exist beneath the insubstantial habiliment, proves accurate. Her makeup is running, washed away by the storm's blast. He is cold and wet despite being fully dressed. Clasping his still gaping shirt, he shudders in empathy while throbbing in anguish.

She leads him down the ladder, kicking off her impractical heels to tramp barefoot down the steel stairway. He winces in sympathy for the punishment he imagines her bare feet must be absorbing.

Soaked to his skin, his shoes start to squeak.

The cold and wet penetrate, and he begins to shiver. He wishes he had worn a hoodie, despite the garment's dark connotations. Usually, he associates the urban wear with inept, lawless, and unsavory cyber behavior, classifying it as something he would never own, much less wear.

But dang, he is cold!

He is well-insulated compared to her. She must be freezing. He marvels at how she manages to resist the elements. Upon reaching the pavement, she pulls him into an all-out run.

He finds himself chasing her barefoot, translucently-clad form through the dark alleys and down the block. Incredulous shouts echo behind them as passersby react; most sound approving, though one voice says, "She isn't wearing a mask!"

Another adds, "Neither is he."

The rain and the thin, wet garb do not dampen her impressive running form. Despite bare feet, she is fast; easily able to outdistance him. He is panting, huffing, and puffing, struggling to keep pace. His heart is pounding from the unaccustomed exertions—her undulating cleavage doing little to calm it. It is obvious she is a fine-honed runner; the realization surprises him.

He has no idea how far they run, his sense of direction disoriented as they zig-zag from block to block, up and down alleys. Unsure why he is following her in this madness, he begins to suspect not only has she spilled her marbles, but he is falling, flailing uncontrollably, footing uncertain in the chaos. Who are they running from? What are they running to? Winded, he considers abandoning the chase, leaving her to whatever fate she imagines awaits.

Still, he is fascinated. Like Alice tumbling into the rabbit hole, falling out of control, she compels him to follow her down this urban warren, whatever the mystery, no matter the danger. He has plunged head-first, powerless.

After many minutes of mad-crazy dashing about, they dart into a dead-end alley, coming to an abrupt halt. Imprecations escape her lips as she searches the backstreet, looking for ... something—an exit, perhaps? Unsure what she is looking for, he welcomes the break. Deep, shuddering breaths wrack his body, causing hiccups as he inhales fresh rain with each breath.

Though confused and uncertain, he thinks they are in the Bowery. She acts agitated, near panic, trapped, looking for a way out—unwilling or unable to reverse course. Pointing at a fire escape ladder impossibly high overhead, she whispers, "You must boost me up!"

He squints up. "What? Impossible!" She stares at him. Shrugging, he cups his hands. Instead of placing her foot in the makeshift stirrup, she shakes her head. "No, you can't lift me high enough. When I jump, you must throw me as high and hard as possible.

It will take every bit of strength we both have. Hurry, our lives depend on it!"

Why 'they' are chasing them is a mystery. Who 'they' are is a mystery. Her imaginary fiend? Does anyone actually pursue them? He hasn't seen any pursuers. Is she merely drawing him into a private, demented fantasy? Are they actually in danger? She is Director—the captivating fantasy he has worked near for many months. Yet the woman before him is so different, so uncharacteristic of the demur, button-down executive; he imagines she is an alien doppelgänger who has body-snatched her in her sleep.

He ponders as she retreats a few paces, studies the ladder overhead, and squints at him. She motions for him to move back and to his left. He bends and cups his hands, gripping them together as hard as possible; they are both drenched. Her short brown hair is soaked and drooping. She brushes the wet hair from her face. Her wispy shift is ripped, soaked, barely restraining her plenteous charisma, much less concealing the rouged headlights illuminated by the cold and wet.

Riveted by her overflowing charms, his awareness slowly embraces her exceptional muscularity. How had he not recognized this before? Subcutaneous padding smooths the feminine form, stealthily masking well-developed muscles.

Besides, an executive does not need muscles; one does not readily see what one does not expect to find. Her muscles ripple and bulge when she flexes and leans forward in preparation for her charge, revealing an astonishing degree of muscular development.

He wonders: world-class barefoot runner and bodybuilder? Fascinating! She takes deep, slow breaths as though steeling herself for a tremendous exertion. "Ready?"

Intimidated, he nods. She leans forward and charges at him like a mammalian offensive guard set to mow him down. He stiffens his grasp for the impending assault. She slams into him, her wet kick nearly knocking his hard-clasped hands apart. Her diaphanous containment, overstressed beyond design limits, rips asunder with her lunge. Her surging, uh, musculature ... slaps his face as she bounds upward. Stunned, he manages to augment her kick with his firm upward thrust as she becomes airborne.

For an instant, he fears the extraordinary leap is ill-timed and misdirected. She has undoubtedly missed the target to land disastrously. In shock and near panic, he squints into the driving rain, searching for her.

To his surprise, she has attained her goal, dangling from the bottom rung of the high, retracted ladder. Noting the height, he marvels at how she has managed to fly so far. He wonders if she pursues a side career as a circus aerialist.

Cirque Du Loon?

Pursued by killers or not, he never imagined anyone could make such an impressive leap—amazing stuff, adrenalin.

Grasping and holding the cold, wet steel is a feat in itself. The quiet, demur Director is an incredible athlete. Who knew? Stunned, he stares open-mouthed as her dangling limbs dance on thin air.

Barely hanging from the ladder's rung, she appears in danger of falling. He positions himself to catch her. The height is dizzying. At first, nothing happens as she holds on; the ladder remains unmoving. She swings back and forth. Nothing. She jerks her body up and down in a series of mad chin-ups, her biceps bulging from the effort. Nada. Switching her grip to overhand, she begins even more demanding pull-ups; she slams her entire body forcefully on each downward stroke, encouraging the rusted hulk to move. He marvels at how she manages to keep a grip on the wet metal. Her hand strength must be incredible.

She jerks and bounces back and forth, up and down, and climbs to no immediate effect. Her tortured garment, caught on the ladder by her struggles, disintegrates. The rain continues pouring as he whiffs a pungent scent. Imagination? The natural stench of the alley? Or? He moves to one side so as not to be directly beneath her.

Finally, the ladder moves with a noisome creak and grind. With a metallic scream of protest, it begins to descend, shuddering as it drifts downward. It stops above his head, his companion's lower body pressed against his face. She is pale, cold, and shivering violently, barely conscious, holding the ladder rung with a white-knuckle death grip. Leaping with all his muster, he grabs the ladder rung, his added weight pulling the stubborn contrivance to full extension. Her feet touch the ground, and she collapses in a heap, his grip alone now holding the ladder in extension.

He wants to assist her but dares not release the hard-won ladder. Instead, he nudges her with his foot. She grunts as she heaves several deep breaths, her pale, blue-tinged bosom rising with each inhalation. Seconds slide past as she recovers and, with effort, regains her feet. Shivering with the cold and wet, she moves to tuck her endowments into the failed garment. The measure proves pointless given said garment's shredded condition.

In frustration, tinged with anger, she rips the remaining fabric from her body, tossing it away like a soiled tissue. Frigid rivulets of rainwater drip from her hair, flow along her neck, and merge as they plunge between swells of pale blue skin.

Still weak and panting from her exertion, she nods at the ladder. "Climb. Fast. We have seconds—if that."

He shakes his head. "I gotta hold this lest it retracts. Ladies first."

She eyes him, sweeps her eyes down her unclad form, and grunts something which might be a cynical laugh. Without another sound, she mounts the ladder. He politely closes his eyes as she climbs past him, though she is unaware of his gentlemanly deference.

She ascends to the first level, and he proceeds to climb the ladder behind her. Predictably, having expended so much effort to extend the ladder, it now refuses to retract. He bangs it with his hand and shakes it, yet it remains extended. Questioningly, he peers at her.

"Pull it up if you can, else it will betray us."

He removes his belt, loops it around a rung, and pulls. With a groan, the ladder moves, ascending to the retracted position, resisting every inch. He cannot retrieve his belt now. He tries a second, a third time to release the belt from the rung. Finally, she whispers, "Leave it. They probably won't spot it. It was thoughtless to leave my shift down there too. Too late anyway. Let's move before they spot us; get to the roof."

On attaining the rooftop, they pause to catch their breath—the rain, driving hard at times during their run, halts as though turning off a shower. A sudden, tense silence descends. Their exertions have offset the cold, though it returns with a bite as they halt. Shouts echo from below. Exhausted, panting, still catching her breath, she does not react to the voices. He moves toward the sounds, but she pulls him down, finger to her lips, signaling silence. He crawls stealthily to the roof's edge. Peeking over the parapet, he spots two familiar forms. Arguing like predators whose prey has escaped, they appear to be nearly turning on each other. A moment of imprecation-peppered searching, and the agitated forms race into the darkness. Were they the cause of her panic? Are they a credible threat?

After a few moments of recovery, they cross to the next building. No alleyway, the chasm to the next building is an easy, if dangerous, jump, particularly in the wetness. He follows as she crosses the roof and tugs the roof-access door. Locked. The rain returns with a renewed vengeance.

She sighs and motions him toward the next building. Again, they risk a dangerous crossing to the neighboring tenement. Reaching the roof access door, they discover it is unlocked.

Opening the door slowly, she whispers, "Come."

At least they are out of the rain, if not the danger. The stairwell is warm. They pause and sit on the stairs for a moment. She squeezes water from her hair and uses the side of her hand to squeegee beads of water from her skin, shivering as she shakes away the droplets. He tries to collect his thoughts as he similarly dispels excess water from his face and hair; he wishes for a towel.

He leans close, and whispers, "Who's chasing us? Is anyone chasing us? WTF is going on?"

She leans near his ear and replies, barely whispering, "We must reach a Dojo nearby; I will explain then. No talking until we are safe. I think we lost them, but let's not give them the chance to reacquire us. We are in grave danger."

He notes her use of the term Dojo. He is not the first to consider the risks of the game. Tabling the thought for something more pressing, he starts to speak, "Clothes ...."

She places her finger on his lips, shaking her head. "We are running for our lives. Let's go."

Descending the stairs quietly, they reach the top floor. The stairway is at the other end of the building. As they creep down the hallway, an apartment door opens. He is surprised beyond words as—too late to retreat—she pulls him to her as though embracing, his body covering hers, masking her lack of clothing. He freezes for a moment before yielding to her embrace.

They assume the position of oblivious lovers as a teenage girl emerges from the apartment. She wears the tats and piercings of rebellious urban youth, ragged bell-bottom jeans with holes in the legs, and a slouchy deep V-Neck nearly as translucent as the recently discarded tattered shift in the alley.

She walks past the intertwined pair, eyes on her palm. As she passes, she does a cartoonish double-take, belatedly noticing the unclothed form against the wall. The two exchange knowing smiles, the older giving the younger a wink. The wide-eyed teenager continues walking, and her voice is audible in the distance as she speaks to her palm. "Hey Twig, guess. I spotted another one. Yeah, right here in the building. Yeah, in the hallway. Bold as brass. Nah, didn't hear the chopper; shellshocked me. ..." Her giggling echoes faintly as her voice fades in the distance.

"At least the kid didn't snap a picture," she whispers. He nods in agreement, recognizing the undesirability of having one's photograph taken in such a situation, doubtless to circulate on the Internet forever. Although, while concerning insofar as it applies, he is as yet ignorant of the far greater danger.

Still shielding her with his body lest another observer should appear, he whispers, "Ya wan my shirt?"

"Yeah, but porky-piggin it doesn't help—besides, we've no time, and you shirtless would draw unwanted attention too. Anyway, we must avoid being seen at any cost lest the C'thulhu spots us. Speed and stealth over modesty. They will kill us no matter what I am wearing. Or worse. Now come on, let's move!"

They descend the stairs floor-by-floor without further encounters. As they do so, he wonders who, or what, she means by 'Kathuloo?'

*More information about my stories and projects, along with free-to-read short stories and more at my author's website.*

# Chapter Eight

# Inside the Crypto Cavern

*Sensory stimuli trigger activity in brain regions that process sensory information. Constant stimuli cause the brain to tamp down its response. This process, called habituation, enables people to tune out the routine to focus on the new. Autistics tend to develop habituation slowly and imperfectly.*

"HOLYHOBBLINGCROCSONACRUTCH!! WHAT THE HELL?" The skinny kid's reaction borders on cartoonish as his eyes goggle at their sudden and unconventional entrance.

"Language! They were waiting for us," she replies. "I had to improvise."

"Some improvisation." The speaker gawks wide-eyed at her egg-bare, dripping-wet skin.

"Manners, Twit, and language! Eyes on my face. I'm freezing cold! Get us some towels," she commands with blistering authority, an assertive tone he has never heard Director use. "Crank up the heat and bring us those coveralls from the laundry. The hairdryer, too—we need to get dry and warm. We're both cold as bricks."

"Sorry, Professor," he croaks as he jumps from the Air Chair and disappears into another room. His sudden movement startles a beautiful gray feline, causing the animal to rocket past them with a panicked yowl.

"Putain, je suis crevé, you'd think the kid never saw an unclothed woman before," she grouses softly, to no one in particular. She turns to face him and speaks more purposefully, "Here, let's get you out of those wet things." She starts helping him unbutton his shirt. He balks at the prospect of joining her sans-culottes.

"For the love of cheesecake," she mutters. "You were willing to show me everything and pay in Dogecoin for the privilege an hour ago, then chased my naked bang-tail halfway across the city, and NOW you're shy? Knock off the prudeasso and get those freezing, wet clothes off."

He jumps in shock at her words, nearing a freeze from the stress. Her tone snaps a military cadence demanding willing, correct, and immediate compliance. He suspects, if motivated, she might blister paint at twenty yards. He is terrified, unused to such a command presence, especially from a woman.

Hands shaking, he complies, unbuttoning and dropping various items. He hesitates at his briefs, but at one arched eyebrow, he doffs those as well. He fervently hopes she recognizes the cold and does not form any lasting impressions, but if she develops an impression, lasting or otherwise, she gives no sign. Later, in hindsight, he wonders whether dropping his briefs was indeed called for.

They are standing egg-bare in the center of the room, dripping puddles on the hardwood, when Apprentice reappears with two extra-large, fluffy towels. Failing heroically at restraining his gaze, the kid mumbles something incoherent, relinquishes the towels, and disappears again. Finally, they dry themselves, and, with relief, he wraps himself in the towel—though she appears starkly unaware of his nudity or her own as she calmly hangs her towel on a chair to dry.

Struggling, eyes carefully focused on her face, Ritz sputters, "M-Maybe the k-kid h-hasn't. H-he appears to be at an awkward age."

She puzzles a half-second before she tracks his meaning and sputters a chopped-off laugh. "With all the imagery on the Internet, I should think he is familiar."

He shrugs. "IRL{In Real Life}? Pictures are one thing. A living and breathing human: another. He acts a bit disintegrative."

Her eyebrows pinch in thought. "The kid's weak in social interaction, nerdy, and geeky, but not enough to reach a diagnosis level. He's extremely talented in cyber. You may be right, though. You would know, I'm sure. Shush now."

His mouth falls open, unsure how she thinks he might relate to the kid's possible diagnosis. However, before he can engage, Apprentice reappears with a giant hairdryer and an assortment of combs and hairbrushes. She grabs the appliance, uses it with dispatch, and hands it to him. He does likewise, relishing the warm airflow. He considers luxuriating longer in the warm air before deciding the towel is sufficient.

With the copious hot air from the gadget, the bone-chilling cold begins to dissipate. The room is warmer, too, as the central heating system blows warm air. Finally, his teeth stop chattering, and the shivers subside.

Apprentice returns once more, this time bearing a pair of jumpsuits, thin coveralls one might wear over street clothes while playing mechanic. The ringing "Tilt, tilt, tilt, tilt...tilt" of sensory-overload fades as they dress; at least the jumpsuits are dry and calm the modesty reflex.

Apprentice grabs a mop and squeegees their puddles, and disappears again with his sullied and soggy clothing.

Looking toward the doorway, she raises her voice. "Bring the Assbook to the den. Coffee, too."

"Right away, Professor," echoes from the next room.

Puzzled, Ritz asks, "Uh, 'cuse me?"

She inclines her head toward an open doorway to yet another room with a low table and comfortable chairs. Tugging his borrowed zipper, he follows her lead into the den, a perplexed expression floating above the coveralls.

They settle in the den. Moments later, Apprentice appears with a massive binder and lays it open-faced, sliding an elegant chess set to one side. Moving quickly, he vanishes again only to return within moments carrying a tray with a steaming carafe with cups and utensils. Errands complete, Apprentice settles in a third chair and turns the binder to a middle page.

Turning the book toward him, she explains, "Assassins Codex, a picture book of evil. We keep dossiers on high-functioning sociopaths of every stripe whenever we can. We group them into collections based on their penchants and proclivities. You almost met some of them tonight, though you had no reason to recognize them. This book is our register of highly dangerous assassins. In other words, the Assbook."

Turning to her companion, she announces, "Twit, I'd like to formally introduce you to Ritz Pringle, possibly the most extraordinary White Hat in the inhabited universe. Ritz, I'd like you to meet my apprentice. We call him Twit. Twit is not a nickname; it's leetspeak, 7w17. Not to insult him, but because it is his 1337 handle.

"It means **T**ech **W**izard **I**n **T**raining—we use leet handles rather than IRL names. 7W17's a budding young Indigo of outstanding skill, aligned with our cause. He is also my ward and majordomo. To which point, this is the last time you use your IRL name in leet company."

Ritz shrugs. "Hats don't use leet names. That crayolia's for posers."

"True, within the Agency," she admits. "But you have a life outside the Agency."

He stares at her blankly, unsure where she is going.

"I don't mean IRL. But, Ritz, do you think I would recruit someone without a thorough vetting?"

He continues staring, hiding his rising panic behind his best dumb look. He prides himself on his dumb look—it's almost as exceptional as his blank stare, something he has polished to perfection.

She stares at him; her look is anything but dumb. Instead, her glare reflects growing exasperation.

She turns to her apprentice. "Would you like to explain it to him?"

"Professor, I don't....."

She sighs, "It's all right." Her expression hardens as she speaks. "He is one of us. He merely doesn't understand it yet. Tell him."

Apprentice glances at him deferentially, ducking his eyes as though apologizing for some impending act. "Um, there are, um, some bad people on the net. People who will do anything, no matter, um, how evil. Some of the worst are, um, in this book." He squirms and nudges the massive binder.

As he does so, his face transforms, he gains confidence, his manner becomes focused, his thin nerdy voice lowers a register, and he speaks slowly with focus, confidence, and authority.

Unfortunately, with the transformation, he becomes the most annoying lecturer, the slow-talker.

"Those listed here are assassins who kill people for money, ideology, or pleasure. They enjoy it and harness their sadistic bent to fund a lifestyle and further goals. These are not merely sociopaths. Those who are insane are usually caught by law enforcement rather quickly. These are not out-of-control murderers like the Unabomber or the Zodiac Killer. These killers are brilliant and firmly in control, often with massive resources backing their every move. They sell destruction, deception, and death—their tools are stealth, intimidation, and fear. Their customers are wealth, power, and politics. Especially politics."

Director impatiently shifts as though wishing her apprentice would talk faster. Indigo 7w17 has assumed the rostrum now, and he speaks slowly with precise grammar, careful diction, intense focus, and without deviating from his course. When in the zone, interrupting him risks his ire; a glowering stare is guaranteed.

"Their murders are seldom recognized as such. When someone prominent dies in an odd accident or ill-timed natural causes, it is possible, even likely, that one of these people is behind it. They will, without hesitation, take down an aircraft killing all on board to eliminate one person. Although they do not shy away from such high-profile charges, they prefer simpler, smaller, more surgical strikes.

"Sudden illness, heart attacks, and drug overdoses are more commonly their modus. Think of a prominent person dying of supposed natural causes under suspicious circumstances or a high-profile personage dying unexpectedly. It remains impossible to prove these mysterious deaths are, in fact, assassinations. One hallmark of their work is the crazy way the official ranks close against attempts to investigate. Autopsy results deemed classified, information embargoed, and theories floated ignoring established facts to blame the victim. Persistent investigators meet with unfortunate accidents. Suspicious death allegations dissipate into the realm of conspiracy theorists as the puppet masters and their media meat-puppets shout down any opposition. The more fiercely the attack against anyone questioning the official line, the more likely the death was, in fact, an assassination."

He waves his hand expansively. "Stealth is the hallmark of these people. Stealth along with political alliances. If an official is openly, publicly assassinated, it probably was not someone in this book behind it, though there are others to consider; they're not the worst."

Unable to constrain her impatience, Director interjects, "The worst are those hidden master puppeteers who employ these people. We don't have a picture book on them, as they are unknown, recognized only by the shadows they leave. We call them *The FAANG* to distinguish them from the assassins, but we do not know they are a different organization; we merely differentiate them by their methods."

Her rapid-fire interruption has earned a steely stare from Indigo 7w17. He sits quietly until she finishes, and silence descends, unmoving, staring. He vehemently despises interruptions.

She mutters a soft, "Sorry. Please continue. You're doing fine."

7w17's hardened stare softens, and he resumes the narrative. "Our job, mine, and others, is to track these people, unravel their activities and communications. We do not address their crimes. Instead, we want to dismantle the organization above them. Once we have neutralized their employers, we will deal with them, or law enforcement will. So, we have the unhappy job of watching them operate, often powerless to intervene, letting them ravage as we search for clues to the IRL identity of those pulling their strings."

Ritz raises a hand, wary of interrupting. He has spotted the shift in personality when the leet operator is in control—a hallmark of a particular form of the disintegrative, mildly autistic-like condition. Twit's intellect is mature and authoritative when focused; when unfocused, the kid is juvenile, nerdy, and awkward. Ritz notes the change as it flits across the youngster's face as Twit, the nervous Sorcerer's Apprentice, becomes 1337 Indigo 7w17, Junior Cyber Warrior. Then he shifts back to become the timid Apprentice again, a startling Jekyll/Hyde transformation once you see it.

He is familiar with the behavior—too familiar. He has often recognized similar characteristics, surprisingly common in other Hats he has worked with, though he is apparently unaware many of those observations might also apply to him. This kid is brilliant when he is on the beam. He wonders why Director isn't aware.

After a moment, the youngster nods as though granting permission to speak.

Ritz responds, unintentionally imitating the kid's precise manner and phrasing. "A noble pursuit, no doubt, assuming the supposed puppet master's networks' dismantling is the result, but what has that to do with me?

"I do something similar for the Agency. Uncle Spook is not wasting my talent on some garden-variety assassination plot; we turn those over to law enforcement or the FBI. Jurisdiction notwithstanding, the Agency sometimes supports high-profile criminal investigations, as we did in the Milk Road case.

"My primary activity focuses on nation-states, particularly those rogue states threatening world stability. I commit acts of war daily, using sophisticated cyber weaponry to attack hostile countries, sabotage missile programs, and disrupt rogue nuclear research projects. We conduct covert campaigns against our enemies, and they do the same to us. We are better at it, of course. Ours are some of the most dangerous cyber weaponry ever developed.

"And we are not powerless to intervene. When I build a case against an enemy, it results in action. Sometimes military, often civil as in the Milk Road case, but always decisive, effective action."

The youngster nods. Touching fingertips and making a tent of his hands, leet Indigo 7w17 reasserts control. "We monitor criminal activity on the web, the 'dark web' I mean, and create dossiers on those operating there. Of course, we are interested in those connected to our targets, but we flag interesting operators of all stripes. We create profiles of anyone potentially useful using specialized device-fingerprinting technology, and our monitors spot them whenever they appear on the net. One, in particular, has become quite interesting. He uses the 1337 handle The Ph3DoRA."

Ritz's dumb expression melts into one faintly reminiscent of a started deer.

Director peers into his eyes and smiles. "We recognize this leet operator is on our side, whether or not he understands it. Like us, his focus is the predator who lures victims using unsavory tactics. He targets many whom the Agency largely ignores. Dark web transactions can be dangerous; citizens who seek minor contraband risk becoming the prey of dark web-based criminals who would rob them or worse. This leet's efforts help us track these villains and expose them to law enforcement. In a manner of speaking, the Agency does the same, but the Vigilante is more direct, as evidenced by the Milk Road case, and more focused on the criminal."

She leans in and lowers her voice for effect, "As Director, I have options. You see, I, too, have a secret identity. By day, I am the Agency's Director of the Cyber Warrior Corps. By night, I lead a secretive cabal and use different tools. The puppet masters we seek to unseat have infiltrated the Agency, which is why I couldn't brief you there, even in a SCIF. They do not suspect my Red Team exists. I only trust my secret Red Team Warriors."

His cape flaps and flutters like a startled window shade as his voice rises to a squeak. "Y-Y-Ya think I have a secret identity? Am I this mysterious leet? AYFKM? I am a White Hat! Why would I ...."

She interrupts him with a sarcastic laugh. "Ha! I don't THINK you are the Ph3DoRA. I KNOW it! Absolutely! Beyond doubt!

We have been watching you, occasionally helping you, for over a year—excellent work on 'Milk Road,' by the way.

"I hate to extinguish your side hustle. However, you provide a resource we can tap without exposing ourselves, an independent foil, misdirection. We have used you most effectively to deflect attention from our activities. That time is gone. Now it is time to join us. I want you to join my secret Red Team."

Still stubborn, not accepting the mantle of the leet Ph3DoRA, he shakes his head and starts to object again. Before he can do so, she moves directly into his face, invading his personal space. He can feel her hot breath.

Her voice again takes on a military snap. "*Rithwick J. Pringle*! Are you still trying to tell me you are not the Ph3DoRA? Give up, man; I can prove you are the leet vigilante! And whether you understand it, I saved your life! No less than THREE Assbook luminaries were out to kill you tonight. If not for 'Trixie' spiriting you out from under their noses, you would be DEAD now. DEAD! DEAD! DEAD! Three times over and ruled an accident with no investigation. And we're only talking about tonight—we will ignore the Hashtag, although I am confident the meteor targeted the Ph3DoRA too."

His cape, unmoored by the shock, flutters to the floor.

He blanches at her use of his birth name. How the hell did she come to learn it? The vague Hindu-sounding name hints at his origins, origins about which he has no clue.

He blanches again when he reviews the mental replay. Was the Hashtag for him? Impossible! Even the darkest, most powerful supervillains do not command meteors. Do they?

She retreats from his personal space. He takes a deep breath and pulls his voice back down forcibly from the stratosphere. "I... Uh... Let's fergit who the leet operator is and ask whether I was in danger and did you save my life." His voice deepens and becomes more robust and confident as his anger surges. "I can think of two alternatives. One idea is they were after you instead of me. Had I abandoned you, they might have left me alone." He pauses a moment, closing his eyes briefly, breathing deeply, forcibly calming himself before continuing.

"Another alternative explanation might be this is all a ruse. You want to make me believe I am in your debt. You said you want me to join you and Twit in your vigilante club. Isn't it possible the only danger lay in climbing fire escapes and rooftops in the cold, dark, and rain? Such impromptu midnight parkour in the rain is certainly high-risk, the only danger I can prove."

Even as he trivializes the chase, he remembers the strange pair in the alley after reaching the rooftop.

She appears shocked by his words—anger boils in her eyes, but only for an instant. Closing her eyes, she pushes her emotional reaction down. When she opens them, she addresses her nervous apprentice. "Push the book over this way, please, and order pizza. More coffee too. It has already been a long night, and I, for one, am hungry. I'm sure our guest is as well."

Twit nods and bolts from the room like a frightened little boy disturbed by mom and dad's fighting; the front door opens and closes.

"I see your point. You are correct about one thing; those chasing us would have been ecstatic to capture or kill me. I am valuable, but the assassins were after you. I doubt they knew who I am. At least not until later. Those two apparently bought my brass nail impersonation, at least initially."

She flips the pages, searching for a moment, and taps a picture. "Here is a terrific guy—a blood-thirsty sociopath with seventeen proven murders for hire and another twenty-three suspected murders for recreation. He relishes killing and takes his time when doing so for personal reasons. For hire, he kills quickly and cleanly. His usual method is to arrange an accident. If not an accident, or convenient natural causes, he makes his victim quietly disappear as though they stepped through a portal to another realm. Either way, he never leaves a crime scene to investigate." She turns the book so he can see the dossier.

Lean, pale, small-boned, pristine suit, blue shirt, bow tie, thick plastic-rimmed glasses. Ritz turns slightly pale as he scans the enumeration of the man's alleged crimes. "I spotted him in the bar. He was checking me out. I thought he was gunna ask for a date; I get that sometimes. I tagged him as an accountant."

"I, too, call him 'The Accountant' for the same reason you did, though I doubt he is skilled with numbers. But, yes, one way he often approaches his victims is with a prospective sexual liaison. He will be smooth, charming, and seductive until the instant he sinks the ice pick into your neck.

"He uses sex as a weapon to draw his prey. He has little overt interest in sex other than as a tool to approach his victims. He uses it on both male and female prey. If sex doesn't work, he is not above a direct assault. He would not likely attempt a frontal attack in your case since you have a considerable size advantage. Nonetheless, if the two of you fought barehanded, he would kill you—sin duda."

She sighs, looking him up and down as though seeing him for the first time. "No offense, you're big, strong, and reasonably fit, but you're not a fighter. He is a highly-skilled fighter, although you might not think so. He would render you lifeless using only bare hands in less than ten seconds unless he decided to savor it. Either way, you would not have had a chance."

"Reasonably fit," he retorts. "I'm in terrific shape. I sweat at the gym thrice a week, even got a trainer."

She smiles, saying nothing. He remembers the astounding physical prowess she exhibited mere hours ago. Perhaps, he thinks, she understands a thing or two about physical fitness.

"What about this one?" She flips a couple of pages. Staring at him is a woman with long black hair, similar in build to Director though thinner, a more substantial Asian influence, and much paler.

He nods, pointing. "She was there too. For a moment, I mistook her for you. But, after the first glance, she never paid me any attention, nor did I, her."

She nods. "Her methods are more subtle, though no less deadly. I call her 'T-K' for 'Two-Knife.' She likes blades. Her favorite technique is to stab her victim in a crowded room. Messier than unicorns playing leapfrog." She waves her hands expansively, pantomiming a stabbing.

He cringes at the graphic overload. Without acknowledging his reaction, she continues, "I was watching her while in your lap. T-K disappeared into the crowd for a moment, and I pulled you out. The Accountant watched us leave but assumed I was a hooker, and we were conducting the usual business. After a couple of minutes, he followed us, undoubtedly intending to do us both in flagrante delicto. We were out the window and down the fire escape before he figured out the dodge. T-K was close on his heels. By the time they realized we had gone out the window, we were down the fire escape and gone."

He softly adds, "I saw them in the alley when I looked down from the roof."

She nods. "They are part of a group we call the Legion of C'thulhu." In response to his raised eyebrow, she adds, "Named after the 'Great Old One' of H.P. Lovecraft."

He nods, "I thought that's what you said, but I didn't follow you, didn't understand it was merely your codename for them."

"Right, though we've identified some individuals, we have no clue who they actually are," she says. "They are purveyors of intimidation, maiming, and murder. They chased us for several blocks, which is why we dodged and zig-zagged so much. I was trying to guess where they were going and go elsewhere. When we ran into the dead-end alley, I thought they had us. I expected a way out but was mistaken. Bad planning. They would have killed us both. Or worse." A flicker of fear crosses her features as she remembers those desperate moments.

She sighs and pushes the book toward him again. "Those are the two I spotted, and there may have been more. Skim through the book and see if you recognize anyone else. There was a third one, your rideshare driver. She was to divert you to a kill-site before you arrived, but you foiled them by walking instead. If you called a car to return home, I am sure she would have again been your driver. I bet they only knew you from the rideshare account and couldn't pick you out from a crowd. That would explain how we were able to escape."

"Believable. The profile pic on the account is a random white dude, but why kill me? Likely they were there to kill you instead."

Apprentice has reentered the room during this exchange. At this question, he inserts himself into the discussion. "I, um, can explain th-that," he sputters. "My fault. I mixed up the credentials and set off alarms. I was at the Hashtag, piggybacking on your Pineapple. I'm so sorry, um, I didn't mean to cause you trouble."

She places her hand on the youngster's arm. "It's not your fault. It was an accident. We can't prove it was the credentials, either."

She turns to him. "As I explained, we were piggybacking on your leetness, using you as misdirection. They detected us through bad luck, poor timing, and bad decisions. We haven't the faintest clue what happened. They discovered us and struck back—hard. We had to drop our Internet entirely to fend them off. We're usually more competent."

"I see," he says. "You were probing these Night Stalkers while pretending to be the Ph3DoRA?"

"Yes, we must have hit a tripwire. But, of course, they thought we were you. Your IRL identity was well-masked, or so we thought. So, we did not believe you were in danger."

"I hit something similar when I probed the address you sent. The attack hit my firewall with crazy badness. They were probing from thousands of locations at once. It was a full-on cyber assault like the massive botnets with nation-state funding."

She gapes at him wide-eyed, then drops her eyes. She responds, "Hmm, that may be a factor too. They may have deduced it was you probing them. They're more dangerous than I believed. So, I set up our meeting to warn you and arrange to bring you into our protection. I had already decided to recruit you but did not suspect there was such urgency. I had been waiting for you to take down the Milk Road."

Please visit the Undercover Alien Reviews Page and leave a nice review.

https://amazon.com/review/create-review? &asin= B09YNG2JD3

*We hope you are enjoying the story thus far. If so, please visit the reviews page and leave us a nice review. Reviews are the life's blood of independent authors. So, please help us out, won't you?*

# Chapter Nine

# Recruited

*In professional settings, the neurodivergent are often viewed as under-performers—until someone notices and is wowed by their exceptional talents. Many of the greatest geniuses in history fell on the autistic spectrum; e.g., Albert Einstein, Bob Dylan, Thomas Jefferson, Mozart, Charles Darwin, Isaac Newton and Leonardo Da Vinci. Perhaps the abnormal lies in the neurotypical, not the autistic merely for being socially awkward.*

R ITZ AND DIRECTOR HAD been discussing their near-death experience and the growing threat of the FAANG. She had explained how she was prepared to bring him into her Red Team and had scheduled the meeting to warn and recruit him.

He ponders her words, replaying them in his mind. *"... I set up our meeting to warn you ... had already decided ... did not suspect ... urgency. ... waiting for you to take down the Milk Road."*

Head spinning, struggling to unpack her meaning, he begins, "Still..."

She is not ready for him to interrupt, so she plows on. "It is clear they are more dangerous than we suspected. While waiting for you to arrive, I spotted these two in the bar. I alerted my crew. Word came back about the chatter. They had put an urgent-kill order on you and named *The Irish Counting-House* as the place to acquire you."

"How'd they figure out I'd be there? Is there a leak in your organization? If they didn't know what I look like, how were they to spot me?"

"I suspect it was the rideshare. You called for a car to take you there, and the chatter popped. We learned from them the rideshare was to take you to a spot where there would be a staged accident. You were to die in a mundane traffic accident. The flap at *The Counting-House* was a panicked reflex action when their primary plan failed. They are never so careless. Someone must want you badly.

"You thwarted their plans when the storm began and snarled traffic made you hoof-it. So, they sent this lovely pair," Director poked the open pages with her finger for emphasis, "to intercept you. Something about your account connects to the Ph3DoRA. They likely don't know your IRL identity and only deduced the Ph3DoRA uses the service by the timing."

"DIVI coin!" he slaps his forehead. "The link is DIVI! I pay rideshare in DIVI coin through a dark web broker." He appears not to realize he has admitted his dark web alter ego. "It's supposed to be anonymous," he adds, almost shocked.

She nods, noting his admission but not commenting on it. "Makes sense. Is the rideshare in your IRL name?"

He shakes his head. "No, a fake identity. I use h0M8uR9 {Homburg} for innocuous stuff like dark-web research and rideshare. The Ph3DoRA only comes out for the real Harry Potter stuff. I set up the secret rideshare identity using Homberg to cloak certain low-level activities from the Agency. Like a secret meeting with a naked coworker at *The Irish Counting-House*. I am careful not to mix my identities—usually. I blew it; what can I say? Fatigue, or a momentary lapse, I guess. Whatever the excuse, I mixed em up. The Ph3DoRA checked out *The Irish Counting-House*—a disastrous mistake, something h0M8uR9 should have done. I have two rideshares, one for general use and another for secret superhero work. The rideshare is anonymous, but the alias' name is the crypto wallet used to pay for it. The name on the crypto wallet is the fake identity linked to h0M8uR9."

She dimpled slightly at his jab but did not comment. "That still doesn't explain how they connected the rideshare to the Ph3DoRA. Or how they recognized you at the pub."

"I think they keyed on anyone who arrived drenched and out-of-breath around the appointed time. We convicted ourselves when we bolted. Had we stayed put, they may have never attacked.

"I bet they approximated the location of the Ph3DoRA the moment he came online. Doubtless, they nailed my block, at least, when I checked the directions. Later, when h0M83R9 called for a ride to the same destination, the rest followed. Luckily, I obfuscated my location using a piggybacked Wi-Fi and gave the rideshare a street corner, not an address. So, they identified my block, at most, not my address."

She sighs with relief. "So, your IRL identity is likely still unknown. Nuke your secret account immediately—retire h0M8uR9 too. The Ph3DoRA may still be unbreached, but let's keep him offline for a while. You cannot go online again from your apartment. Do you have any other leet identities?"

Shaking his head, he is lying with silent lips. What superhero does not maintain a few burners? He resolves to keep d328y {Derby} offline too.

Aloud, he says, "You threw my phone away. At least it's off and locked. I use a strong password too, but we see how easily the Agency breaks into Phones. If they find it, they may be able to unlock it."

She grimaces. "You're right. That is a severe risk." Apprentice jumps from his chair at the mention of the phone. He is halfway to the door as she addresses him. "Send a team to search the alleyway for his phone. We must assume his IRL identity is compromised unless we find and destroy it. But, no doubt, they are already looking for it. So, we must find it first."

"Yes, Professor, on it," echoes from the next room.

She went on, "You're wrong on one count, though. They would not hesitate to kill a hundred innocents to remove a target. They would have killed every person in the bar, if necessary. If they took your picture, facial rec might reveal you, although the Agency tries hard to keep Hat identities secret. You are not in the usual databases."

He nodded but did not add he, too, tries hard to keep a low profile.

She continued, "Also, sending more than one assassin is uncommon. That they sent three is astounding. They want you dead, no doubt about it, and don't care if it gets messy. This is beyond amazing—stealth is their usual method. We never meant to put you in physical danger. I'm sorry.

"I went to the pub straight from the office. I had no suspicion of anything awry at the time. However, I arrived early and was forced to improvise when I got the warning. I cached my bag and office clothes in a storeroom and became 'Trixie' to avoid putting myself on their radar. As a brass nail, I hoped to approach you without arousing suspicion."

He nods. "You were bold as brass and sold the prostitute subterfuge well. So, you have an alternate career to fall back on if you need it. Ouch! I mean acting! Acting, not hooking, stop throwing the chessmen."

He feigns injury and fear until they both start laughing. After a moment, he continues. "You may not have aroused suspicion, but suspicion may be the only thing not aroused. You certainly led me out of there by my, uh, well, um, you led me out. How'd you come up with such a costume? It took guts to wear so little in public, commando no less, without underwear!"

"That was my underwear." He arches an eyebrow slightly, saying nothing. She continues, "That silk chemise was brand new and not cheap!" She pronounces chemise, "she meezuh," French, rather than American in her accent. "Neither was the dress I cached there along with my bag. I hope I can retrieve it. As for being scantily clad, I suspect that establishment has seen plenty of skin."

He shrugs. "Nonetheless, I appreciate your sacrifice on my behalf, but I'm still skeptical. There was no threat, as far as I can say, no one tried to kill me, and until I spotted those two in the alley, I thought no one chased us. I'm still only half-convinced they did. How do I trust you are telling me the truth?"

They are alone at the moment; she arises, dons the Trixie persona and comes to him, settling on his lap and placing her arms around his neck. "Dear child," she coos in Trixie's voice, "I have not begun to tell you the truth."

"Are you trying to 'not arouse suspicion' again?"

She laughs but balances on his knee rather than sliding closer for more intimate contact. Her manner is warm and sexy but falls short of intimate. Her proximity is unsettling and inappropriate. She is Director—his superior. They are alone, there is no need for role-playing or deception. This feigned intimacy is intimidating, predatory, as though she is forcing herself on him, almost against his will. Her tone is all business, although her voice is soft and sensual causing his to wonder about her motives. Her magnetic pull is undeniable.

First, she explains explicitly how their lives were in danger and how her organization has safe houses and dojos around the city. She elaborates on the organization and the enemy they are fighting. Time quickly passes as she briefs him, and yet he grows more nervous with every passing moment. She is scaring him, both with her words and her manner. His anxiety is rising.

She concludes with a warning. "If your identity is secure, you must return to work at the Agency as though nothing has happened. You went to a bar, met a working girl, and had some off-the-books kicks, as far as an outsider might suspect."

"Anyone who knows me would laugh at the idea. I don't hang around bars and don't need prostitutes." He waves a hand over his face. "Do I look like someone who pays for sex?" His statement somehow sounds slightly more adamant than necessary.

She laughs softly, tousles his hair, and leans in close, speaking softly. "Prostitutes serve other purposes than servicing the ugly or homely. Plenty of people pay for sex. Perhaps something on the kinky side indulges a fantasy one wouldn't admit to their IRL friends or merely avoid emotional entanglements. You don't need to buy a working girl dinner or call her the next day. No need to justify it. If anyone notices, leave them to their imaginings."

Crestfallen, he sighs, then with visible effort, his lopsided grin reasserts itself—he winks and quips, "You appear far more knowledgeable of the trade than I." He turns somber again after a moment, "Why 'dear child' me? I get such tripe from boomers or someone of Boss' generation. You're older than I am, but you're not boomer-aged."

She reacts almost as though slapped and appears much older for a fleeting instant. Recovering, she laughs. "Ha! Nice try, but I will not tell my age. Let's merely say I am an illusionist who works hard at her illusions."

"I weren't askin', but challenge accepted," he answers with a mock-evil grin.

Her dimple returns, along with a mischievous twinkle in her eyes. "I do so love teaching a young dog old tricks."

After this brief moment of sunshine, she dons a face dark enough to chase away any hint of a pleasant mood. "We must go to work tomorrow; then we have the weekend. If your identity is compromised, you must stay here in the Dojo. Returning home would be suicide, as would going to work. You are jobless and homeless if they suspect your identity. If necessary, you can stay here the weekend or until we resolve this. This old house has many bedrooms. We use it as a meeting place sometimes. Otherwise, you must act and appear normal and be on guard. The next few days are critical. The Ph3DoRA needs to stay off the dark web."

"Dare I go home?" His tone is as severe as hers.

"We will know soon. We have pwned their chat server; we follow every message. We will alert you if the chatter turns threatening. I will assign you a Boeing Black Phone, so we can reach you if needed."

"Fine, but you and Twit will sleep at some point. I doubt your 'Legion' will stop looking while you sleep."

She straightens her posture and taps her front teeth with her fingertip in solemn meditation. She hesitates for a few seconds before apparently deciding to reveal greater detail. "We are a larger organization than I have implied. We operate in cells arranged in an open pyramid of tetrahedrons. Each cell member has two cellmates and a secure communications channel to at least three other cells and possibly other special-purpose channels. Each can send messages up to the cell above them. In addition, they can send to one other cell at their level and down to at least one cell below."

She grabs a notepad and quickly draws a rough diagram illustrating the architecture. She explains, "Four triangular faces, six straight edges, and four vertex corners. A tetrahedron is the simplest of the ordinary convex polyhedra and the only one with only four faces."

He studies her drawing and smiles. "Revolutionary theory!" he exclaims. "I've read about this."

After another moment's pause, he frowns and continues, "Actually, I think I read it in an old science fiction story. But I didn't understand it then, and I'm not sure it's real. Can you explain it?"

She elaborates. "Each cell has three members. Each member only meets directly with the other two members of their cell. They secretly communicate with two others: their inductee in the cell below and the person who recruited them in the cell above. Anyone else they communicate only using a leet name. All such communications are encrypted. Each triangle shares sides and vertex with other triangles. Each channel communicates with another triangle, not sharing a side or vertex, but need not know where the channel connects to the larger picture."

He studies her diagram and scratches his head. "So, member 'A' at the top of the first pyramid talks only to B1, B2, and B3. Is that right?"

She nods. "B1 talks to C1, C2, and C3, B2 talks to C4, C5, and C6, and finally, B3 talks to C7, C8, and C9. Member C1 has a channel to, say, C4 and C7, and C2 to two others, ditto C3. They all have channels to the one above who recruited them and down to their inductees. Most members have one inductee. A few may have more than one.

"The communications channels and techniques are secret—they are blind about whom they are contacting sideways. They only have a leet handle and no personal identifying information (PII). So, if one turns traitor, he can only betray his cellmates, and the side channels allow the organization to carry on in the face of a breach and repair itself."

He asks, "So, no one in any cell has a clue how many cells there are, right? Nor how many are above or below them, correct? They only know their cellmates and the leet names and contact means of any other operatives, not where or what their cell might be. They do not know the IRL identities, only leet names, though I'm guessing there may be rare exceptions."

She nods, adding, "Yes, except we don't only use leet names. Leet names only work for Cyber Warriors. Others have cell names; we use cell names or leet names, never IRL names or more common nicknames. Ours is a complex organization few outsiders suspect exists."

She pauses for effect. "Our Congress of Elders oversees the functional cell structure. Each Elder heads an autonomous directorate, which manages local Lodges, much like this one. The Lodges put on a public display of meetings, memberships, and charitable works. We are visible and trusted in the community, but each Lodge manages a pyramid of secret cells unknown to most members. The cell members are unaware of the connection to the directorate, nor anything about the organization."

He nods enthusiastically. "It sounds complicated, but perhaps it is the only safe way a clandestine organization can operate and survive the inevitable traitor."

Her chin dips in a quick nod. "You got it. The organizational structure is as old as espionage itself. Cells of three members exchange information by combining modern encryption and old-fashioned spy-craft. The watchword is compartmentalization. What one does not know, one cannot spill."

He smiles, rubs his hands, and says, "I get it. Efficient and robust."

She resumes, "Yes, and a fundamental tenet is cells never gather in a single location. Meetings are kept small and anonymous. Dodges such as anonymizing face masks, leet handles, and nondescript clothing can blunt the risk. Cell members have strict orders about dress codes and speech restrictions.

"Thanks to the pandemics, face masks are a socially acceptable and commonplace fashion accessory—a necessity in the eyes of many! Anonymizing face masks are standard accouterment for secret meetings.

"Each low-level cell has a handler. The handlers also organize themselves into cells with sufficient redundancy to recover a broken link. The cell members don't know their handler, and often, the handler does not know the identity of the cell members. Identities of operatives outside a cell are secret and protected against a breach. Everything rolls up to the Directorate Elder, although the Directorate Elder does not have any public affiliation with the Lodge. The public Lodge Elder is a figurehead, a sacrificial lamb in case of betrayal. Each Directorate Elder is a member of the Congress of Elders, which oversees all Lodges. A given Lodge may have any number of cells."

He says, "You make it sound like a secret society aimed at totalitarian world government. Lodges, councils, and secret meetings—it all sounds conspiratorial. New World Order stuff."

"Oh, yes," she agrees. "We cultivate the image. Also, our public face is real. We are a fraternal order and charitable organization, and most members are confident that is all we are. Only a select few know of the more conspiratorial activities. Few of the cell members are also Lodge members, and not all Lodge members are a part of the conspiracy. The conspiracy theories mask a true conspiracy."

He nods. "Makes sense," he agrees. "Hide a conspiracy inside a conspiracy theory, like 'The Purloined Letter.' Hidden in plain sight."

She nods in agreement. "I am officially recruiting you into my cell, joining my Apprentice, Twit. No one may be aware of anything going on in other cells. I lead this cell with Twit, and now you. He leads a cell and the disciples he has recruited. You will eventually develop a cell and cyber-Dojo of your own. Each of his disciples runs cells of their own. We pass messages mainly via old-school spy-craft. Although we do use secure Black Phones, it is risky to trust technology.

He is surprised at the extent of her caution. Paranoia? Possibly, but there do appear to be genuine villains. It isn't paranoia if they're indeed after you.

Suppressing a grimace, he says, "It is undoubtedly true the Agency can read most forms of encryption, and the BPP {Boeing Black Phones} are not as secure as they might be, and besides, the Agency holds their encryption keys.

"This is my field. Believe me when I say I can show you how to fix that. I have encryption curves the Agency cannot break without the keys. The Agency is not omnipotent, despite the image they portray. It mostly relies on backdoor access to compromised Cloud servers, not brute-force real-time decryption."

With a shrug, she murmurs, "The Agency is not the one we fear reading our communications. We do not understand the capabilities of the FAANG, save they have broken every encryption we have employed."

His cape returns to its proper position and partly unfurls.

He says, "I can set up a secure crypto cavern for trustworthy communications. No backdoors, no Cloud, no compromised data centers. A private, locked-down little server locked away in a closet with the strongest encryption on the planet. They won't break it."

She nods. "Old-school spy-craft techniques do limit our ability to communicate. Information flow is vital. Plus, secret notes and handwritten ciphers can be broken too. The web is dangerous, and the Agency can read any encryption."

He protests. "Not true. No one can break my encryption, not the Agency or the FAANG. Not without a backdoor. I have a few tricks."

She grimaces. Her question, "Are you sure?" hangs unspoken.

Frustrated at her lack of trust in his expertise, he sputters, "T-th-th-this is my field. Tr-trust me, I know."

She asks, "What about quantum computers?"

Forcing a reluctant calm , he responds, "When quantum computing becomes a threat, I will use quantum encryption. The scientists are developing quantum encryption curves in anticipation of that day. But, for now, quantum computing is a field of rainbows and unicorn farts. No quantum computer is capable enough to be a threat. Yet!"

She sighs, and a wan grin cracks through. "If you believe in your ability to encrypt communications securely enough to make the cyber trustworthy, we will experiment with your techniques. No security is absolute. Perhaps yours will be useful, we'll test it. But be aware, the FAANG are highly capable."

As she finishes speaking, the front door opens and closes. She touches his hair again as she jumps from his lap, returning to her chair. "Pizza is here."

Please visit the Undercover Alien Reviews Page and leave a nice review.

https://amazon.com/review/create-review? &asin= B09YNG2JD3

*We have worked very hard to create an entertaining story highlighting the crucial role that those "on the spectrum" play in our world. Won't you please give us a nice review on Amazon?*

# Chapter Ten

# Friday!

*Sensory overload in the neurodiverse may stem from the hyper-vigilant brain overthinking its surroundings. This can lead to crippling anxiety when faced with threatening situations. Anxiety is a severe problem for many on the autism spectrum.*

H E SLINKS ALONG THE busy street. An observer might read the nervous head-swiveling, eye-darting, anxiety-ridden body language as fear. Yet, fear is only the surface, beneath which lies cold anger and a determination to defeat this new enemy.

Despite wearing a plain black face mask, he nonetheless struggles to keep his face calm. His eyes betray a nervous, anxious state, made all the more frenetic by lack of sleep. He will likely need Candy to make it through this day. Adrenaline and caffeine can propel one only so far, despite assassins dogging one's heels. Even Modafinil has its limits. He wishes for some Hard Candy, perhaps some Adderall to help him thru the day.

He slows as he approaches the dark, seething monolith. Steeling himself to confront the sally-port, his heartbeat jitters with faint dread.

"Good morning, Sprocket," he says as he joins the queue of one. His muffled voice competes with the wind and traffic noise without the benefit of lower facial cues.

"What?" she asks.

Pulling down his mask, he repeats, "Good Morning, Sprocket."

"Oh," she says, "Good morning, Ritz." Then, she adds, "Cripes, I hate cold weather," but she too covers her lower face.

"What?" he asks, but Sprocket loses interest in the conversation and turns away.

"Crikey," she grouses to no one in particular, her cup of Bux in hand.

"Wonderful aroma," he says, inhaling the bouquet of her blend. Savoring its richness, he wishes he had one. Pointedly ignoring him, she is not up for conversation today.

Moments later, he gains the portal and pantomimes the security ritual on autopilot. Almost. Today he carries an official Boeing Black Phone. They issue BBPs to high-ranking officials and, rarely, a Hat with extraordinary duties.

Screening is swift and perfunctory. Security scans the BBP without comment, although he imagines the guard treats him with a touch more respect. In his fantasies, he imagines the BBP as the Agency equivalent of a Roman legate's short, white baton, as much a symbol of authority and rank within the Agency as it is a communications tool.

On the 29th floor, he pauses at his cubical to drop his face koozie on the desk and collect his Hak-X logo mug. Caffeine became a priority, a necessity since the moment he whiffed Sprocket's aromatic blend. Cup in hand, he replaces the discarded face mask with a facade of nonchalance. He saunters idly toward the breakroom, wondering if he will survive the day. Professional assassins dogging one's trail is unsettling.

Making coffee mechanically, he spirals into a trance-like dark reverie of fear and funk. Shortly, a boisterous voice breaks the spell, his startled jump sending the coffee sloshing. He dances to restrain the carafe as meandering droplets scale the rim.

"Good morning, young man, good morning," bellows Boss. "My congratulations on the promotion. I just got the word. I guess we are peers now." His eyes fall on the BBP. His expression falters. Boss does not carry a BBP. He covers the minor stumble with his mug, holding it out for a fill not yet offered.

Willing his shaking hand into obedience, Ritz extends the carafe, pouring the deep black liquid into Boss's extended cup. "Here, ya go."

"Thanks, kiddo; I find a fresh cup of coffee helps me mimic socially acceptable behavior." Boss laughs at his witticism, almost as though it were funny.

"Thank you," Ritz responds to Boss's previous comment. "I suspect management has confused me with someone else, but who am I to judge?"

"Modesty is invisibility, young man. To be seen is—to be! So be proud of your accomplishments, and be modest about what you don't know, not what you do—tut, tut. Your record shines for itself; you will go far. I've had my eye on you. In fact, I recommended you for this promotion."

He smiles, recognizing Boss is playing at self-aggrandizement, vainglory ever his hallmark. The pomposity of his manner grates the Hat's already overstressed nerves, but he forces a smile through his facade.

The promotion came in the small hours of the morning as a ploy to give him a phone. With his leet identity at risk, the ability to communicate is now essential. He imagines pulling him away from the meddlesome Boss is a factor, too, although Director did not say so. It would not do to tip the Machiavellian intrigue, especially not to Boss.

Rather than challenge the man's questionable assertion regarding his imaginary role in the promotion, he smiles and assumes his best dumb look; he is a world-class dumb-looker. "Why, thank you, Boss. Kind words. I appreciate your sage advice. I wondered who my anonymous champion might be. It came as quite a surprise. I understand I should expect interesting new work."

Boss breaks into a toothy grin, relieved at the ready acceptance of his deception. "Count on it, my lad, count on it. And do feel free to call me if you need help. Yes, sir, I'm betting on you."

Slapping the younger man on his shoulder, Boss sloshes a few drops of his own. Then, oblivious to the mess, he turns and bounds from the break room.

Ritz stares at the doorway as the forced smile fades. Finally, he shakes his head, grabs paper towels, and sops the spilled brew.

Alone, his expression returns to one of dark reverie, holding his mug and staring into space—but only for a moment. He shivers and downs a hearty slug, refills his cup, and retreats to his cubicle.

His eyes fly open with a start; the buzzing BBP crashes his feigned concentration. A message from Director requesting his presence violates his power nap. Has a coworker spotted him napping and tattled? Has his IRL identity been compromised? He represses the urge to stretch as his stifled yawn screams silently for coffee. In response, he slams his last cold dregs in desperation before heading for the corner office.

As he approaches the privileged domain, the slightly too-ornamental assistant glances up. "Good afternoon," he says, eying the BBP. In a soft, almost breathy voice, he adds, "Congratulations on the promotion, sir. Director is expecting you; go right in."

He knocks politely on the partially closed office door, nudging it open. Director is standing behind the desk, pacing, on the phone, not the Agency phone on her desk, but a BBP, and she is talking soft, furtive, almost a whisper. She waves him in, motioning to close the door. His exceptional hearing automatically tracks her words. Though not intending to eavesdrop, he cannot help but overhear her side despite the conspiratorial tone.

At first, the call sounds innocuous.

"Yes, Alex, I'm quite certain."

"No, we retrieved the phone, as well as the clothing. Yes, everything. We overlooked nothing ... I AM certain!"

He realizes the call is not about Agency business but their extracurricular adventure, piquing his curiosity. So, whom can she be talking to? No one in the Agency, he guesses. So, who the heck is Alex? What role does he play in this game?

"I know, Alex. It was a risk we had to take. I had to take!"

He is surprised to note her deferential demeanor. She is not talking to a random subordinate but someone she highly respects.

It dawns on him that perhaps "Alex" is not the other party's name but a cell name used to mask his identity and protect his conspiracy role. Since it is not a leet handle, the other party is not a Cyber Warrior but someone of high executive rank. He questions the significance of the first initial. Does the letter 'A' denote the cell's organizational level? Plausible, he decides. He wonders about Director's level. That she is high in the ranks appears evident, but how high? How far does the conspiracy extend? Is 'A' the top?

She is still talking, "Yes, I was in grave personal danger, something I should never have permitted.—Yes—No!—Alex, please—I understand my value to the mission—They forced my hand; we mistimed the portal. I had to improvise. Fortunately, they thought we escaped through it, or else they would not have abandoned the chase so easily. The alternative would have been to sacrifice a valuable asset."

She glances at him, then dips and closes her eyes as the other party silently speaks.

"I consider that unacceptable. This isn't Chess."

The conversation continues in this vein for several more exchanges. He idly wonders what she is talking about. He tries not to listen but cannot help himself. Finally, chagrined at the suggestion someone is reprimanding Director for saving his life, he diverts his thoughts from the conversation to focus on her. He studies her appearance. She reflects no deficit from their adventuresome sleeplessness. Every crease, every hair is perfect.

What surprises him, though, is not her impeccable appearance or the pristine Brooks Brothers Tuxedo Dress. Brooks Brothers is de rigueur. The classic dress or its interchangeable pantsuit is typical office wear for high-ranking female executives in any field, though she sticks to dresses. He imagines a closet crammed with dozens of near-identical, expensive dresses.

She never wears pantsuits. She never changes things up. Ritz imagines she must wear the same outfit every day so as to make as few decisions as possible about unimportant matters. Instead, she saves her decision-making energy for her work.

What surprises him most is her hair. She always wears it waist-length, straight as though ironed, and glossy black. Today is no exception. As Trixie, her hair was short and reddish-brown. Without thinking, he assumed she cut it for the masquerade. Now he realizes she must incorporate a wig into her wardrobe. He doesn't understand but is impressed. Was her short hair the wig? Or is she wearing a wig now? Stumped, he cannot decide, cannot explain it.

As the call continues, his mind wanders to the brass nail persona. Director had suggested the chemise 'Trixie' wore, in fact, was her office underwear. Moreover, Brooks Brothers are renowned for the heft and weight of the fabric employed in their flagship creations. So, wearing a luxurious silk chemise under the hefty, crisp business dress makes sense.

She did not claim the chemise as her sole undergarment, although it appears all Trixie wore. His imagination skips to a logical conclusion. "None of my business," he reminds himself. His mind niggles at the detail although he resolves never to mention it. A gentleman does not notice such things. "Am I a gentleman? Can I at least pretend?" he wonders.

His preoccupation with her, and especially her wardrobe, is nigh ungentlemanly. Her pull is magnetic; under her influence, he is flailing, veering out of control. He sighs, wishing last night had not happened. He is discomfited and prefers to maintain a safe distance from the object of his fantasy.

The call concludes, and she drops into the chair, head in hands for a moment. She sighs, shakes her head, and stands again. Wordlessly, she comes to him, leans against him, and leans into him. Unsure how to respond, he places his arms around her shoulders. She is a big woman, tall, taut, and muscular. He is a bigger man. They fit together well as she rests her head against his body.

He is confused and unsure of what she expects of him. She says nothing, does nothing, but merely stands and leans against him. A quiet moment spent doing nothing, each listening to the other breathe and sensing the other's heartbeat.

Abruptly, the spell is broken. She steps away, digs deep, and draws forth the will to continue. She sighs and whispers to no one in particular, "Some days, it doesn't pay to get out of bed. Not that I've been in anyone's bed in a long, long while."

She passes her eyes over him, slowly, as though she has forgotten his appearance, finishing with a long sigh and a dark face. "Sorry, I should not let you see my moment of weakness. I deserve a proper dressing-down for the risks I took. Not your fault, mine. You did nothing wrong. I made one poor decision after another, putting our entire mission and many lives at risk. I am an irresponsible fool, but I would take those, or worse, risks again, given the circumstances. I believe you are far more valuable to our cause than anyone suspects."

"Call me 'Neo' then," he quips. He pauses, waiting for her to react to his reference, but she ignores his cyberpunk wisecrack, and a momentary pained expression slides across his face. Fortunately, it does not linger.

He continues in a more somber tone. "I appreciate your saving my life, although I was initially skeptical. In any case, the deed is done. Life has no 'undo' button."

She flies up a wan smile. "How did you get so smart?"

"Lots of sleep, fresh air, and long naked midnight runs through the city."

Her smile deepens for a brief instant before turning solemn. "We were lucky. Incredibly lucky. Trust me. You have no clue."

"Then give me a clue. Let me in on the grand story."

"I cannot. Must not. Compartmentalization protects the lives of those involved. No one person knows more than necessary. I have already shown you too much."

He smiles at the weak double-entendre, wondering if she was acting coy or her words were unintentional, an accidental choice bereft of deeper meaning. After a moment's hesitation, he asks, "You act as though you have the full picture. Or am I wrong?"

She sighs, "You're not wrong, which is why my going into the field as I did was so foolish. That is why I earned a thorough chastising and deserved the dressing-down I received. I would have pinned back the ears of anyone under me who exercised such bone-headed judgment. I am one of the few people in the universe with broad and substantial knowledge. Few others are at my level, and most are elsewhere, beyond our enemy's reach. I alone am foolish enough to go into the field, placing myself at risk. Had they merely killed me, it would have been a horrible disaster to the organization, aside from my personal interest. Had they instead captured and extracted what I know, the loss would have compromised our mission and cost many lives."

He has no response other than standing mute, waiting for her to continue.

She stares at the abstract painting on the wall for a moment as though gathering her thoughts. She turns to him, and as though a curtain has fallen, she is all business.

"The promotion is official. You are now a White Hat First Class. I need you to swear your commitment."

"Do I need to sign a contract?"

She shakes her head. "Human Resources will want the official paperwork relating to change of title and bump in pay, and doubtless you will sign endless pages of bureaucratic gobbledygook, but for the real contract, the agreement between you and I, no. Such is the nature of our specialty that we may not commit the agreement to a written contract. This transcends the Agency and our official duties. Your word will do. You report directly to me and are accountable only to me, personally. I need your sincere, verbal promise and understanding."

"What do I need to do?"

She plants herself in front of him, intruding on his personal space. "You are now officially my highest-ranked Agent and Number One cyber soldier. Your rank and title extend throughout the entire Agency. Within my organization, you may treat anyone, including your former boss, as assets. You also bear the responsibility for the consequences of doing so. If you delegate a task to someone, and they fail, it is your fault. If your orders cause them to fail to complete another task, the fault is yours. It is your fault if you share information with another, and they compromise it. Do you understand?"

He nods, "Yes, I understand. I will use care and judgment in asking others for support but will use them as needed."

"I ask you to swear to carry out such duties as I assign without fail."

He appears puzzled but responds, "Although not told what my duties may be, I swear I will give my all to carry out whatever duties you may assign."

"Now, here's the kicker, and think carefully before agreeing to this. You no longer work for the Agency when you leave this office. Technically you do, as the Agency still pays your salary, and Agency resources will be available. Still, in a sense, I am embezzling you from the Agency for my purpose. Your work, your projects, and your loyalties belong to me personally. Whatever work you have done for the Agency, whatever remains unfinished, is now someone else's concern. Unfinished work falls to your former boss, and I will so inform him. You work for me and me alone, in whatever capacity I assign. Is that clear?"

He freezes, eyes narrowing; a somber tone overtakes his voice. "If... If I agree, you can require me to paint your apartment or clean your bathroom?"

She nods almost imperceptibly as he strives to read the evasive social cues, parsing her words for hidden meaning. He finds the subtle language of facial expression and body language challenging, although he has learned to focus well enough to usually wrestle order from the chaos. As he struggles, a fluffy smile tugs at the corners of her mouth, and his fear melts. Face splitting into a wide grin, he adds, "Well, que sera sera. I have never been the 'not my job' sort. I accept that from this point forward, my talent, my abilities, and my talents are dedicated to you alone until such time as we may mutually agree to cancel the agreement or until one of us is deceased."

Her eyes widen at his words.

He continues, "I would beg the proviso that the agreement is terminated and not assignable upon death. My allegiance is not a property that may be passed in a will or estate or used to pay off a debt. I am a willing volunteer soldier serving you alone until my services are no longer wanted or needed."

Her face shows surprise. "That you add the proviso suggests you fully understand the agreement and mean it. This proves you are the 'One.' Proviso accepted."

He beams at her belated acknowledgement of his nerdy cyberpunk humor. His cape flutters.

Her eyes twinkle as with a sly smile, she adds, "Til death do us part."

"Ha!" His guffaw breaks the solemn mood. "I feel like I should buy a ring."

# Chapter Eleven

# Hell

*While rare, some have exceptional abilities far above the norm. We don't know the causes, and although there are theories, no single explanation addresses all cases. Estimates are that 10% of autistics have a degree of exceptional abilities. Some start demonstrating their capabilities in early childhood, while others acquire them, even as adults.*

"**S**O, WHERE IS SHE?"

"IRL or online?" comes the surly response. Apprentice is insolent today. Ritz and the kid have been circling one another for days, not unlike dogs sniffing each other.

"Both, I guess—she wasn't at work."

The youngster leans back from his desk, stretches as he tenderly strokes the gray feline curled in his lap. The cat briefly opens one eye to acknowledge the gentle touch. Feline and teenager—two solitary and territorial animals, neither especially well domesticated.

He still wears the dirty Tee and cutoffs he had over a week ago when they first met. Ritz resolves to influence the kid, to guide him gently. This nerdy kid needs a switched-on mentor. Someone to teach him not only ways of the cyber but also the art of dressing — bathing too.

"IRL, I haven't a clue, prolly at another of her homes. Otherwise, she's in the Hell forum. Or was—we're catphishing."

"I see. So, Director doesn't exclusively live here? I thought she did. Who are you trying to hook?" Looking over the kid's shoulder, Ritz notes he has been creating and fielding leet identities on the dark web social site. Working with two others, they have been trying to engage the lieutenants of 7R1LBy {Trilby}.

He shakes his head, non-verbally dismissing the first question. He adds, "We baited 80w132 {Bowler} and p02kp13 {Pork Pie}, but they ignored us. Dunno how we're tipping our hand. Last I knew, she was still at it, but I jumped out a while ago and started developing a new profile without reusing any old bits. A total fresh start. Check this one out."

Ritz leans over the desk and examines the credentials and avatar Twit has assembled. "Sweet avatar. Steal it from The Verge?"

"Nah, Gizmodo. The waist-length flaming red hair is my idea. Sexy, doncha think? I tweaked the face and figure and traded the pink crayolia for the bitchin' leather. No resemblance to the original image. Almost. Was debating adding some tats and piercings, but boss-lady is not into that sort of thing."

"Not even a tramp-stamp?"

Twit shakes his head, his expression reflecting disdain. Evidentially he is not into that sort of thing either.

Ritz said, "She doesn't have red hair, either."

Twit shrugs. "Professor has any hair she wants. Tats and piercings, too, if the mission demands."

"You may be right."

"I am, trust me. I've known her longer than you."

It is Ritz's turn to shrug.

"You sure she shouldn't have a tat or two?"

The youngster waves a hand at the image. "Going for a low-key Wiccan theme. Keep it simple; simple is sexy. She likes to dress up and role-play; she doesn't like tats. Plus, she's too old for tats."

Ritz's expression turns thoughtful. "Interesting," he muses. He is silent for a moment. "Hey, Twit, what's your real name?"

"Why?" he asked, suspicion rising. "We don't use IRL names in the dojo."

"You know mine; I wanna know yours. I promise not to use it. I want to know."

Twit studies Ritz with suspicion. Seconds pass in awkward silence before the younger man gives in. Finally, he relents. "Milner, IRL—*Milner Fitzroy Stone*—Don't you dare repeat it! In the system, they called me *Millie*. Later, in high school, I became *Mill Stone*. I hate both nicknames!

"Everyone calls me Twit! You call me anything else, and I'll start calling you Rithwick." He pronounces the hated name with an equally hated fake Hindi accent. Twit continues, "I would promise you a punch in the nose," waving a fist, "but you're too damn big."

Ritz boggles momentarily at the unlikely name, as unlikely as his own. Then, he laughs.

"Truce! Truce," he says, laughing. "I promise I won't use Milner, Millie, or whatever if you promise never, and I mean never to call me 'Rithwick.' Ritz is not bad as a nickname, short and masculine, but Rithwick sounds effeminate, especially when you say it like that. Seriously, though, a world awaits out there, away from computers, Twit. So, you may want to cultivate your IRL identity and let some people meet you." Grinning, he adds, "You could use 'Fitz,' it's short and macho, like 'Ritz,' only not as virile."

Twit shrugs without comment.

A few seconds pass as Twit manipulates the image on his screen. Then, pointing at the spectacular avatar, Ritz asks, "Have you given her a leet handle yet?"

"Tried out a couple. Does boss-lady look like an 47h3n4 {Athena} to you?" He spells out the leetspeak numbers and letters.

"Athena! The Greek Goddess of War! Perfect! I like it."

"You know, she sometimes uses Greek goddess names with her secret friends."

"Huh? Secret friends?"

Twit becomes exasperated. "You know..."

"I do not know. Director has not seen fit to tell me anything yet."

Twit sighs. "The secret meetings, C-names, the Order," he whispers.

He asks in a normal voice, "What is the Order?"

"Shhhh," he shushes. "Be quiet! Please.... don't say it. Never use that word."

Ritz throws up his hands, exasperated. "What are you saying? No one told me. Will you get into trouble for telling me? I don't get this C-name stuff. Leet names I get, sort-of, but C-names? How are they assigned? Who oversees them? Is there a rank? Who are these secret friends?"

Twit shrugs — doesn't answer — then repeats himself with a grimace.

After long moments of non-response, Ritz tables his questions for another time. Finally, he continues, "Don't change a thing. Going catphishing now?"

"Yeah. Try this out and see which wolf whistles. She's different from any bait I tried before."

"You do know they will think IRL she is a fat middle-aged nerdy dude sitting around in his underwear. No one will believe there's someone built like that behind the avatar."

"Or worse, prolly NIFOC, yet another media-driven nerd-trope. They may doubt, but they'll bite. It's not for nothing I made the image as seductive as fire. They may doubt, but they'll bite out of pure lizard-brain curiosity. She'll seduce them by telepathy."

Responding to Ritz's raised eyebrow, the kid continues, "I mean it! She has magical powers. You must have noticed."

Now it is Ritz's turn to shrug.

The kid rolls his eyes before continuing, "If Professor decides to meet them IRL, the avatar will match if she wants. They will pow in their pants."

Ritz laughs. "She does have a capital-P personality."

Twit smiles. "You might call it that! Seductive and deadly like a cobra."

After a few seconds, Twit asks, "Want to join me in Hell and salt the space a little?"

"Okatoe. I'll chat you. Maybe we can raise the heat."

He is hovering over the youngster's desk. After a moment, the juvenile points an eyebrow at the other desk. "In the Matrix..."

"Grok that." He settles into the second Air Chair. He takes a moment to admire the massive eight-monitor setup—significantly more impressive than his massive workstation at the Agency. Naturally, he is envious and wishes he owned such a system. But, despite, or perhaps because of, his dark-web alter-ego, he makes do with an inconspicuous clamshell—primarily for safety. Such a colossal system would draw attention, and would not be portable.

Moreover, in this age of crypto-crackdowns and cyber terrorism, such high-powered systems fall under the rubric of munitions. As such, they can draw assault-weapon-style scrutiny. As a highly-skilled Hat, he could create chaos with almost any system. Any system is merely a tool; the danger rests with the mind wielding it.

Another reason to set up a secret dojo, he muses—no reason to keep suspicion-inducing hardware in his tiny apartment. Moving the locus of his clandestine activities away from where he sleeps is also a compelling motive.

With a sigh, he assaults the keys. For a while, the only sound is the furious clacking of gamer keyboards, punctuated by an occasional grunt. Occasionally a giggle flies up, but otherwise, loud, raucous key-clatter reigns.

This is the true nature of cyberspace—mind-numbingly boring. Boring to see, tedious to hear. Romantic portrayals of cyber criminals ignore the mundane, rote aspects of the work. Policymakers and LE often issue aggrandizing press releases couching cybercrime investigations as targeting sophisticated cyber rockstars, making cybercrime appear lucrative and exciting when for those involved, cybercrime is no more glamorous than any other monotonous office job. This is why TV never shows the real action. There is no action.

Instead, TV writers invent silly animated avatars, like Pacman, wending their way through a 3D maze meant to represent a firewall or other defenses. Instead of chasing ghosts and power pills, they leave skulls and crossbones images. The leet crowd chuckles at how silly it is as the techtarded devour it. The false media's ridiculousness makes the leet audience giggle; genuine cyberspace is boring.

The participants are engrossed in the virtual world, absorbed in what's going on in their minds, cyberspace, and the deep web hangout called Hell. Hours pass—the colorful avatar and leetspeak peppered conversation designed to attract their prey. They are so focused they do not hear the door open and close but subconsciously recognize an observer has joined them. She settles on the couch and pays rapt attention to the non-activity—she sits quietly, waiting for a break in the non-action to explore what's happening.

Several times Twit interrupts the action to ask Ritz to explain a trick or dodge he has used. At first, grudgingly, then with growing awe, Twit begins to understand the depth of skill and knowledge which distinguishes a professional White Hat—this White Hat in particular— from the ordinary Fascination.

At last, Ritz lets loose a long, loud "Wheeee!" Glancing at their silent companion, he winks and, in a slightly more subdued tone, adds, "You hooked him, now reel him in."

Moments later, the Apprentice pushes back from his desk, shaking his hands as though restoring the circulation—every computist is well acquainted with the tingly hands of excessive qwerty tugging.

"Done!" he exclaims. "We meet IRL at The HashTag. I think his toes curled when I told him to watch for the avatar. Said he'd be wearing a gray fedora with a red feather in the band."

He glances at the quiet observer and becomes addled. "Um, Hiya Professor. I think we, um, hooked a live one. His handle is kr4k3n {Kraken}. Want to reel him in?"

"Hell, I presume?"

He nods. "Yeah. I made a new handle and avatar, and we double-teamed on 7R1LBy's new Lieut. He would not have bitten, except we double-teamed and played him. Between the two of us, we sucked him in." He points to Ritz, "This one is quite the Sensei; played him like a violin. All I had to do was set the bait, hold the sack, and whisper, 'here, snipe.' Now we go cozy up to him IRL and land him."

"I suppose you have a plan to do that. ..."

"Uh well, you see, Professor. ... I kinda made this sexy, um, avatar, and uh, played it up. So he helped, and well, the um mark is expecting her."

"Let me guess. ... Impossible ratio waist to hips to bust size, cartoonishly large head, tiny ankles. Am I right?"

Ritz sits silent, his eyes intense as he studies their terse reciprocity. He puzzles at their relationship. She acts cold, indifferent—he appears disrespectful, resentful—an undercurrent of ironic respect too.

Love? A reach too far, he decides. He wonders if they're biologically related, a possibility he rejected that first night. He'd surmised fellow travelers in cyberspace, yet their coarse interplay hints at more. Perhaps not blood, but indeed history. He tries to imagine what events might have conjoined this strange pair.

Twit squirms under her gaze and gulps. "Uh, you um see, well, kinda. With long, um, red hair. But it worked!"

"So, Barbie's titian-haired today! I saw the avatar and thought it looked like your handiwork. I've seen the porn you like." His mouth opens and closes in a wordless response, but she continues without pausing. "When I saw you had his attention, I left the cantina and came here. I'm guessing you want me to play 47h3n4 IRL and seduce this flunky. Do you have a plan for what to do once we have him?"

"Um, well..."

"What I thought! So what do we do? Do we kidnap him and torture him for information? How far do we go? Do we kneecap him?"

"Uh, I haven't prepared a, um, strategy."

She lays a hand on his shoulder and speaks softly, showing a warmth Ritz has not seen before. "Think of our Chess games and the nature of strategy. It is not enough to pull off a brilliant move. You must plan and anticipate your opponent's reaction." He touches her hand and smiles. He speaks not a word, though his body language is eloquent.

Ritz's face is a study in amazement. One moment she mothers him, another, she treats him like a menial, and still another, she acts cold, almost contemptuous. He realizes respect and admiration are rare, but they do shine through. In those precious moments, the kid turns into a wiggle-butt puppy. Ritz realizes with a start that the kid worships her, but she is either oblivious or indifferent. She is cold to him, challenged to communicate so much as a modicum of human warmth. At least not in the presence of another.

Finally, Ritz inserts himself into the conversation. "A snatch and squeeze won't net us anything. This is a valuable opportunity; one we can't waste. We must go for the long con, but a long con will require scrambling. We will have to build a foundation quickly; we must craft a build-up, and we need a Convincer."

She sighs. "Fortunately, I have been planning since before we started catphishing. So, what do 7R1LBy's people want? What currency can we offer to draw the mark into our con?"

The youngster asks, "Access?"

Ritz responds, "What access can we offer them? Access to what? Or who?"

She is silent for several moments. "The Agency is their target. It is the one thing we still control which they want. Mostly, anyway."

Ritz asks, "You say they've already penetrated the Agency?"

She nods. "Yes, on multiple levels. Low-level stuff, but serious enough. So, let's offer them a new level of access as the Convincer."

"Like what? What do they not already have that we can offer? And what happens if we get caught? I like fresh air and sunshine."

"You," she answers. Surprise plays across his face. She continues, "The former you, I mean. More specifically, access to White Hat tools and data. We honeypot your former position and give it to him."

"You're proposing to hand out tools and encryption certificates for the Agency network? That's a significant breach. I believe I mentioned I like fresh air..."

"I don't think it's necessary; I'm sure they already have them. We will offer credentials for a single, high-value Cyber Warrior account, along with the tools and exploits of a White Hat. Or rather, a sanitized version of one, a honeypot. Plus, if they bite and use their previously stolen encryption certificates, we can identify the compromised certs and invalidate them, blocking future access. The exploits we give them will, of course, be old ones of trivial value, vulnerabilities already fixed and useless, such as the Heartbleed tools or the Neurotic Kitten exploits."

"Do we let Boss in on the game?"

"Absolutely not! We've no idea whom they have compromised."

"Boss is a fink?"

"No, heavens no, of course not!" she answered emphatically. "Rufus is family, I trust him implicitly, but we must tell no one in the Agency. Someone has, or, more likely, several someones have turned quisling and betrayed the Agency. We must find the Brutus and anyone they have seduced and deal with them."

He is disturbed by this answer. He has come to accept the Agency is penetrated and trusts Director's extracurricular work to unmask the traitors. Yet the prospect of risking sensitive information via unsanctioned pursuits troubles him. Even though it is a sanitized honeypot, the idea makes him nervous. Nevertheless, he reminds himself Director is his boss, and this task is no different than any other she might assign.

"You two get busy backstopping the identity for the approach while I get dressed for my date at The HashTag. We don't have a lot of time."

She leans over Twit's shoulder and studies the avatar. She turns it and examines it from different angles. "She needs some tats, I think. Fiercely Wiccan!" She quickly adds a pentagram encircled by a crescent moon to one wrist, a triquetra to the other, and a dragon on her exposed back with a clawed, three-toed foot reaching up the neck. "Give her those." Without further discussion, she disappears into a back room, leaving their mouths agape, eyes swinging alternately in her direction and at each other.

"Uh, all right, Sensei, you create a sanitized honeypot for Professor to play in while I polish the IRL 47h3n4 identity."

"I can't believe she's good with this."

"Toldja; she likes to play dress-up. She became Trixie Bang Tail instead of calling in the cavalry. She's an exhibitionist who likes to role-play and will use any excuse to indulge; she might have stalled until we could get people there, or she could have called the cops. Instead, she chooses to risk everything to role-play a hooker in her underwear. Or minus."

"Hmm," he muses. He believes there are flaws in the kid's analysis but refuses to think about it right now. Pushing aside his misgivings, he tackles the immediate task. Silence again falls save for the frumious dueling of gaming keyboards.

They are still furiously clattering hours later when she returns. They are oblivious until she clears her throat rather loudly.

"Well? Will this do?" She appears nothing like the button-down Brooks Brothers-clad executive. Instead, she matches the avatar right down to the tats.

"Uh, um," answers the youngster, wide-eyed and speechless.

She stands taller, leaner, with unrealistic, impossible curves. The burgeoning curvaceousness beneath the too-tight classic V-Zip leather vest captivates the eye, as does the ultra-short, skin-tight leather micro-skirt.

Ritz is uncharacteristically eloquent. "When a woman wears a leather dress like that, a man's heart beats quicker, his throat gets dry, he gets weak in the knees, and he thinks irrationally. He reacts this way because, with all that leather, she smells like a new truck."

She breaks her pose to laugh, at which point Twit joins in. After their laughter subsides, Ritz adds, "If the mark is male, the only access he will think about is biological, not tech. Scratch the 'if male' part—I highly doubt the appeal is so limited. Impressive."

Ritz's observation is not wrong. The capstone to the illusion is the luxurious waist-length titian barnet. Did she dye her coal-black hair to that shade, or is it a wig? He realizes her coiffure must be artificial; nevertheless, he cannot spot the slightest tell. The result is an unfettered male fantasy abandoned by reason. Yes, she should hook any quarry—human or otherwise.

# Chapter Twelve

---

# Hashtag

*Many can function normally in life, drive a car, get married & even pursue managerial careers. However, that they can cope does not mean their challenges are minor. They can experience crippling anxiety and paralyzing sensory overload that renders them unable to follow through on even simple tasks.*

S HE TURNS TO HER Apprentice. "I want you to go in and scout the field for us. Especially watch for Assbook luminaries." She fiddles with his phone, carefully positioning it in his shirt pocket with the camera peeking out. "Your phone is on live-feed, so we can see too."

"Yes, Professor, on it." He nods, fiddles with his phone for a moment, pokes his BluePod several times before exiting the vehicle.

He asks, "You're not trusting our contact to be legit, I presume."

She replies, "Not likely. They may have been catphishing us as readily. However, I'm taking no chances. After Twit verifies none of the identified C'thulhu are present, I want you to take a turn looking for anyone else from that night at the *The Irish Counting-House*. I will not risk myself until you both have cleared the field." His eyebrows lift at her statement—he is not facile with faces—but he says nothing.

They lean over the screen, watching Twit's bouncing, nausea-inducing video feed. They are looking for anyone suspicious, as well as their quarry. Ball caps and hoodies are ubiquitous; fedoras, with or without a feather, not so much. The fedora is old-school haberdashery. The *HashTag* caters to a younger, punker crowd.

"We're early," she whispers. Ritz nods in silent agreement.

It's a busy night in *The HashTag Cyber Cafe and Gaming Emporium*. Despite the damage, or perhaps because of the meteor's publicity, the place is packed. Visibility from the pocket-borne phone camera is erratic. Band-Aids of rope and yellow tape cover the scars of the destroyed cafe seating area, keeping patrons away from the construction zone. With the cafe out of service, the bar picks up the slack, serving fried foods to baked clientele. The gaming arena draws the crowd, and although itself packed, the bar is somewhat less boisterous.

A Fortnite tournament is in progress on the giant screens; it is week two of the World Cup qualifiers. Competing teams occupy the pits, with each avatar's FPS view onscreen. The atmosphere is noisy, and every arena console is taken. Observers line the pit, and the bar reflects the overload, empty seats a rarity.

The crowd is mixed. Reflecting youth's invulnerability, fully half the attendees wear bare faces. *Agent Twit* prowls the floor, repeatedly intruding into some patron's personal space to capture a clear facial image. Finally, he whispers, "I don't see anyone. No one who is a threat."

"Come on back to the van," she says. "Let Ritz take a pass. I don't think our mark is here yet."

"Yes, Professor, on my way."

Ritz adjusts his face mask, positions his phone as the other had done, and pokes his BluePod. With video streaming, he heads into the cafe, passing the youngster on his way out. Like trained undercover spies, neither acknowledges the other.

Taking his turn around the competition floor, he pauses, briefly watching the tournament. Scanning for familiar faces, he wishes he had the time to play—almost salivating as he marvels at the millions of dollars in prizes, the largest ever for an eSports event. He has every right to think of himself as a contender. His hyper-focus gives him an edge, although No-Skins and Bots don't rise to this level.

Clan Echo is in dire straits, outnumbered, and outgunned behind enemy territory. He longs to engage, savoring the challenge of pulling their fat from the fire. He had once considered such competitions vital. Part of him would like to join this one. Since joining the Agency, he has been privileged to play a bigger and more exciting game.

After a couple of minutes, he shakes his head in futility, turns from the arena, and enters the bar. He sits and is about to order something from the barman when he spots a gray fedora with a feather in the band, unaccompanied, sitting on the counter.

Apprehensive, he scans the nearby patrons.

Spotting the target, he changes his mind about drinking.

In shock, he studies the mark for several minutes, observing while avoiding a direct line of sight or eye contact before deciding to retreat. Finally, he moves away from the bar as quickly as possible without attracting attention.

He heads for the door, whispering, "Prepare to abort!"

He exits the cafe, fairly runs to the van, climbs in, and shuts off his phone, motioning to the others to do likewise. "Let's go."

She guns the van, and they hit the street. She takes a few evasive turns while watching the rearview. Twit is looking at every car. Once certain no one follows, she slows and begins a circuitous route in the direction of the Cyber-Dojo.

Noticing how visibly shaken he is, she pulls over, parks, and asks, "Speak! What prompted the panic?"

"Our mark is at the bar, all right. Complete with a gray fedora and a red feather in the hatband. But he is not some dark and mysterious villain. Instead, the mark is someone we both work with. I don't think he recognized me, given my black chin koozie and the dim lighting, but I almost gave us away."

Busily watching the mirrors for any sign of pursuit, he says nothing more for several seconds.

Patience exhausted, she finally asks, "The lighting may be dim, but I don't want to be in the dark. Who is it?"

"Boss! Boss is there. I almost failed to recognize him even without a face mask. He didn't act like Boss."

She gapes at him in shocked disbelief. "Rufus was there? Wearing a gray fedora with a red feather in the band?"

He nods.

"He was acting oddly, somehow different than his normal persona?"

He nods again.

She says nothing. Then, she repeats herself.

After a long moment of strained silence, he speaks. "Sorry, I got rattled. Boss has never impressed me as an operator. I understand he was in the field years ago...

"Bu-but he wasn't wearing the fedora; it sat on the counter, so only those nearby might spot it. He would have seen you long before you spotted him. What rattled me was his manner. Cold, confident, and calculating. I nearly didn't recognize him. Instead of his daily flustered disheveled persona, he was confident, well-dressed, and meticulously groomed. I can't explain it. Like he was not Boss but his James Bond-like evil twin from the mirror universe."

She nods. "Evil twins and mirror universes are science fiction plot devices, but that sounds like the Rufus I know. Any number of reasons might explain his presence here, including an interest in the tournament. Dressing nicely isn't a crime, nor is wearing a fedora, though perhaps it should be. Nonetheless ..."

He interrupts her rambling with a soft cough. "One more thing." She stares straight into his eyes, waiting for him to continue. "I spotted a bulge in his jacket," he said.

She cocks an eyebrow.

He quickly adds, "I mean, he was armed, and he wasn't trying to be subtle about it."

"Rufus likes to carry a dangerous antique. Did you spot anyone watching him?"

"Not that I could see. Why?"

"Perhaps we go for a snatch and squeeze."

"Did you hear the part where I said he was armed?"

She grimaces without speaking. Moments pass in silence.

"Might you be mistaken? Could the bulge be something else?"

He shrugs. "It was too obvious like he meant it to be spotted. Of course, it might have been something else, but the distinctive shape and the shoulder holster strap convinced me. The weapon is not a petite lady-gun."

She asks, "Can we grab him before he can pull it?"

"What happened to the long con? Did the fact that the mark turned out to be Boss upset your plans?"

"Of course! Rufus knows us both. Anything we try will give away the game. He cannot suspect his target works for the Agency."

Her pent-up exasperation explodes. "This is impossible!" she states flatly. "I have known Rufus since he was in, er, for a long time, know him well. He is family! There is no way he is our quarry. No possible way! There must be another explanation."

Ritz replies, "Maybe, but he is here; he was in Hell; he answered our phish and has the fedora. So, we must assume the worst and play it out."

She sits in silence, her hands unable to find a place to rest as she wrestles with possible choices, possible reasons for Rufus to have crashed their plans.

Finally, Ritz breaks her introspection by asking, "Does he know Twit?"

Wide-eyed, she gazes at the young man, biting her lip in thought. Would he remember? The kid has grown a lot, and Rufus has stayed distant, given the circumstances. She decides to gamble.

"Twit," she begins, pausing a moment before continuing. "How do you feel about approaching the mark?"

Blank look! His mouth opens and closes as though dumbstruck. His mind went from brilliant to BSOD. Finally, he manages to squeak one word. "Huh?"

He gulps a couple of times. "Wha-what do you want me to do?"

She checks the time on her phone. "Glad we came early. We still have some time. Here's how it is going to work." In hushed and hurried tones, she briefs the youngster on his re-imagined role.

Minutes later, streaming as before, Twit returns to the bar.

"C-Cool fedora," he stutters. The mark turns and studies him for a moment before responding.

"Not mine," comes the response. "It was there when I sat down. I presume the owner will be back for it."

"Th-the red feather sets it off. Too bad it's not yours; it would be stylish on you. My friend," he nods vaguely in the direction of the door, "likes it."

"Tell your friend to come and join us. If no one claims it, he can have it."

"Nah, it wouldn't be quite the same on her."

"Ah. Perhaps much better. Where is your friend?"

He waves expansively. "I dunno, over there somewhere. Prolly went to watch the tournament. You can't miss her long red hair."

Wordlessly, he picks up the fedora and tucks a tiny device into the hatband. The mark eyes him but says nothing. He returns the headgear to the same spot on the counter, adjusting the position meticulously.

"Uh, a small present for our uh, mysterious uh hat." The mark cocks an eyebrow as the youngster takes a deep breath and continues in a calmer, steadier voice. "A small cryptographic puzzle. Perhaps our absent friend will find it amusing."

There is a quiet click. A rather ugly piece of hardware is in the mark's hand, stubby nose pointing at the youngster's belly button. The Fitz Special is not amused.

Without a hint of humor, Rufus asks, "What mask do you wear on the dark web?"

After a near freeze, the youngster stares blankly before rallying to reply, "A Netmask!" He suspects his life may have depended on the response. Fortunately, despite the shock and fear of the moment, he remembers their earlier online exchanges.

Rufus asks, "Who are you?"

"Wha-wha-why the gun? I-I-I'm unarmed, no threat." The young man is pale and shaking, nearly passing out from fear.

Outside in the van, Director is gripping her companion's arm so fiercely as to induce intense pain. However, he does not register the pain, as he, too, is focused. He moves to exit the van to intervene.

"Ain't nobody safe on the battlefield," she mutters, restraining him. "Let it play out. He's got this." She lowers her voice to a whisper, "Don't lose your cool, son. It's only Rufus. You've got this. Make Nana proud."

Ritz boggles briefly at her odd use of 'son' and 'Nana,' as though the kid were her progeny. Shaking his head slightly and discarding the question, Ritz concludes Director is not old enough to have a grandson, and he has seen no evidence that she has any children. He tries to figure out how old such a hypothetical offspring might be, deciding Twit is close enough to the right age. If Twit is her son, why wouldn't she have said so? He discards the thought entirely.

Inside the bar, one hand holds the .38 steady, and the other picks up the fedora. Instead of placing it on his head, he puts it over the gun. "Maybe, but where are your friends? Where's the other? Let's wander outside and grab some fresh air, shall we?" The two exit the bar. The youngster is calmer and more in control by the time the two reach the parking lot. The gun is not in sight.

"I'm Dun53l," using the online handle he'd used when cat-phishing, with Ritz playing 47h3n4. He speaks slow and measured. "I came ahead to give you the hash fingerprints of the merchandise she is offering, a collection of tools and certificates collectively referred to as *Crypt 21*. Vet them, and 47h3n4 will complete the deal."

"How do I confirm their validity?"

"Up to you. You said you had contacts. Use them."

The mark grunts. "You might be a bit confused, but I will take this anyway. Tell 47h3n4 to meet me in Hell." The weapon is again in his hand. "Turn around and lean into the wall and meditate while I vacate. I'm a crack shot, so don't move too soon!"

Please check out the Nathan Gregory Amazon **Author Central** page.

https://amazon.com/Nathan-Gregory /e/B00QZHIIBK

*Check out Amazon's Author Central for my other books, both fiction and non-fiction. Undercover Alien is a prequel for the 'Chromosome Adventures' books. If you enjoy this story, check out the continuing adventures of the characters in Chromosome Quest, Chromosome Conspiracy, and Chromosome Warrior.*

# Chapter Thirteen

# Non-Offensive Conspiracy

*The neurodiverse often struggle to place themselves in another person's position and experience challenges interpreting others' nonverbal cues and facial expressions.*

RITZ IS COAXING THE Jura into crafting a brew of extraordinary amalgamation when Boss appears. His bungling, peter-pinnacled persona is once again driving, albeit somewhat subdued today.

"Hiya, Ritz. Do you have a few minutes for a private confab?"

Ritz nods, tilting an eyebrow in question. He offers the carafe of fresh brew.

Boss responds by raising his empty mug. "Make with the jitter juice, my friend," he begs cartoonishly. Again sober, he adds,

"I stumbled into something on which I'd like your opinion. Something private."

"Sure thing," Ritz replies while pouring. "Is this related to a case? Or something a bit more, ah, sensitive, perhaps personal?"

"Highly sensitive," comes the reply. The man's voice is subdued and soft, unlike his wonted booming expansiveness. "But not specifically case-related. Nor personal either—it could be explosive if it leads where I think. I stumbled into it last night and am unsure what sort of skullduggery I've fallen upon. I need another perspective."

"Might I suggest we take it elsewhere?" He rolls his eyes in pantomime as though to impart a more expansive meaning than words alone might carry.

Puzzlement flits across the older man's face, he appears surprised, but he nods. "Perhaps that would be wise," he agrees. "Let's go to the park and take a walk. It's a beautiful day."

Ritz agrees and adds, "Let's discuss it. If we decide it belongs under an Agency seal, we'll schedule a SCIF."

"Perfect. Shall we go now?"

Reaching for his BBP, he answers, "I need to make a quick call first. Let's meet at the park in a half-hour, alright?"

"See you there."

Boss executes an abrupt whirl and bounds out of the break-room with surprising alacrity. Ritz's eyes widen with mild surprise, unaccustomed to seeing the man move energetically. Although he emits every sign of sloth, the man can move fast, and he appears trimmer and more confident than Ritz had previously believed.

He stares at the empty doorway a moment, then, with a slight shake of his head, turns his attention to the BBP.

First, a text, "Secure call?"

A moment later, "K."

He taps the screen furiously, invoking his particular brand of arcane encryption magic. He is confident no one will eavesdrop, including the Agency. Especially not the Agency. He configured the encryption curves himself, and this is his field.

Hitting the speed dial, the other party answers on the first ring. He speaks scarcely above a whisper, lest his voice carry.

"Guess who I had an interesting conversation with. Yeah, waltzed right in and asked for my help with some big secret."

"No, I diverted him off-site. Not taking any chances on the walls having ears."

"I will handle him, don't worry. Heading out now. Will I see you this evening?"

"Terrific. I'll brief you later."

"Right. Got it."

The call ends: He taps furiously for a couple of seconds, and his BBP is once again a standard Agency-issue secure phone. The non-standard app and encryption comprise the only hint of unofficial capabilities.

He takes a deep breath and places his hands on his hips. His cape floats high behind him as though driven by a gust of wind.

An unremarkable exit dance with Security; minutes later, he is walking toward the park. He would happily walk or run the entire distance, though it is a few blocks. He can often make better time afoot than a vehicle in congested city traffic and doesn't mind the exercise. Despite this, he opts for a ride though he is a touch apprehensive—not surprising, given recent experience. He is about to launch the officially-blessed rideshare App when he spots Boss at the curb, approaching a limousine. Boss has a more luxurious bent.

He shouts, "Hey, share a ride?"

"Perfect timing," Boss responds affably, "Climb aboard."

The ride to the park passes in fractured silence interrupted with small talk. Ritz is silent, save the occasional grunt. Boss chatters about a TV show. Something about a robot cyber-criminal and a cybersecurity engineer with plans for anarchy: this may not be entirely correct, but it is what Ritz understood. When Boss describes the robot as the protagonist's father, Ritz emits a small groan. He is thankful their destination is at hand. Willing suspension of disbelief is one thing, but. ...

He realizes Boss is comparing the cyberpunk adventure to the matter he wishes to discuss. Unfamiliar with the show, Ritz senses he has missed a crucial element.

Debarking the limo, they head into the park. Though far from unpopulated, the mid-afternoon timing means the uncrowded park is ideal. Within moments, they are sufficiently alone to converse without undue concern for eavesdroppers.

"So, what's the deal?"

"As I explained, I got interested in your class of modern-day cyber-criminals because of the TV show. Espionage has changed since my days as a field agent. My tradecraft is old-school, not all digital and computers like your world, but still espionage, mind you, and much is the same." He shrugs as though expressing the self-evident nature of his words.

Boss continues, "Technology, especially the dark web, has brought new elements to the craft, but one thing remains the same. Humans. I set up a dark web identity and started trolling around the forums for a lark. I was merely having some fun until I started noticing things."

"What sorts of things?"

"Well, people, I mean."

"People?"

"Yes, what I mean is, I realized despite the assumed mask of anonymity, privacy is largely nonexistent. I recognized someone."

"How's that?"

"These days, with leet handles and digital identities, we forget real people, real humans, are behind the avatars. We fingerprint our every move, with every word and gesture--everyone uses words and phrases unique to them. This technique is forensically valuable, often used to identify the authors of historical manuscripts, for example. Have you read about the controversy concerning the real identity of Shakespeare? How various scholars now attribute various works of William Shakespeare to Francis Bacon and Edward De Vere?"

Ritz raises an eyebrow. He is unaware of the supposed controversy—he takes no interest in conspiracy theories. Such things are not within his wheelhouse. Besides, he hasn't the time between his White Hat responsibilities and extracurricular pursuits. The idea Shakespeare wasn't Shakespeare sounds ridiculous. He mulls the concept for a moment before discarding it.

Boss continues, "Shakespeare himself may have been a semi-literate actor paid to mask the true authors. Some claim to identify the real genius via such techniques. As a field agent, I learned to spot and note such subtle tells, to use these techniques to uncover spies and moles."

Ritz has donned his trademarked blank stare. His cape clings protectively around his body.

Boss continues without noticing. "There was this character who used the leet handle kr4k3n, trying to procure suspicious digital items. She used an expression in the chats I have heard only one person use in everyday speech. Cripes."

Ritz raises his eyebrows in surprise. "Cripes?" The expression is familiar, but for the moment, he cannot say from where. He carefully reasserts his blank stare.

"Yes, cripes—as in a mild curse word used by someone who would not blaspheme by saying 'Christ' instead. Non-offensive swears—which I find amusing. Like non-alcoholic beer or decaffeinated coffee. What is the point of swearing if you're not willing to piss off someone, especially a deity? So how can you insult someone, much less a god, with a non-offensive swear?"

Boss laughs, adding, "Genteel folk use a sophisticated style of cursing that befuddles and amuses we coarser souls."

"I see," Ritz muses, choosing his words carefully. "So, you spotted someone you believe you can identify because they used a non-offensive swear word? Lots of people express creativity in their swearing, avoiding traditional Anglo-Saxon monosyllables. Isn't this awfully circumstantial?"

"It is, of course. Once I keyed on the expression, I began noticing others. Not limited to Cripes, but Crikey, Flickin', and several more. The formal term for the technique is stylometry. Using word choice, sentence structure, and idioms to identify someone is archaic but effective. The words and phrases used in the chat match closely those of someone I know. Someone YOU know."

Ritz's blank stare flickers and nearly extinguishes. He carefully nurses it back to life.

Boss continues, "The more I lurked, the more confident I became, but it is not merely the person's possible identity behind the avatar. I mean, who am I to care if an employee spends her spare time hanging around dark web forums? The proposition of trading in digital munitions is what raised my hackles. Until I put that together, I was merely having a bit of amusement observing the players."

Ritz hauls out his best, heavy-duty, most practiced blank expression. "True; we must investigate anything that is a potential security threat. Is that all? Or is there more?"

"Oh, I have more, a lot more. As I said, this kr4k3n was looking to trade in sensitive goods, and others were sniffing around—two in particular, but kr4k3n blew them off and left the forum. So I played a prank on them. I pretended to be kr4k3n and arranged a meet. Fooled em easier than I imagined possible! Talk about dorkus erectus; what a pair of dime-store Zorros!"

Reaching into an inside pocket, Boss pulls a print photo and hands it to Ritz. Although badly exposed and askew, apparently taken from a hidden camera, the face was recognizable.

Ritz struggles to keep his face passive and manner mildly curious. "So, did you meet them? What happened?"

"They showed alright. That one did, anyway. I'm not sure if both were there or not. Bought the whole sham too. Gave me this." Boss produces Twit's digital storage device that, as Dunsel, he had tucked into the fedora. "It is proof that the enemy has a collection of digital munitions. Or so he claimed. Sensitive property of the Agency that, if verified, would convict these traitors. That is the part where I need your help. These are the tools and weapons you use every day. You should be able to verify the claim."

Ritz asks, "You refer to this person, kr4k3n, as female. Who do you think she is?"

"I'm surprised you haven't figured that out. Given that you and she were quite close a few months back."

Surprised, caught off-guard, his face contorts into a caricature of his tactical forced passivity. The wonted blank stare has fallen away, forgotten. His cape shrivels and hides.

Boss chuckles at his expression as realization dawns. Priceless.

Ritz fairly sputters as he responds, "Y-You think kr4k3n is Sprocket! Are you kidding? She acts a bit short on intellectual firepower to be a mastermind, doesn't she?"

Boss smiles and slaps him on the shoulder. "Does she now? Or does she merely understand the value of being underestimated? You may have slept with her, but I've managed her for years. Trust me, she's more capable than she pretends. She may or may not be a mastermind—she may be the driver or a sockpuppet. I am unsure how deep this goes, but I do not doubt that she has not shown all her cards."

Ritz cringes at Boss' abuse of the old USENET term when he means meatpuppet, but he does not point out the distinction. His restraint is heroic. He deflects by pretending to examine the photo and shrugs, implying he doesn't recognize the subject. Not a facile liar; he doesn't trust himself to speak.

Unaware of his inner struggle, Boss hands him the device. "Check this out and tell me what you find. I am supposed to meet these jokers to complete the deal. I plan to take them down the next time they show."

Reasserting his feigned passivity, Ritz returns the photo and responds, "Alright, let me see if I understand this. So, you went trolling around a dark web forum for fun? While there, you spotted some inhabitants talking about cyber-munitions."

Boss nods and adds, "The other two used the handles dun53l and 47h3n4. Athena had quite the avatar and claimed to match it in real life too. Unlikely! I never spotted her, though. Only Dunsel—just a punk kid. I almost felt sorry for him. I'd bet this Athena is another punk kid. The avatar was the work of an adolescent mind. No way was that pimple-faced kid I met hanging around with a *femme fatale* like that. Athena is probably another punk kid."

"So Dunsel and Athena were looking to sell cyber-munitions to Kraken?"

Boss nods again.

"But Kr4k3n wasn't interested and blew them off."

Boss nods once again.

"And you believe kr4k3n is Sprocket."

Boss bobs his head once more.

"Do you have any clue who Dunsel and Athena are?"

Boss shook his head and replied, "No, but we will use Kraken to draw them out. We will get them, trust me."

"They were bold enough to carry on this exchange in an open forum where anyone might see, rather than use private messaging?"

"As I say, Kraken wasn't taking their overtures seriously. She was buying, but not from them. They went to private messaging, where I pretended to be Kraken and picked up the conversation; they were so oblivious they didn't realize I wasn't the same player. When 'Kraken' engaged them that they took the bait and fell for it like a ton of titanium. No wonder she brushed them off." He laughs, "What a pair of dorks!"

Ritz is aflame but keeps his face placid, thanks to his well-practiced blank stare. "Flock of Black Ducks!" he thinks. "How did Twit and I completely miss a change of player? Leet operators! Ha! How will we live this down? Director will be thoroughly bashed."

He fumes, hoping Boss doesn't spot the steam coming from his ears. Aloud he says, "Sounds like an inept crew. Weren't you concerned about meeting them alone, IRL?"

Boss' eyebrows waggle. Ritz translates, "In Real Life."

Boss drops eye contact momentarily in acknowledgment. Leetspeak is not his vocabulary. "Of course, I took precautions; I came prepared, armed, and ready. In hindsight, it was unnecessary against the kid, but I was glad I carried a weapon at the time."

Turning the device in his hand, Ritz asks, "So what do you think this is?"

"Ya got me," he shrugs. "Dunsel claimed it is a 'cryptographic puzzle' meant to amuse Kraken. I presume it is proof of the cyber-munitions they were peddling. I will leave the analysis to you; it's your wheelhouse. Tell me what it is, and I will lay a trap, and the Agency will arrest Dunsel and Athena."

"But what about Kraken? I mean, Sprocket? Doesn't she merit attention too? She was the one soliciting the contraband. And why would she do so? She already works for the Agency. True, she's not a Hat and doesn't have access to that sort of thing, but if she wanted it, why buy it on the dark web instead of simply stealing it from work? She is capable of manipulating someone into giving her access."

Boss shrugs again. "Other than some questionable dark web activity, which I might add, we have no hard proof Kraken was her despite my expert assessment; she has done nothing illegal. I will watch her going forward, but I will be content to arrest these obvious would-be traitors for the moment."

The unexpected turn of events leaves Ritz dejected. It would be difficult to screw things up more thoroughly. After a moment's thought, he asks, "Aren't you suspicious of a larger conspiracy? Maybe instead of focusing on dun53l and 47h3n4, we should work up a sting to capture whoever is behind them. You yourself said they seemed little more than a couple of adolescents. Perhaps there is a Mr. Big who we should worry about more."

"Maybe. Or not. Until I have evidence of a larger conspiracy, I'm not concerned. Tell me what's on the device, and I'll take it from there."

# Chapter Fourteen

# Dejection, Defeat, and Intimacy

*Rumination and self-flagellation are common. Depression often comes easily to those on the spectrum—as with non-verbal social cues and facial expressions, rejection and life's reversals can be immensely challenging.*

A PAINED MUTTER OF vituperation escapes his lips on each slow, shuffling step of the nearly five-mile walk to the Dojo. Mask-less, absent his usual forced cheeriness, scarcely looking beyond his feet, Ritz's body language bespeaks defeat, dejection, and disappointment.

Director glances up from her reading as he trudges into the den and flops in an adjacent chair; Twit is nowhere in sight.

"We're a pack of fools. We were played."

"So, your meeting went poorly, I surmise?"

"You might say so. You might; I won't be so kind. However, I will say it was the worst-planned outing since the Donner Party, one we, and by 'we' I mean I, screwed up magnificently. I need to hand in my formerly White Hat for this. I have stained it beyond repair; any possible amount of burnishing will but leave it tattered and dingy."

She rises from her chair, sits on his knee, and places her arm on his shoulder. He leans into her for comfort. She asks, "Got your head handed to ya, huh? Happens to us all. Remember the morning I received a thorough ass-chewing for allowing Trixie out? That you're breathing and not in handcuffs argues it is not so bad. Tell me about it."

With threatening tears, he relates the tale of the afternoon's interview. Though painful, he does not spare the ego-bruising details. He is too dismal to whitewash his failings.

"I see," she says as he finishes. "Well, let's list the positives. One," she ticks items off on her fingers, "We know—or have an indication of—the identity of kr4k3n. That, my friend, is a definite win in any universe."

"Two," she raises a second finger, "we have reason to believe your old boss is not one of the conspirators. Such a high-level traitor would be unthinkable. Though not the least surprised, I am especially relieved, as I have known and worked with Rufus all his life and trust him implicitly. The idea he might be a traitor is as horrific and unimaginable as it is ridiculous."

He reacts to her words with surprise.

She briefly pauses, closing her eyes, oblivious to her accidental revelation. She is too self-absorbed to note his surprised expression as he replays her words and considers that she might be older than Boss, despite appearing perhaps half his age. Illogical! Impossible!

Raising another finger, she adds, "And three, we now have a clue why your attempts to phish kr4k3n have been failing. Sprocket knows you intimately and, therefore, your tells."

His shoulders droop; his face falls.

She places her arm around his shoulder, fingers his tightly-buttoned top button, and adds, "Having a tell recognized by the opposition can be a disastrous leak. Yet, in our profession, the right response is to treat it as an opportunity. In any counterintelligence operation, as soon as you find a source of your adversary's information, you never burn it—you use it to feed misleading information."

He sighs in feeble agreement.

"Yes," she says, sliding closer and unbuttoning his top button, "It hurts to have been duped, but it might have been worse. We will regroup and run at them again. Perhaps we will bring Rufus in on the chase. He will love being a part of the adventure. I think you underestimate him. He plays the role of a bumbling middle manager around the office, but it's an act. He loves having the Hats underestimate him."

With a shrug, he agrees. "I've heard he was a competent spy years ago, but technology has obsoleted the old ways, hasn't it?"

Emotion bubbles up hot and ripe; her voice takes on a biting edge. Through clenched teeth, she asserts, "The Agency is heavily compartmentalized, and you are not supposed to know what goes on. Your job requires you to focus on cyberwar and cyber weaponry. Whether you realize it or not, old-style tradecraft has become cyber-weaponized, and Rufus is a top master of weaponized tradecraft. When he's not busy playing Pointy-Haired Boss for the Hats' benefit, he is ass-deep in Fancy Bear and the GRU, along with their counterparts in other repressive regimes."

She checks herself with a slight shudder and takes a deep breath. "Rufus is far more involved in the cyber war than you imagine."

Her caustic tone dissipates as quickly as it had risen. Her playful, seductive manner returns as she fingers his shirt buttons, unbuttoning a second one as she talks.

Calmer now, she says, "Different combinations of cyberattacks, data theft, and disinformation have been a common tactical feature of repressive nations' influence operations. One particularly salient technique is 'Hack and Hype,' when stolen data fuels a disinformation campaign. Hack and Hype, a tagline encapsulating extortionate nations' manipulation of cyberspace for soft power projection, must be understood to combat such attacks. Rufus specializes in this intersection of old-style tradecraft and modern cyber warfare. He uses Hats as specialized tools to uncover whatever information he needs. You are his favorite, and he delights in his office role-playing. But never forget, his experience with espionage is deeper and broader than most of us can imagine."

She unbuttons another and slides her fingers inside his shirt. They sit together in shared intimacy for several minutes; her frustration is palpable; it is no accident that they are alone; Twit is unaccountably absent.

Best laid schemes, or so it appears...

Refusing to concede failure, she sighs as she reaches out and takes him by the hand.

Rufus stares after the young Hat, a thoughtful expression clouding his features. Was he too quick, he wonders, to dismiss the Hat's concerns of a greater conspiracy? Replaying it in his mind, he realizes he had focused narrowly on the juvenile miscreants and not adequately considered who might pull their strings.

"You must be slipping," he mutters to himself. "Didn't the cold war teach you anything?" He sighs, realizing the Hat is right.

He castigates himself for being short-sighted. They were such obvious bumbling fools; he had not credited them with intelligence enough to be dangerous. Instead, he had dismissed them as kids who had stumbled on something they thought might turn into a payday, regardless of the damage it might do. Opportunism and treason are often intimates.

Was he a fool, falling into a sophisticated trap? Has he grown complacent, overly confident, ripe to be downed by a foe pretending to be less than they were?

The crimson-haired avatar, too, he had dismissed. He considers the image likely the infantile imagination of the kid, dun53l, but what if 47h3n4 is the actual mastermind? The kid did claim her appearance mirrors the avatar! He had thought it teenaged bluster—that such a person does not exist—but is that indeed the case? Belatedly, he realizes he knows actual operatives, one in particular, capable of bringing to life the stunning presence the avatar implies and with the mental and physical attributes to mastermind a fiendish plot.

He imagines a woman with the skills of a White Hat and physical attributes analogous to the avatar would make a formidable adversary. If intent on skulduggery, she could effortlessly bend those susceptible to her charms to her ends. He well understands how powerfully the female aura can influence the unwary male.

Rufus muses about this and other things as he strolls the park. Finally, after a while, he sits on a bench, brow furrowed in deep thought, sitting quietly for several minutes, idly watching passersby in the park. When no one is in view, he reaches beneath the bench and gropes around the cavity beneath the seat.

He withdraws an antiquated flip phone, flipping it with rapid-fire finger jabs before it fully unfurls. "Rendezvous. Penthouse. Twenty-Three," he states in clipped tones and flips the phone shut.

A couple walks into view. Rufus disappears the phone like a magician palming a coin.

"Thou art God!"

Her thunderous outburst startles him, breaking his focus. He stumbles briefly in his own quest but quickly recovers. Her body flushes as she vacillates near her plateau's edge until she is pushed over by his sudden forceful, final slam. As they sail over the peak together, he echoes her unconventional exclamation.

"Thou art God," he proclaims. Though he is unsure of her meaning, it resonates as they collapse in each other's arms. Minutes pass as they float earthward on a gently drifting pillow of ecstasy. Finally, she giggles softly. He whispers, "Wow."

She recovers and declares dibs on the bathroom. Moments later, the sound of the shower intrudes on his post-coital reverie. Without waiting for an invitation, he joins her under the warm stream and gently massages her shoulders.

"That was amazing," he whispers. Her only response is a wordless purr. He tries a few times to engage her, but she is not receptive to conversation, though she does welcome the massage. Only sometime later, after the shower, she begins to act open to discussion.

"You surprised me. I've heard the throes of passion elicit a deity's name, but I have never before been called one. For a moment, I was unsure of what to say."

"Orgasms fill me with existential angst, another tell, I suppose, which betrays my age."

He studies her appearance. Although she is older than he, she doesn't show it. Instead, she appears almost equal to his age—perhaps younger. And yet...

"But what does it mean?"

"It means I should not be bedding jailbait! Especially when said youngsters technically work for me."

"Jailbait!" He exclaims, "I'm pushing thirty, you know—hardly jailbait."

He muses that for an older woman to be with a younger man is a bit socially awkward and carries a stigma. Such women are called names like puma and cougar, but stigma and derogatory labels seldom deter couples who want to be together, and he is comfortable with the social stigma. It is almost like an old friend. He believes their age difference is trivial.

"I wish I could even imagine thirty," she whispers.

"You're older than I, admitted. You appear more mature in the office, though your amazing athleticism proves you're not as geriatric as you imply. What gives?"

"I do make an effort to project an appropriate illusion of maturity commensurate with my job, but there too, I am selling a lie, presenting as younger than my true age."

"Yet here at this moment, you pass for twenty-five. If an illusion, it is a masterful one. How?"

"You're so sweet to say so. You're giving me a girl-boner. The how is unimportant. Call it magic if you wish. The question you should ask is 'why.' Why do I try to appear attractive and seductive to you?"

He is unsure of how to respond. The mere fact Director seeks his attention shocks him. He leans in and examines her skin, her flawless, smooth face, and her waist-length deep-black hair. Dyed? He can't tell. Her skin from head to toe is as smooth and unwrinkled as a child, but she would appear much younger if not for her mature mammalian endowment. Nor do her hands reflect the age she alludes to.

After a moment, he responds, "Whatever the effort, it's working. Still, I am mystified. No amount of willpower will smooth the skin to such a perfect silkiness." He touches her cheek and lets the tips of his fingers slide down her neck to end in a soft cup and caress. "I marvel at what your daily skin-care regimen must involve. I suppose this is one more item on my list of your conundrums."

"So, you're keeping a list," she says with a tease in her voice. "Can I seduce you into divulging what you find so list-worthy?"

"I'm not easy, but I can be had," he answers, eyes twinkling. "Start by telling me about this 'thou art God' salutation. It sounds fascinating."

About to reply with a flippant answer, she peers into his eyes and checks herself as she realizes the depth of his seriousness. She ponders her response before continuing.

"A movement long ago, from the beginnings of the counterculture revolution."

He nods to encourage her to continue; he does not grok the reference. What revolution? Counterculture? Is she talking about Weed? What does legalizing marijuana have to do with any of this?

He resolves to research the subject later. For now, he smiles and nods as though he understands.

She continues, "The reference is the juxtaposition of God, organized religion, and humankind's place in the universe.

"The premise claims God created the universe and the world. Not only this world, infinite worlds, in infinite dimensions, but God is still God, alone in his vast creation. His creation had no one besides himself to appreciate it."

He nods again. "So, God split himself into an infinite number of pieces, spread himself, or herself, or perhaps itself, throughout creation. Each piece became a man or a woman or other sentient being. God, no longer alone, could share his creation. A creation filled with an infinite number of sentient beings, and they could worship him. Every God must have worshipers; it's a natural law."

He smiles but does not interrupt. She continues, "Thus the greeting 'thou art God' is mere acknowledgment, the recognition of one of God's particles encountering another."

"I wonder if the idea coincides with using the word 'piece' for sex." Her eyes roll imperceptibly, though he does not see. He smiles as he ponders the thought. "I think God invented humans to amuse Himself because He didn't have television."

"I feel like a stranger in a strange land," she muses, staring at him with a quizzical eye. She is amused at his casual dismissal of an entire generation's philosophical meanderings, but she had lived it; he had not.

He continues, oblivious. "It sounds like hormone-driven teenage angst, not something thinking adults would waste time on, but I can see how the meme might go viral."

He leans back and stares at the ceiling. "In any case, it links the questions of life, the afterlife, past lives, and reincarnation. It defines the soul on a quantum level. The trend must have flamed out without my awareness, though. I wonder why the meme presumes God spread his sentience throughout the universe? Why not Earth alone? There is no evidence for sentient life beyond Earth, is there? So why the leap?"

"Perhaps the meme's originator is an extraterrestrial."

He guffaws, looking her straight in the face. "Yeah, right!"

She sighs. "I should be quiet. You think I'm full of hooey."

"Or say more. I'll listen, although I am not convinced. If you didn't want to get it off your chest, you wouldn't have mentioned it."

She dimples. "There's nothing on my chest."

"To my wondrous delight. I was speaking metaphorically."

She touches him. "Well, stop it. It ruins the mood."

"Bare your soul then. Dear one, I know I am younger than you and don't care a whit. You, however, appear deeply bothered by our few years' age difference. You're the one wrapped up in angst as though you were a thousand years old. Unburden yourself and let me in on your secret for staying forever young and so wonderfully strong, or leave me to my illusions. Please don't keep tormenting me. It distracts from more important matters at hand, like this...."

His fingers begin teasing a convenient anatomical feature.

She smiles and closes her eyes for a moment as his fingers touch and tease. After many seconds she opens her eyes, slowly focusing on her companion. Her fingers locate another convenient anatomical feature to tease and touch.

Dreamily, "Perhaps I am a strange visitor from another world, able to bend steel with my bare hands and alter my appearance at will. Perhaps my superhuman shapeshifting abilities are what allow me to make you believe I am young."

"Now you're pulling my leg."

"Oh, is that a leg? I must don my bifocals." Giggling ensues.

He throws a pillow at her, but not with force. "You're welcome to pull anything you want, but I don't believe in aliens, extraterrestrials, or shape-shifters."

She is intensely occupied for a few moments, then asks, "Do you believe in that?"

"Thou art God!"

Please visit my Facebook page for various odd posts, old family photos and more.

https://www.facebook.com/nathan.gregory.923

*I am active in various Facebook science fiction, fantasy, and writer's forums.*

# Chapter Fifteen

# Penthouse

*When people think of the stereotypical aspie, they
think of some clueless, reserved geeky guy with a
math/science-based or otherwise weird obsession. They
might have problems with facial expressions and
expressing their emotions. People see this and assume
the person is disinterested in emotional validation.
But, of course, this isn't the case—they're not clueless
and are often hurt when others are patronizing.*

"**S**HE HAS NO RIGHT!" he shouts, oblivious to the 'inside
voice' concept. "She put our entire mission at risk. Worse,
she endangered our entire populace. Had they captured and
broken her and extracted her knowledge, the C'thulhu would have
wiped our leadership from the face of the Earth," he expostulates,
waving his arms expansively. Fuming, he paces the penthouse
living room like a caged tiger. "They would have systematically
eliminated every Asheran!"

"Calm yourself, Alex. You'll have a coronary," Rufus says, trying to mollify the younger man. His much greater age gives him a calmer perspective than the more impetuous youth. "What's done is done, and she succeeded, you must agree. It was indeed a crazy thing to do. She took a dangerous path when the far wiser course would have been to cut her losses and sacrifice the Hat. Foolish! I agree, but you know our Phryne."

"Yes, Rufe, I do, all too well. I also know she doesn't care for that name. You've known her much longer than I, but she is my mother. She will drive herself to any extreme, take any risk, grasp any thread, no matter how fragile, rather than admit defeat. Her compulsion to win at any cost will be the death of us all. Had she only endangered herself, it would have been bad enough, but she endangered our people, not only we Elders but our entire community. Not forgetting the threat to Earth's humanity if the FAANG are allowed to succeed."

Alex slowly calms enough to sit. Then, placing his head in his hands, he forcibly tamps down his surging emotions, reaching deep inside for a calm that isn't there.

With a sigh, Alex says, "I am sorry to be so bashed. I have unloaded my frustrations on you, and I am sorry, but darn it, she nearly got us all killed and doesn't act the least bit contrite."

Rufus erupts with sudden emotion. "Contrite? Her! Contrite? When has she ever been contrite, unless... u-unless contrition was part of her latest scam? For endangering her whole species, she doesn't know the meaning of the word! I knew she focused on that Hat for some purpose; I had no clue it had gone so far. Ha! Want to bet on how long until she beds him?"

Alex pushes as though pushing Rufus away. "No bets. Although he is not her type, 'type' has never stopped her before. He's such a dork. Isn't he autistic or something? I wouldn't expect his dark skin to slow her down, although I am unaware if she has broken that taboo before." He laughs, "Ha! Taboo might be the only 'virginity' she has left. Miscegenation was a crime when I was young, but the societal taboo over skin fell away decades ago, so that doesn't count. Still, I would have expected such unbounded social ineptitude might put her off."

Rufus sighs. "He's not exactly autistic, more like Asperger's, which does place him somewhere on the spectrum. But unfortunately, society is getting itself all wrapped up in terminology these days. One can't voice any opinion without some ninny getting his panties in a wad over some word they don't like. The proper term these days is neurodivergent, as opposed to neurotypical. But whatever you call it, the guy is a genius, off the chart, especially when put in front of a computer. And yet, in some ways, he is inept and bumbling. I've met many smart humans...."

Alex interjects, "Voltaire, Goethe, Galileo, Leibniz, Tesla..."

Rufus flips the bird with a laugh. "At least I'm not still wet behind the ears."

Alex continues, "Ha! But you're right; he is not her usual type, although, in recent decades, she has grown less and less picky." Winking, he adds, "Senility, I suppose."

Rufus nods in agreement. "Especially as Earth's natives have relaxed about such things. This last century has changed her. As her youngest son, you're much too young to appreciate our progenitor's sexual limitations. As in, she doesn't have any. I've been around much longer than you and watched her far longer. She's always been impious, but her criteria these days appear limited to a pulse and working genitalia; either style, she ain't picky. Nevertheless, she has been scheming, and whatever her plans, he's a part of it." He sighs. "I wish she would involve at least one of us, if for no other reason than to have us watch her six." He draws his .38 Fitz Special and waves it for emphasis.

The two men sit in silence as their emotions subside.

Rufus resumes the conversational thread. "These last few years, the Agency has uncovered an increasingly sophisticated pattern of crypto criminal activity. You're undoubtedly aware of the escalating number of breaches, the stolen databases, and the ransomware. Whole cities held hostage—it's all over the news."

Glumly, Alex nods in agreement.

Rufus continues, "Historically, ordinary cybercrime has been the province of organized criminal gangs, but the most sophisticated attacks have always originated from state-sponsored, military units. Few recognize the extent to which it has become open cyber warfare. You are probably unaware the Agency has been losing ground against the newest Black Hats. The Hat you called a dork is the only effective weapon we have left.

"We are in a war! Nation-state-funded attacks have been a factor for years, but lately, they have displaced organized crime. We are literally in World War Three, and that war has a new combatant. This latest enemy is different; they are more advanced than the most sophisticated APT or Hades group. We have tentatively linked these new warriors to the group we have named the FAANG. At least the few we have identified. Their decryption capabilities significantly exceed Earthly capabilities."

Alex's expression displays questioning disbelief. Rufus spreads his hands, nods, and says, "Yes, World War Three has gone Interstellar. We are in an Interstellar war with the FAANG!"

Rufus adds, "We believe they have quantum computers at least two generations beyond our most advanced research. Quantum computers are not simply faster computers. Whereas classical computers switch transistors on or off to represent data as ones or zeroes, quantum computers use quantum bits, a.k.a. qubits. Because of the crazy brain-fucking nature of quantum physics, qubits exist in a superposition state, where they can be both 1 and 0. Superposition enables each qubit to perform multiple operations simultaneously. Not like a multi-core computer, but multiples within a single qubit. Thus, compute power grows by the power of two as more quantum-entangled qubits are added to a quantum computer. Its computational power can grow exponentially instead of linearly. The advantage appears minor with the few qubits our most sophisticated quantum computers possess. Noise and random errors limit our systems now, but once we scale to millions and billions of qubits, it will be to our most powerful supercomputers what they are to a mechanical adding machine. It will change data processing in ways we cannot imagine."

Alex asks, "How did you become such an expert on quantum computers?"

"I'm not," Rufus answered with a laugh. "I've just been hanging out with the Hats, discussing the cyber threats they fight every day; them and Professor Google.  However, that isn't what prompted my call. There is another matter and a couple of new players. I initially dismissed them as kids playing at something they don't understand, but the more I consider it, the more I think there might be a larger conspiracy. I need your help."

Rufus elaborates on his encounter with Dunsel, the backstory of Kraken, Athena, and the rest. He concludes, "After talking it over with the Hat, I concluded I might have been wrong to dismiss them. However, I need your help to identify this kid, Dunsel."

With this, he hands the photo to Alex.

Alex examines the photo and freezes. He recognizes the face, for he is familiar with the young man, unlike Rufus. For a moment, he is surprised Rufus doesn't recognize the kid, but Alex remembers Rufus had been off-planet for over a decade. He has probably forgotten the child.

"Rufe, you're telling me you don't know this kid?"

Rufus shakes his head.

"Oh! Man! You're gonna be petchy when I tell you. Don't pop an aneurysm.  He is your son! He is Milner. Whatever conspiracy you have stumbled upon, your grandmother is behind it."

# Chapter Sixteen

# Refractory

*Asperger's is considered obsolete terminology, and we now merge the behaviors into the broad term Autism Spectrum Disorder or ASD. The 'Disorder' part is waning too, as only extreme cases are considered a disorder. Simply "autistic spectrum" or even "on the spectrum" is generally preferred.*

H E WHISPERS, "YOU KNOW, I am captivated by you. I have observed you for months and noticed your little habits, clothing choices, and more. I knew you quite well in some ways. Then 'Trixie' shocked me, showing a facet I never imagined. The running, climbing, and athleticism exposed yet another version of you; I found I knew you not at all." He pauses a heartbeat and gives a half-wink at his intentional weak double-entendre.

She grimaces as he resumes. "And now this! Shocking again, but in a wonderful way, though I will no doubt be accused of polishing the brass rail. I have always only thought of you as 'Director.' Usually, at least I learn the proper name of my lovers. But, if we are to continue as intimates, I need to call you something other than 'Director.' The company roster lists 'Director Novak.' Is that even your real name?"

He begins ticking off a list on his fingers. "You are Director, Trixie, Athena, and Professor. Have I forgotten any? Which, if any, of those is your given name?" His voice softens and turns almost sullen as he adds, "I don't know your right name."

"Why do you assume we'll be lovers?"

"It appears that ship has sailed."

She sighs. After a pause, she continues in a soft voice. "It is wrong. Pleasurable, but wrong. Not your fault. Such interludes are zip, zilch, nada, and rare in my life. I had a lapse in judgment and should not have allowed it."

"This is a cliché," he grouses as his face falls; a dark cloud descends. Eyes down, unable to meet her gaze, he appears close to tears. With a visible effort, he rallies, squares himself, and, with discipline, meets her eye to say, "Then it never happened; I will punch in the nose anyone who suggests it did—Director."

"Gwen"

"Huh?"

"As Director, my given name is Gwendolyn; I use Gwen among friends; never at work! Always 'Director' in the office."

"Gwen," he repeated. "Sounds soft and feminine."

Smiling, she smacks him on the arm as though in faux reprimand. "Are you suggesting I am not feminine?"

"Far from it. I only note the contrast between 'Gwen' and 'Director Novak.' The latter somehow sounds masculine in the abstract."

Her twinkle blossoms as she laughs. "The title would once have been Directress. Society and language once distinguished gender in such titles. A Director is male, and a Directress is female. The words are still in the dictionary, but usage and society's view of such things have changed. Now we castrate the terminology and make speech gender-neutral. I am a female Director, but that's not correct either; one would never think of someone as a female Director. It suggests a female is somehow conditional, provisional, or less qualified. I am the Director; the title stands alone. The shape of my genitalia and what I do with them is on another plane of relevance."

She extends her foot, spreading her toes. "But," she says, "if a director has six toes, it would never occur to anyone to refer to them as a polydactyly director. Unrelated. Gender is, thankfully, now merely another physical attribute."

"*Now there's a twist,*" he thinks, surprised he hadn't spotted this before. He contemplates the uncommon digits for a moment, then grunts in frustration. "I don't care how many toes you have." He massages and kisses the perfectly formed if uncommonly endowed appendage.

"I do not want to rehash the battle of the sexes, but I do not want to return to solely seeing you as 'Director' either. I want more. I want to do this again. And often."

"So do I, dear child, so do I, but I can give you a hundred reasons why it is a bad idea. So, I am 'Director' in the office and Gwen in private for now.  Not in front of Twit, though; he does not know me as Gwen."

"Oh?"

Silence. She ignores his questioning gaze.

After a pause, he continues, "Let me see. You are Director or perhaps Director Novak at work, and in private, you are Gwen. Is that even your real name? Or should I call you Poly?"

His quip evokes a sardonic laugh, although body language suggests she is far from amused; she's probably heard it before. Dryly, she answers, "I suppose it's better than No-Pants-Novak."

Words lie, body language doesn't—even he can see the lady is annoyed! Pressing the matter irritates her. Eyebrows elevated; he pushes further.

"But to Twit, you are?" He ignores her self-deprecating slut-shaming. Then, sensing a prickly nerve, he resolves to avoid further digs involving supernumerary digits.

"I was introduced to Twit as 'Hazel Stone' when I accepted custody, but he never called me Hazel. Something about that name upset him. Instead, he calls me Professor, and I call him Twit. Typical nerdy, hormonal sociopathic teenage behavior. His given name is Fitzroy, though he hates the name. He is officially M. Fitzroy Stone; the M. is short for his most hated Christian name—Milner. I know the kids teased him about Milner when he was young. I'm unsure where he came up with *Professor*, and he refuses to use Hazel; he's never said why. You can call me Trixie if you want; he heard us refer to it as an alias. Although, I imagine he would accept 'Gwen' as merely another alias."

"So, I'm to think of you as a hooker?"

Her vexation softens; she laughs, throwing a pillow at him. Then she turns pensive. "I am many things and have played many roles. If the hooker persona bothers you, then forget it. I won't remind you of it again."

"It doesn't bother me; it is only that the contrast between your staid office persona as Director is so stark. The brass nail surprised me. Yes, she shocked me, but that does not mean I imagine less of you for it—the opposite, in fact. I want to know more about you. What other roles do you slip into with such ease? Who else is hiding in there?" He touches her forehead. Then he strokes her foot. "What other surprises are you hiding?"

"More than you would believe, my love. Trixie is not my first courtesan gig. But enough of my deformities and surplus personalities. We need to talk about your adventures."

"You said 'custody' a moment ago. Are you Twit's legal guardian?"

"Yes, I caught him in some petty dark-web criminal activity. I was impressed, so instead of arresting him, I adopted him and have spent the last three years reforming him. He's a good kid at heart but had a rough life after his mother died. His father wasn't around, so I took him in. The system is hard on bright kids."

He wonders why she would take on such a burden for one unrelated, but before he could ask another question, she adds, "I'll tell that story another time, but he will be home from school soon, and I need to know more about what happened."

"I've told you everything. And there is nothing deformed about you. Pants or no. I shall call you Athena, for you are my goddess. In private, you shall always be Athena to me."

She says, "You know, according to Greek mythology, Athena was noted for advising/mentoring heroes, but she never had a true lover, no one to hold her, embrace her, and love her. She had a loving mother and father, and most of all, brothers and sisters—but it was hopeless that she would fall in love. Is that the fate you foresee for me?"

Startled, he begins, "My love..."

She sighs and places her finger to his lips before he can continue. "It is more appropriate than you know. Yes, I am your warrior goddess Athena, and you are my Perseus." She snuggles closer to him, and they lay in silence for several minutes, cuddling in a lover's embrace.

Finally, she says, "There are mysteries, unanswered questions. For example, you expressed disbelief that Sprocket might be a criminal mastermind."

"Harrumph," he grunts. "Surely! She is staid, dour, and unimaginative. We had some moments together, but she is uptight and prim, and her intellect does not shine so brightly. Boss claims she is acting; she is brighter than she appears."

"It is not uncommon for a brilliant woman to play dumb, particularly in the presence of strong men."

"Am I a strong man?" He asks, genuinely surprised.

She smiles but continues as though he hadn't interrupted. "Part of the mating dance, I suppose, but a woman who intimidates men gains a reputation as a ball-buster, a barrier many find hard to surmount."

He shrugs. "If Sprocket intends for others to underestimate her, she is succeeding."

"Could she be a foil for someone else?"

He shrugs in frustration. "I don't know. That Sprocket might be someone's meatpuppet is more believable."

"What about your old boss, Rufus? You remarked about how different he appeared in the field."

"Well, I agree, he did act capable in the moment, but a few moments of confident demeanor don't invalidate his workday personality. But act or no, I have problems seeing him as the mastermind type."

She sighs in vexation. "Rufus' record is one of outstanding competence, and as I explained, there is much you do not know. He intends for people to underestimate him."

"Besides, there is much more to espionage than cyber weaponry. Ultimately, it's about human beings, not computers. Rufus is the best—and I mean the very best—espionage agent that I know, and he doesn't need a computer to infiltrate his targets. His specialty is manipulating humans, not computers—he's primarily a social engineer. For example, Rufus owns uniforms for every delivery service, utility, repair service—you name it, he's got it. With the right uniform and persuasive social skills, he can walk into almost any office building in the world and be accepted as belonging there. Once he's penetrated the building, nothing is off-limits. You can't do that from a keyboard."

"I suppose," he agrees, spreading his hands, palms down. "He does appear well-versed in traditional spy-craft, but old-school stuff is out the window in today's cyber world. I don't see him as having the technical competence to mastermind much in today's world."

Her face turns stony as she struggles with the rising frustration of his persistent dismissal of the Agent's abilities. Finally, biting her tongue, she asks, "Could either—or both—be a puppet for someone else? And if so, who?"

He grimaces. "Boss used 'sockpuppet' to describe Sprocket, and I almost gagged. I chalked it up to his lack of Cyber experience."

One eyebrow lifts, but she says nothing. He continues, "When someone is a dupe for someone else, it is fair to call them a dupe. We refer to them as deceived or otherwise serving false ends. Calling them a puppet may be accurate, but it implies a willingness to be used. A sockpuppet is a different thing, a fictional person created to obfuscate the identity of the hand inside the sock."

She laughs dryly. "The idea has been well-known ever since Benjamin Franklin used the pseudonym 'Mrs. Dogood.' Doubtless, it was not a new idea then. Although the slang in this context is more recent, it is an 'old-school' idea, and I'd be shocked if he didn't know the slang and its usage. But remember, I have known him much longer than you."

He stops cold. The idea of a 'sockpuppet' outside the Cybersphere is something he has not imagined until now. He practices his blank stare for a couple of seconds.

He asks, "So, if the idea of a sockpuppet should be well-known to him, why would he misuse the term? Is it intentional? Is it possible he is deliberately doing so to appear inept?"

She shrugs. "The term is relatively new, but the concept is ancient—technology changes, as do methods. Underlying principles do not. Being underestimated can be incredibly useful—Rufus was merely ensuring you would continue to underestimate him. There's much more to Rufus than you know—not all fools are foolish."

"Hmmm," he muses as he considers the idea.

She leans in. "You're brilliant, too, you know."

Shocked, he blinks. "I suppose I can be a little better than average on a good day, downhill with a tailwind. But only when I can concentrate. I block out the world and life's distractions when I focus. My hyper-focus has enabled my cryptographic success as a Hat. But, outside of cyber, I have always struggled to be merely average—sometimes painfully. People, especially, make me feel stupid. I never quite know what people expect of me. Sprocket once told me I catch what others miss in the cyber realm, but IRL, I miss what everyone else intuitively grasps. For example, I always found eye contact tiring. I learned to read at a young age but didn't look people in the face when we talked. Sprocket taught me I must learn to read faces like a book. It never occurred to me there could be linguistic information on a face. I suppose, like dogs, I interpreted staring someone in the face as threatening. But I did learn to read faces and body language. It isn't easy and doesn't come automatically, but I can do it when I focus."

She nods. "I suspect you are undiagnosed with mild ASD, the way your mind works," she says. "You have an unparalleled memory for detail, are truthful to a fault, have highly logical, if nonlinear thinking processes, and solve challenging problems easily. But, further, you talk little, mostly only when relevant, and become easily distressed. All these are hallmarks of being 'on the spectrum,' as they say."

As she talks, he is looking down, not meeting her gaze. Finally, she reaches out and touches his cheek.

"What you have is God's gift to you, but what you do with it is your gift to God. You have a tremendous talent for the Cyber, a talent this world desperately needs."

Facing his long-denied reality hurts; his head droops. ASD? Perhaps he already knew it on some level, but it shocks him for her to state it boldly. He sighs deeply, shakes his head slightly, and softly says, "I did not have a happy childhood; it was pretty rough, actually. I was always the odd kid, a target for bullying. No one understood that, for me, social cues are not intuitive; I tend to take things literally. Words, as spoken, should say exactly what they mean, but that is often wrong; people often do not exactly mean what they say and frequently mean all sorts of other things instead. It took me a long time to figure that out. As a result, I was bullied quite a lot and the target of cruel jokes."

He pauses for several seconds, eyes down. Athena waits for him to continue, fearing to break the spell of intimacy she has worked so hard to foster.

Finally, he looks at her face, but his gaze is distant, as though he is on another plane. "I retreated from people. Read a lot of books, lots and lots of books, and watched a lot of movies. It took me a long time to understand things that most people grasp intuitively."

She says, "I wonder if, in a way, it was a gift, inasmuch as brains are plastic and neurons flow where the action is. Suppose the external world and the social cues others spend so much mental energy obsessing over are partially cut off. Perhaps that enhanced your ability to understand the world inwardly in ways others don't."

Grimacing, he says, "From a technology standpoint, I found value, for I found it rewarding to spend all night programming computers by myself. Most people don't enjoy typing strange symbols into a computer alone in the night—programming in solitary without distractions, all night. Most people think that is not fun, but I liked it, so I would program all night by myself. I found that enjoyable. I now realize that is not normal, but I find it compelling to be alone with the ones and zeros. I feel like I am in a warm, creative fog and free of material concerns."

She says, "It's a riddle to people how you see possibilities more broadly than others."

He continues, "I was absolutely obsessed with the truth. That is why I studied physics because physics attempts to understand the Universe and what are the truths that have predictive power. So, I find physics and information theory fascinating. I wanted to be a physicist but lacked the education. I wanted to be an artist but found I lacked the visual sense of what makes art. So, I learned to program ones and zeros. Programming alone and at night is not glamorous, but it paid the bills and opened a growth path to cybersecurity."

Softly, she says, "You, my love, are a true artist, and the network is your canvas. Many great pianists have played bordellos to buy food, and world-class photographers have paid the bills by photographing weddings. But artists are not remembered for what they do to survive."

He shrugs. "Networking and security became my passion, and I suppose I have found traction in engineering that eluded me in art and science. Facts can be slippery demons, and reasoned opinions are never equal to the cold logic of ones and zeroes—I found I have a gift for cold logic. Ambiguity defeats me."

She nods. "Math doesn't change with prevailing opinions. Science requires diving in, wrestling the demons of belief, opinion, and personal bias, and nailing them like jelly to a tree. Too often, one latches on to supposed facts supporting a pet idea only to see them slither away, leaving only the tears of denial."

He nods in agreement. "Disproof is the final destination of beliefs. Never proof. The most solid theory is always subject to falsification. But ones and zeros are absolute. They either add up, or they do not. They never change. Opinions, bias, and belief affect them not."

"Belief," he expostulates, "Belief is the greatest enemy of rational thought." Emotion rising, he takes a deep breath and continues, "Scientists used to think heavier than air flight was impossible until an empirical engineer showed them how. The math that describes aerodynamics came later. The airplane flies the same no matter what opinions the scientists espouse."

"Scientists!" she interrupts him with a snort. "Most 'scientists' are bottle-washers and button sorters. Scientists come in three flavors: Politicians, bottle-washers and button-sorters, and competent scientists. The latter is exceedingly rare."

Her unexpected passion startles him. His mouth begins forming words, but voice rising, she charges on before he can engage.

"Science, regardless of the question, is the one true path to knowledge for those able to walk it, but it is a rigorous and demanding path. The scientific method is humanity's most outstanding achievement, although it is only valid when practiced without bias or agenda by those competent with the tools and methodology. Few are able.

"Many so-called scientists are merely disguised politicians! They invoke holy 'science' to hammer those with an alternative viewpoint into submission. They invoke the sacred name of 'science' to silence opposition, end discussion, and browbeat opponents into accepting unsupported claims on faith without evidence."

He stares at her as though she has grown two heads. She doesn't notice.

On a roll now, her voice takes on a tinge of passion. "The politicians who disguise themselves as scientists are easy to recognize once you understand them. Anyone who dismisses data without examination, insists the 'science is settled' and attacks those who question pet conclusions; no matter what advanced degrees they may hold, no matter how impressive their title, such a person is not a scientist. A Ph.D. does not a scientist make.

"Science is, or should be, a collaborative, self-correcting process from observation to testing predictions based on a hypothesis, to reproduction by the scientific community." She continues. "When this happens, you eventually arrive at a theory you can begin to trust. Sadly, it does not occur as often as we imagine. Mistakes, human error, and political machinations often confound the results.

"Take, for example, the University of Hawaii Math glitch some graduate students stumbled across."

His eyebrows tilt in question.

She dismisses his puzzlement with a wave of her hand. "It was in the news. A graduate student attempted to verify his study's calculated data prior to publication. His results did not match the results of a similar study by another professor. When they dug into the math, they discovered 'professor bottle sorter' had used an ordinary spreadsheet.

"Spreadsheets are barely suited for business arithmetic but never for scientific work. Remember, computers cannot do math with their built-in instructions. Even math co-processors or accelerators are merely streamlined and optimized variations on conventional instructions. At best, computers only do limited arithmetic, addition, subtraction, etc. Complicated programming is necessary to turn those elemental capabilities into real math, and there are specialized tools and math libraries for doing so.

"Common business tools such as spreadsheets perform their calculations using double-precision floating-point as defined by the IEEE. This fact is well-understood."

He nods as he realizes where she is going; he interjects, "Double-precision floating-point math can hold the equivalent of about fifteen decimal digits. This digit limit leads to meaningless rounding errors in a business calculation but deadly errors when doing scientific math. Any competent scientist understands this; button-sorters, perhaps not so much."

"Right," she says. "The student used a more sophisticated set of tools based on quadruple-precision floating-point, able to work with twice as many digits before encountering rounding errors. Unfortunately, rounding errors had ruined the previous calculations." She makes 'bunny ears' with her fingers as she continues, "This 'glitch' invalidated the conclusions of over a hundred research studies and an equal number of scientific papers. Of course, the popular press blamed it on the computer, but the scientist was the glitch. There was nothing wrong with the machine; it was the scientist who failed."

He continues, "Once you disqualify the blatant politicians-in-scientist-clothing, those who remain, who appear sincere, still often fail due to confirmation bias and other human failings."

She nods and adds, "The biggest enemy of science is confirmation bias. Scientists are human beings and thus blind to their beliefs and biases. Science is incredibly hard. Science is a process of leaping from one wrong hypothesis to another. Each new hypothesis requires more effort to test and disprove than the last, but inevitably, each falls, replaced by a more resilient one. Eventually, we develop a hypothesis that survives all our falsification efforts. We eventually call this most challenging hypothesis a theory and begin using it to make predictions. So, the discovery of the math glitch in Hawaii disproved many solid-seeming theories."

He nods. "Right! Hypotheses and theories are fragile things. Anyone who claims a pet theory is proven and not subject to debate is so nutty their farts smell like Jif and is certainly no scientist."

She grimaces and interjects, "Thanks. One more comfort food that I will never again find comforting!"

Whether he ignores her jab or is merely too focused for the interruption, nonetheless, he continues, "Trust the science, not the scientist. Judge a scientist by the questions asked, not the answers given. Science may light the way, but engineers are more honest. Engineers find ways to improve things, but engineering is never disproven, unlike science. The engine either works, or it does not, the bridge stands, or falls, the airplane flies, or it does not. So, you can trust an engineer."

She rolls her eyes. "I know a few bridges which have fallen, but I take your point. Science is always subject to disproof, whereas engineering is the definition of empirical proof. Engineering may be refined and improved, but not disproven."

He nods. "Engineering proves science, and math explains engineering. The three are inseparable. Until an engineer builds a bridge, an engine, an airplane, or a computer program that reliably operates as predicted by theory and conforms to the math, conclusions based on theories alone are but unicorn farts—pretty ideas and idle fantasies unsupported in the real world. Math and science give us the tools to understand why engineering works. Math is useful in describing the empirical world but fails at truly proving anything, and science without derived engineering is mere speculation. With a collective body of engineering, a theory may become a law, as in the laws of thermodynamics or the law of gravity. A theory may have evidence, testing, and expert consensus behind it, but any theory is suspect, provisional, and untrustworthy until it successfully predicts the real world."

She nods and adds, "Yes, anyone who uses a theory, even a well-supported one with strong consensus behind it, to make long-range, big budget decisions is risking a comeuppance when the theory later becomes falsified. So you opted to embrace the cold logic of computers and engineering rather than confront the ambiguities of art and science. That makes sense. You prefer certainty over uncertainty."

He glances down in silence for several seconds. Then raising his head and meeting her eyes, he says, "I suppose you're right. I find order and beauty where the rules do not change. Science shifts on the whims of confirmation bias and the Dunning-Kruger effect. Ones and zeroes are rigid, predictable, and don't change with opinions. I prefer solidly proven engineering principles over malleable scientific theories."

The slam of the front door interrupts their interlude. Athena says, "Twit is home—I would prefer he doesn't know we are lovers. I will go downstairs and distract him in the kitchen. Can you sneak out, then come back in, so he thinks you've only just arrived?"

# Chapter Seventeen

# Ph3DoRA

*The modern-day medical community considers neither Asperger's nor autism a medical condition requiring treatment, nor are they any longer considered different things. Instead, both are simply manifestations of intellectual development on a scale of cognitive ability, similar to physical characteristics such as height. A 4'10" person may suffer challenges relative to a 6' person but is not labeled disabled merely because of their size.*

"Easy! Slow down!" Ritz's voice fairly squeaks as he grabs at the dash. He is uncertain how he volunteered to let Twit drive—two inexperienced drivers behind the wheel of Professor's van, one with a scarcely used license, the other with a freshly minted learner's permit. What could possibly go wrong?

"Relax, grandpa," Twit says, "I got this."

"I hope you do cause I sure don't. This imaginary pedal don't do nuttin." Ritz is an uneasy rider. He prefers mass transit or rideshare, preferring to place his trust in the training of professionals who spend long hours behind the wheel.

"And who are you calling grandpa?"

"Only socially acceptable handle I could come up with for a big ugly guy banging Professor! Or am I supposed to close my eyes and play dumb?"

Ritz fumbles about as he searches in panic for his best blank stare. He and Athena have been meticulously discreet—how could Twit know?

After an awkward silence and two more death-defying turns, "We're the posers, ain't we? Fighting over a woman who uses us as her pawns!"

Twit shrugs. "Hey man, no fighting over her! I don't give a Dogecoin if you bang her. You ain't her first big squirt; if I know her, you won't be her last. I'd be jealous if the whole situation weren't so damn Oedipal. She's hot for her age, but trust me, she ain't human. She's cold, like a psychopath. Or a praying mantis. She'll bang you today, then behead you tomorrow without so much as a tear. Don't lose your head!"

Ritz grimaces, his blank look shattered—although it is unclear whether he is more distressed by Twit's graphic-verbal depiction or his unhanding the wheel while emphasizing the words with expansive gestures. Grabbing the dash again, Ritz says, "Truce, man, I get it. She's hot, and you're drawn to her; we both are. Of course, any man with a pulse would be, but still, she's essentially your mother..."

Twit fairly shouts, "SHE AIN'T MY MOTHER!" Then more softly, he continues, "She's a cop who took pity on me when I was in a bad way and pulled me out of the system. Although even Google can't say why!"

"Easy Twit, I didn't mean anything."

"Sorry, Ritz, I get testy about my mom. She died, and I never knew my father. So, we spent years bouncing from one foster home to another. Nixie and me, I mean."

"Nixie? Oh, the cat? He's yours then?"

"Yeah, he was a kitten when mom died. He came to me when she first got sick; he moved in and adopted me. Mom said he was a guardian angel sent to care for me when she couldn't. He and I have taken care of each other since."

Twit's unexpected soul-baring leaves Ritz at a loss for words; such raw emotional forwardness makes him acutely uncomfortable, and he doesn't understand such strong emotions or how to respond. So he doesn't; they drive in silence for several blocks.

Twit says, "I still don't see how Rufus usurped our chat. We hooked Kr4k3n, I am sure of it. Not some interloper, especially not some analog boomer. It doesn't make sense."

"Boss may be old school, but he burned that schoolbook long ago and hangs around the new school. He's nobody's fool; I learned the hard way. Director says he enjoys playing the bumbling pointy-haired boss, but it's only an act. He likes it when the Hats underestimate him. Maybe Sprocket is Kraken like he says, but we were trolling others. What about Trilby?"

The padawan tugs at his weak stubble idly, as he hasn't quite embraced the daily shaving habit. "7R1LBy must be the leader, I think, not Kr4k3n. And don't forget 80w132{Bowler} and p02kp13{Porkpie}; they were in the room too."

"Yeah, Bowler and Pork Pie were Trilby's associates. I am sure of that. I don't see how Sprocket fits into their triangle. She was involved, but in what capacity?"

"Let's find out!"

"Don't get us killed before we do. Easy on those turns."

"Relax, see, we made it with no bent sheet metal," Twit says as he turns the van into *The HashTag* parking lot. Despite the hour, cars fill the parking lot. Ever since the meteor impacted the Cafe, the notoriety has drawn a new, more daring gaming crowd.

Ritz relaxes visibly as the kid parks the van with skill and precision, perfectly centered in the tight space.

"We're here," says Twit, "although I still don't see why it was necessary to come way out here when we have a perfectly secure cyber-dojo."

"Call me paranoid."

"You mean instead of grandpa?"

Ritz blew a raspberry; then continued, "A little dash of paranoia is a wise habit when dealing with cyber villains. Especially these characters. These people play rough. I don't want any meteors smashing into the dojo."

"That can't happen! Besides, they wouldn't use a meteor again, would they?"

Hoisting a middle finger, Ritz laughs and responds, "I'm fresh outta cockney farts; here's a finger salute instead. Twit, I know you think you have sufficiently obfuscated the dojo location and misdirected its network hookup through multiple VPNs plus layers and layers of firewall security. Still, I'm the White Hat; this is my day job. So, if I say it ain't safe, I know what I'm talking about. Our best protection is to be in a crowd, in a public venue, and get in and get out quickly. Very quickly!"

"How do you expect to unmask Trilby so fast?"

"I'm not necessarily aiming just for 7R1LBy; I'll lay out my wares for 80w132 and p02kp13 too. Then, if any of them fall for my munitions, we'll plant the seeds for their later undoing. We'll drop a few breadcrumbs tonight and see who sweeps em up. Trilby is too smart for our tricks, but maybe 80w132 or p02kp13 will bite and lead us to Trilby, or perhaps we'll get nothing. We're in a game of chess, and it's our move. How will we take a rook if we don't risk a pawn? The HashTag is our pawn."

"Uh, all right, Sensei, I get it. The most we risk is exposing the *HashTag* as our haunt, which I suppose they already know. You gonna use the 47h3n4 identity again? Or do you have another trick?"

"Oh no. Not Athena for this. She may or may not be compromised; we can't take that chance. Besides, they ignored her last outing. So nah, tonight we're gonna use the one identity we know they have a boner for."

"You mean Ph3DoRA? I thought Professor made you stop using him."

"Yeah, well, let's not tell her. Keep this our little secret; what she don't know won't bring out her scary drill sergeant persona. Hey, why do you call her Professor?"

Twit shrugs. "I don't know. I was angry. Mizz Stone didn't feel right. Heck, I still don't know whether it should be Mrs or Miss. Until you started banging her, I never seen a sign of a husband or any man in her life. Plus, she's old and talks like a professor. So I started using Professor. She tried to get me to call her Hazel, but I couldn't. My mother's middle name was Hazel, and anyway, I didn't want to use first names. Plus, she kept calling me Milner, which made me angrier. So I told her I was Twit and called her Professor, and we kinda got stuck like that."

"She appears to genuinely care for you, as though you were a blood relation."

"Well, I didn't ask her to! She's a part of the system I've endured since my mom died. I can't wait to be old enough to fend for myself. Nixie and I don't need any cops running our lives."

Ritz grimaces at the kids emotional pain. At a loss for something to say, he mumbles a barely audible "Uh huh" as he fumbles in the back of the van for their gear.

Ritz passes Twit a heavy backpack. "Here's your clamshell, the Pineapple, and the firewall package we cooked up. I already fixed the Hashtag's firewall. You wouldn't believe how lax they used to be or how simple it was to break in and tune them up. But it's solid now. Trust me; I did them a huge favor — I did what a White Hat does. With that and the WiFi Pineapple, we should be well-armored. So your job is to monitor that firewall and instantly kill the whole network stack, if necessary, on any indication of collapse. Don't wait for them to break through; I'd rather crash the HashTag's entire network than let them penetrate our defenses—the moment that outer shield turns red, kill everything!"

Twit settles his spit-diaper into place, shoulders the bulky bag, and hesitates, watching Ritz as he gathers equipment. Noting the kid's waiting stance, Ritz nods and points his elbow. "Go ahead and grab us a booth. Order us some chips and jitter juice."

Ritz begins atonal whistling as he grabs various items, stuffing smaller items into his bulging shoulder bag and a couple of objects into a plastic shopping bag. Glancing at his haul, he locks the van, dons his mask, and heads into the Cafe proper. He notes that the meteor damage is now fully repaired. Given the hour, the Cafe is busy but not crowded; several open tables are in the back. He begins walking toward where Twit has staked out a workspace and pauses. Hesitating, he motions to Twit as he takes another table. "Let's not sit there," he says.

Twit shoots him a WTF expression, but silently gathers his clamshell and other gear and moves to the table Ritz has selected. He arranges his work area and boots the computer. Finally, he asks, "Ya gonna tell me what was wrong with the other table?"

Ritz says, "Nothing, I guess. Just bad vibes."

"Oh, I think I get it. Isn't that where the meteor hit?"

Ritz soberly nods as he boots up his clamshell. "Let's not tempt fate."

The distinctive dragon logo materializes as the server appears with their order. Perfect. Ritz jolts down half a can of go juice and grabs the basket of chips as he settles into typing posture. Several minutes of furious key-banging ensue as the pair prepares their field of battle. Then, Ritz stands up, stretches, and glugs his can empty. He waves it at the caffeine steward and settles back into a keyboard hunch. "Ready, Twit? Now let's see who we can knock up, shall we? Pay attention, my youngling; here's your job. You're in the firewall, right?"

The kid nods. As he does so, Ritz examines the work area Twit has configured. He has a tablet shagged to his clamshell as a second screen, showing the firewall dashboard. The login screen in Hell's Forum is waiting on Ph3DoRA's credentials. Twit has anticipated Ritz's next ask.

"Perfect. You go to Hell and bounce around the general forums as Ph3DoRA; if the evil minions pop up, let them steal this." Ritz hands the kid a thumb drive. "This is our trojan horse, the collection of burned Cyber Warrior crayolia we planned to use as bait. It also contains a surprisingly sharp fishhook, a sweet piece of munitions that, hopefully, I can track. While you're trying to bait them, I am taking a run directly at the C'thulhu, or possibly the FAANG themselves. I'm going port-knocking on those VPN tunnels Ph3DoRA spotted the last time. Given some time and a wedge of luck, I think I can crack at least one. Last time, they unleashed a tsunami that burned down my firewall and nearly got me killed."

"Isn't that risky?"

"Yeah, I suppose, but there's two of us, and now we have better tools. Thanks to *HashTag*'s gaming infrastructure, we have a much more robust network than the dojo, and we've created a far better firewall than I had that night they attacked me. Plus, I have you in the overwatch seat, ready to pull the plug the instant things get exciting. That night of the assassins, I wasn't expecting such organized cyber power, and they had several minutes of concerted blasting at my defenses before I realized it. They didn't penetrate, thankfully, but they came much too close and had lots of time to analyze my metadata and dispatch the assassins. So you will focus on our defense while I go on the offense. I'm betting this time we can grab a few bites of their lunch before they notice, and as soon as they begin to counterattack, you will yank my chestnuts out of the fire."

"But what happens if, or rather when, we come under fire?"

"See that traffic indicator on the firewall dashboard? That yellow bar reflects suspicious inbound traffic, pings, pokes, probes, and such. See how it flickers consistently at a low level? In addition, I installed a blacklist of over two million identified cybercriminals. As a White Hat, I have that sort of thing at my fingertips. They're blocked, of course, but any blacklisted probes show as orange blips. Any dramatic increase in yellow or orange likely means an attack. Then there is the green indicator for two-way traffic between whitelisted sites. It shows the routine, regular traffic to anything from Google to Wikipedia and, of course, the gaming servers. So usually, we would see a ton of two-way traffic and a steady background beat of malicious inbound traffic. The firewall drops malicious inbound stuff, so it's only a minor annoyance. However, the bad guys are constantly scanning; thus, we always see them, and the firewall drops their bits, which is why we need firewalls. But the bad stuff happens when that annoying inbound probing begins receiving answers from inside the firewall, indicating someone discovered a pinhole and is trying to exploit it and turn it into a breach—or already has. So the dashboard displays that sort of thing in red. An onslaught of yellow or orange will herald attackers hitting us, but red means they're getting traction. When you start to see two-way red traffic, pull the plug quick before they can turn a pinhole into a gaping breach."

"So, fine, I pull the plug on the connection. Then what?"

"Pull the plug, yes, and when you do, we grab our stuff and vacate this lovely establishment. Fast! Got it? Be prepared to bolt, to move fast."

"Why? What do you think they will do?"

"Well, dropping a space rock on our heads sounds extreme, but they tried it once. Don't forget the lovely T-K and her paramour, the Accountant. So, I dunno, let's not take chances."

"If they kill us, it's been nice knowing ya, grandpa. Give me a moment. ... Got it, I'm in. Let 'er rip."

There ensues nearly an hour of conversational silence filled with frumious typing. After a while, Ritz stands, stretches, and waves for another jolt of jitter juice as Twit continues banging away. Another half-hour passes. Twit's typing has slowed, and he appears almost bored. Finally, after yet another half-hour, drinks and chips having evaporated, Ritz calls a halt.

"No one home. Sign says, stay away, fool, don't bother to knock." Ritz's frustration is palpable.

Twit nods. "Hell is half empty. Slow night, I guess. No cyber-villain minions, no cyber-mastermind Trilby. No one even slightly interested in stolen cyberwar matériel."

Ritz pushes his spent drink can aside, muttering, "Yeah, it's a bust. Let's pack up. Want to get something to eat before we go?"

Twit eyes the now empty chips basket he had scarcely participated in emptying. "I could eat," he admits. With a grimace, he adds, "You sure it's safe to hang? Meteors, assassins? Bad vibes?"

Ritz shrugs. "We didn't stir things—no reason to believe anyone spotted us. Besides, those burgers smell palatable." He motions to the server.

While Ritz is ordering food, Twit begins packing the gear, arranging everything for a quick exit. "I'll have the Bitcoin Burger," he interjects while packing the bag. Finally, he asks, "Well, grandpa, this walkabout was a bust; what's our next move?"

"Nix the grandpa crayolia. It was a funny haha the first time, but it kinda bombs in the reruns. I get it; ya don't approve. Well, here's a newsflash; I don't either. You're right; she's irresistible, like a flame to a moth, and, like it or not, she's in charge—she's pwned both of us. I would promise to keep it zipped, but we both know that won't fly if she has other ideas. And I kinda like her other ideas. So, suck it up. We gotta focus on the villains, you know, those bastards trying to kill us."

"Sorry, Sensei, I didn't mean it like that. I can't help it. It's how I feel, and I know I can act like a jerk, but I don't mean it. Truce?" Twit hoists a fist bump.

"Truce." In response, Ritz awkwardly waves his fist in Twit's general direction; Ritz doesn't quite grok fist bumps.

"Ya know, Twit, I've been thinking about your handle. I get the acronym, but TWIT sounds a little derisive. It was fine for a prepubescent teenage wanna-be, but you're nearly an adult now, and your skills are Hat-worthy. You need a handle for real-life use. Something monosyllabic and masculine."

Twit replies, "I hate my name. Milner becomes Millie, or Mil... Not exactly masculine, is it? My middle name isn't much better. That sounds sissy too. Prolly I should change it entirely. I mean legally, with a court and everything."

"I get it. People change their names. Legal name changes are not uncommon, but usually, it's enough to merely reformat them. You know, parents often name their children with a purpose. Often it is a namesake for a beloved parent or ancestor. Sometimes it is because the name has meaning. For example, Jahi means bright, shining, and dignified in Swahili; I don't speak Swahili. That sounds like it should be a good name, but as babies are cute, their commonly used name becomes a cute baby name. Until we grow up; then we find ourselves wanting to throw off babyhood and choose more adult-seeming names. So, we will commonly settle on something strong and monosyllabic, or at least reduced to the minimum number of syllables. It's not limited to us guys wanting to sound more masculine. An Elizabeth might be Lizzie as a child and become Liz or Beth as an adult."

Twit interjects, "Yeah, and Rithwick Jahi becomes Ritz. I like being Twit online, but you're right; it doesn't carry the same weight IRL. I didn't care because I spent my life online. The net is my world."

"I know. But you're grown now. So, let's see if we can make you a better handle, at least IRL."

"I've played with diminutives and initials. Milner, as bad as it already is, becomes Millie or Mil. My middle name becomes Roy. Sounds like Boy! Using initials becomes M.F., not exactly what I am going for either. So, I am Twit. I like it!"

Ritz counters, "I still like Fitz—short and masculine. In leetspeak, it becomes **eff-one-seven-zee**. So, we could be Ritz and Fitz. We'll start a company, 'Ritz and Fitz, Cybersecurity Services, LLC.' How do you like that?"

"I dunno. Almost sounds like I am drafting on your handle. People will laugh at Ritz and Fitz as much as Millie. I don't think it works. Besides, when I was in the system, one bully called me Fizzy, and I hated that horrible nickname. It thoroughly ruined Fitzroy."

Ritz laughs. "Yeah, Fitz as an adult nickname is fine, but corrupting it into a child's variant of Fizzy should be a capital offense. Ha! All I'm saying is to consider it. I think it is time to leave Twit behind and adopt an adult handle. I said it before, and I say it again. Fitz suits you."

Tech bags packed, burgers devoured, and the last jolt of jitter juice drained, the pair prepare to head home to the dojo. Ritz surveys their surroundings and freezes; he nudges Twit and points with his chin toward the bar. There sits Rufus, wearing a gray fedora with a red feather in the band. Boss isn't alone either. He is chatting up an Asian woman with long black hair in a business suit. T-K! Boss is engaged in a public conversation with their mortal enemy!

Twit whispers, "Wha... What is it? She's T-K, the C'thulhu assassin, isn't she?"

Ritz whispers, "Yeah, and he's Boss! Rufus."

"Yeah, I know him. He pointed a gun at me! I won't soon forget. Does he know who he is talking to?"

Ritz shrugs. "Darned if I know. How can we warn him? Dare we risk it?"

"He met me as Dunsel. I can't let him see me, but he works with you IRL, so you can 'coincidentally' bump into him and not appear suspicious. He knows you hang out here sometimes," Twit explained.

"Maybe, but I told him I don't come here anymore. Still, you're right; we can't let him see you—that would be un-good. So, you duck out through the arena, take our stuff to the car, and wait for me. I will see what I can do. If I don't come out or text in ten minutes, go on home by yourself, don't stick around. I will use rideshare if need be."

Twit objected, "But I need you; I don't have my license yet."

"I know, it's a necessary risk. Try not to get stopped, but if you do, ask to call your guardian. Director will know what to do, and I may need her if the worst happens. But don't focus on that; I am sure I will be fine. See you in ten minutes."

"Professor will be thoroughly cheesed if I call her to get me out of jail."

"She'll be worse than that if either of us gets killed. Now go!"

After Twit safely exits via the Arena, Ritz circles the establishment. He is apparently wandering aimlessly but with a purpose. He is trying to spot any friends T-K might have brought to the party, especially her co-assassin, The Accountant. Fortunately, no one appears evident; if present, they are skilled at staying hidden, or at least more skilled in spycraft than he. Perhaps she is alone. As his wanderings take him toward the bar, he intentionally steps into Boss' line of sight. He tries several times to make eye contact without letting T-K see him. Finally, Rufus stares directly toward him and shakes his head ever so slightly. Ritz concludes that Boss has the situation in hand or thinks he does and doesn't want interference.

Ritz wrestles with the dilemma. Should he abandon Boss to his old-school ways or hang close for backup? Torn, Ritz decides to talk with Twit. So, careful not to let T-K spot him, he ducks out the side door and heads to the parking lot.

"Boss gave me the go-away signal. I take that to mean he thinks he has things under control. Should we leave, or should I call Director?"

Twit shrugs. "Maybe text her."

Ritz laughs. "Phone calls are obsolete, huh? Well, mostly they are, but this is a bit more urgent. You call; as her ward, you're less likely to be on the radar."

Twit pulls out his phone and starts to text. Ritz raises his eyebrows as if to say, "WTF?" Twit shifts the phone and dials.

Almost as though talking hurt physically, he blurts, "Rufus is at the Hashtag with T-K. We're worried; what should we do?" He listens a moment, then, "Got it." He abruptly hangs up and puts the phone in his pocket.

At Ritz's questioning expression, he shrugs. "She said we should leave him, go to the dojo and stay away. She is already on the way; I think Rufus, or somebody, called her. They will be here in a few minutes."Ritz shakes his head in growing anger. "I can't abandon Boss. I'm going in there and keep an eye on them. I don't care what Director says, Boss needs help. Stay here." Ritz begins preparing to return to the HashTag.

Twit responds, "I'm coming with you." Ritz turns to object, but before he can speak, the kid continues, "I'll stay back; I won't let Rufus see me, but I'm not staying in the car." He jumps out and locks the van, although Ritz is objecting, trying to convince the kid to stay.

As they argue, a car slams into the parking lot at high speed and screeches to a stop, nearly blocking the front door. Director and a tall athletic-looking man jump out and bolt inside. The driver turns off the engine and chases after the others. Just as he reaches the door, a commotion erupts. People begin spilling out every entrance—gunfire reverberates within.

# Chapter Eighteen

# Caucus

*The ASD Spectrum ranges between neurodiverse and neurotypical. The deeper into the neurodivergent side of the spectrum, the more challenges the individual must overcome. The line between merely experiencing a few challenges and a true disability is a slippery one.*

RUFUS AND ALEX FACE off across the kitchen table; the Penthouse atmosphere is one of seething anger. Although Rufus appears outwardly calm, Alex is a raging behemoth. The two standing men tower over the lone, seated woman, but she shows no signs of intimidation. If anything, they are intimidated by her.

Rufus grits his teeth as he berates the woman with a dangerously deceptive calm in his voice. "Damn it, Phryne; I had her! I cracked the code. She was giving up valuable intel. So why the hell did you interfere? Between your pet geek and the kid getting in my way, and you and Alex scaring off the quarry, you are giving advantage to the enemy!"

Alex practically yells, "Rufus, you were in way over your head. T-K is a cold, brutal assassin; she fully intended to kill you. The only reason she was giving you intel was to draw you in. T-K only met with you to find out who you work for and what you know. If Mom hadn't called me when she discovered your message, you would be dead now! Or worse!"

"You don't know that! I had things under control! Plus, I was armed."

Without a hint of submission in her eyes or voice, Phryne coldly responds, "They appear unaware of we Asherians, and we can't afford to draw attention to our presence. That sawed-off Fitz Special of yours will be your undoing, Rufus. That antique is dangerous. You're lucky you didn't shoot someone—or your own foot—when it accidentally discharged. If you had shot her, I wouldn't have minded too much, but you risked bystanders' lives—unforgivable. That's the problem with that snub-nose pocket protector; without a trigger guard, it's far too easy to discharge accidentally. As it is, we lost her."

Maintaining a forbidding calm, Rufus counters, "Yeah, it's a feature, not a flaw; it's meant to be easy to draw and fire quickly. That's the point; it's a close-quarters defensive weapon. If you two hadn't charged like the Marines at Omaha Beach, she wouldn't have bolted and slammed me with the table. But, as I said, I had things under control until you two butted in."

Alex throws up his hands in an emotional display of his frustration. "You had NOTHING under control! She was playing you. Her companions were standing by, ready to grab and stuff you into a van. Or, more likely, kill you in the alley, depending on what beans you spilled. They would have killed all Asherans on Earth if she had suspected your real identity and tortured you into revealing everything you know."

Phryne says, "Calm yourself, son. It's not the disaster it might have been. True, Rufus took an awful risk, but we are in a risky business."

"Yeah, Mom, this goes for you as much as Rufus—more, as you are even more valuable. You, too, take ridiculous risks, going out to midnight meetings disguised as a hooker! Then to be running naked through the Bowery, jumping from rooftop to rooftop! You could have been killed or arrested even if the FAANG didn't capture you. How would an Agency Director explain to the cops why she was running around the city naked as an egg? What if the press got hold of THAT juicy headline? You and he are alike in that regard, with no heed whatever for the danger you place the rest of us in. If they had captured either of you and extracted your knowledge, they could have wiped out every Asheran on Earth. You can't take such risks. Neither of you! If you don't start using some sense, I will retire and go live on Nekomata. I could use some peaceful relaxation."

Rufus, mockingly, "Well, if you do, watch out for the Velociraptors. They're hungry this time of year."

"Boys! Boys! Yes, we took some risks. Admittedly, things don't always go as planned, but plans change, and we must be willing to take risks to fight this enemy. We can't afford to pussyfoot around. It requires bold action to beat them."

With dark emotion leaking through his forced calm, Rufus almost growls, "That bold action yielded essential data. We now know that The Accountant is her boss, perhaps more. I believe he's the big kahuna, the boss of the FAANG. Could be he's the entire FAANG. She's awed and deathly afraid of him that much is certain, and yet they are close, possibly lovers. Anyway, he certainly appears to be the head guy. We also know that the assassin we call T-K and the dark web Kraken are the same. So, I think I owe Sprocket an apology—I had wrongly believed she was Kraken."

"So you say," Alex Interjects. "She may or may not be Kraken. I still say T-K was playing you!"

Rufus nods. "Yes, Sprocket's mixed up in this at some level, but I believe now she is merely a witless pawn, not a willful traitor. We must directly engage her and find out what her involvement is. If we can turn her, she can become a valuable asset. Can we use your geek play toy to turn her? I know they were once lovers."

Phryne sighs and shakes her head. "Don't be disrespectful. Ritz has supreme skills that we need. He's not one of us, but he is a valuable ally. I know you boys disapprove of my libido, as though somehow, as your mother and grandmother, that my age should put me above such things. I am ancient, yes, but I am not old."

She waves her hands in animation. "On the contrary, my libido is vigorous, which I know makes you kids uncomfortable. Youngsters are inherently uncomfortable with their parent's sexuality. Yet, I need human touch as much as anyone. I may be ancient, but I am only human. So, it is hypocritical of you to sit in judgment of me when you both leave unwed mothers and unregistered orphan babies everywhere you land. At least when my dalliances accidentally produced offspring, I raised them. Women can't bang and run away like you boys; we must bear the consequences of our carelessness."

Both men hung their heads at her words. They knew that their liaisons had scarcely been less irresponsible.

"Rufus, if you hadn't dropped Milner on that poor girl in Idaho, her death wouldn't have left him an orphan. Good thing I finally found him and took him in. Alex, have you uncovered any lead at all on your young Lex? Another orphaned and abandoned child of Ashera to be found and cared for. You can't keep it zipped, yet you judge me? It's not fair! At least in my case, I am no longer at risk of making babies. Women have a finite supply of eggs and can't make more, but you guys keep going and going, like...like...that damn pink bunny, spraying gametes everywhere you go."

Alex says, "Mom, I think you're being a trifle dramatic. Yes, you raised your children; but you knew they were born—an unavoidable biological reality. Most Asheran children are well cared for; only a few have fallen through the system due to factors we couldn't control. So, we're not as careless as you imply. Rufus had no clue that kid existed. Nor did I, Lex. I didn't suspect I had a son until his mother appeared in the psychiatric unit, screaming for her son. Thank goodness one of our agents was there. I still don't know for sure he is my son; that will require a DNA test, which first requires finding him.

"In both cases, the mothers kept that knowledge from us; otherwise, things would have been different. And I know you certainly remember where Rufus was and why while Milner was growing up. But, yes, the kid's mom died; that was tragic. However, thanks to the Asheran network, he is now in the fold. I am still searching for Lex, and when I find him, I will bring him in too, even if he is not my son. We have never intentionally abandoned our offspring, and you know it. You're just overreacting because you're angry. I think we're all angry because we're scared. Scared of the C'thulhu, scared of their ruthlessness."

She sighs. "Alex, my son, you always were the wisest of my children. You're right; we have taken dangerous chances." She focuses squarely on Rufus. "Grandson, you know the risk you took last night, as surely as I know the risk I took with Ritz. In hindsight, we both think the risk was worth the reward. I could no more sacrifice Ritz than you could pass up the opportunity to extract information from Kraken. But we have to be more careful. We are too valuable to the Asheran people, and we each know too much that could put other people in danger. We must be more careful."

Alex responds, "Mom, I initially thought you took such a risk for him because I saw him as no more than a conquest. I accused you of allowing your gonads to dictate your priorities and taking risks for your sex toy. I was wrong, and I apologize. Not that you weren't motivated in part by sexual desires, but in that there was another, higher purpose I didn't then see. He is indeed a talented cyber warrior, and, as such, his skills are valuable to our cause. I owe you a partial apology for that, at least. He is a valuable asset. However, I still doubt he will prove worth the risks you took. There are lots of geeks and nerds. There is only one you."

"Son, please be more respectful. Yes, Ritz has social challenges. So does Twit, though not as strongly. Ritz is what we call neurodivergent, which is more acceptable now than Asperger's or autism. We would once have called him a savant for his unique abilities, but that term is also now considered disparaging. He does not recognize that diagnosis; he is in denial. But his powers are extraordinary, and we need such incredible people on our side in this conflict. When in cyberspace, he can move mountains. He is not of Asheran blood, but he is so extraordinary that he is an honorary Asheran as far as I am concerned. So, desist that geek and nerd language, and treat him respectfully. I mean it."

Both men looked at each other, slightly shocked by her words. They had just been spanked and knew it. After a moment of silence, Rufus responds, "You're correct, Gram, we have been disrespectful behind his back, and it's not right. I admit it and apologize. But I will add that I have publicly treated him with nothing but respect. You are correct when you describe his abilities when he occupies the Air Chair. He is unquestionably a superman among Hats."

Alex says, "Okay, I give in; you're both right, he is a valuable asset, and we need to treat him better, though I've never actually met him. But what's this 'Honorary Asheran' stuff? You're not planning on telling him about our people, are you? That would be stark insanity."

She shakes her head. "I don't plan to tell him anything he doesn't need to know, but he is brilliant and given time will probably deduce the truth. I can only lie to him so much. He has already seen much that challenges his incredulity. Don't be surprised when he does."

Rufus counters, "Gran, you can't let that happen. The Asheran presence on Earth is our most closely guarded secret. We don't let natives in on it, ever!"

"Oh, BS! We have allowed others to know. Yes, it's unusual, and we don't do so lightly, but it's not unheard of. But enough of this;

It's late and I must get back to the dojo and debrief him after the night's fiasco."

Sucked into a hacked Battle Royale, Twit is fighting for his life. Ritz is gunning for him, and he is running out of gambits. It's not just that Ritz is a fast shooter—he can also build at lightning speed, and his strategic twists are a labyrinth of unending surprises. Twit might have fared better had he focused on the fighting instead of studying Ritz's technique. Instead, Twit is more interested in learning from the more experienced master gamer than beating him. Just as Twit succumbs to a fatal curtainfire barrage, the front door opens, and Director enters, bearing an armload of loaded pizza boxes.

"So, who's the winner?"

Twit pushes back from the keyboard and hooks a thumb at Ritz. "No contest!" A half-heartbeat later, "Pizza! Wonderful! It's been hours since that burger."

As the aroma permeates the room and draws his attention from the game, Ritz realizes Director is bearing food. He pushes back from the workstation and jumps to assist her in safely landing her cargo. Twit, realizing the sudden appearance of cheezy comestible, rushes to retrieve plates and utensils from the kitchen. As the heavenly slices distribute themselves among the human contingent, a non-human participant joins the queue. Nixie, anticipating cheese, takes a position intended to ensure his share, parking his furry presence in the chair closest to the cheese and sitting at attention, ears up and eyes alert. Twit pulls out a cat-sized bite of cheese and a cube of ham and, grabbing a paper plate, places it in front of the cat. "Don't worry, Nixie, we'll share. No one goes hungry when Pizza's in the house."

Athena objects, "Maybe you shouldn't give him that. It's not exactly cat food."

"Nonsense. Nixie's a pure carnivore; meat is his proper diet. Ham is fine, although its sodium content is a little high; thus, it wouldn't be ideal for him daily, but it's fine as an occasional treat. The cheese might be a little challenging, too, as some cats don't tolerate dairy too well. Fortunately, Nixie has no such problem. So, in moderation, he will be fine. Plus, he loves it! Trust me; I wouldn't give it to him if he weren't used to it."

At Twit's words, Nixie emits a strongly worded trill and head-butts Twit's elbow. Twit strokes the cat lovingly as he makes purring noises into the cat's fur. Twit's devotion to the animal is striking. The two are nearly inseparable, even sharing the same bed.

Athena glances at Ritz and smiles.

Ritz asks, "So, what happened at the Hashtag? Your driver chased us away, so we left without knowing what had happened. We were a bit worried. That was a scary situation, with the gunfire and all, so tell us what gives."

She shrugs. "The gunfire was a misunderstanding. Rufus had his weapon in his pocket. When we moved to intercept T-K, she kicked the table, slamming it into him, and the gun went off. The only casualty was a .38 caliber-sized hole in the Hashtag's floor. But, of course, the gunshot caused mass panic, and in the chaos, she got away."

"I bet that ruined a few games," Ritz says.

"And underwear," Twit quips.

"Oddly, the gamers in the arena didn't react until later. They were so engaged in a game firefight that one more gunshot was nothing—they played through without a bobble. Only the patrons in the Cafe panicked and ran."

Twit interjects, "I bet it adds to the Hashtag's reputation. First a meteor strike, and now a real gunfight! Gamers will be fighting to play there."

Director reacts with a momentary expression of horror. "You're probably right. Anyway, Rufus garnered some valuable intel from our assassin friend. We have called her T-K because of her love of knives, but she identified herself as simply Mary. Of course, the Legion of C'thulhu is our name for her group, and we did not learn any new name for them. She did drop "The Council," but that of itself is meaningless."

Ritz says, "Council of what, I wonder..."

She says, "Exactly, we don't have a clue, but she and The Accountant are not peers. That much we learned. He is the big boss, and she meets with him but rarely. Instead, she receives encrypted text messages with necessary instructions. They don't know that we compromised their chat servers, which shows us that they are not superhuman. Unlike her, he isn't a local and only comes to town when something important draws him here—he spends most of his time elsewhere. We are not clear on what their relationship is, but he often recruits her to work directly with him when in town. She is the only Earth-based C'thulhu to have met him in person, all the other assassins take orders via messaging, or through her. She is his top lieutenant on Earth, or at least so we infer from what she admitted to Rufus, and the texts we have intercepted. From what Rufus gleaned, he is far higher in the organization than we would have believed, perhaps the very top. We now think he is almost a one-man operation, or at least, any other upper echelon members do not interact with Earth-based resources."

Ritz asks, "So, does that mean that he's not C'thulhu?"

She nods, "Only that I suspect he is FAANG instead of C'thulhu. Or both. We know so little about their organization, but we have never identified anyone as FAANG until now. They have always been elusive the elusive masterminds, impossible to pin down.

We're not sure they exist as a separate organization. Because of their different behaviors, we separate them in our thinking with different code names. The FAANG appear to be the puppeteers and operate behind the scenes, whereas T-K and the others wade in and get their hands bloody on nearly any excuse. That the Accountant enjoys killing is why we counted him as C'thulhu. But I wonder if that is wrong, and there is only one circus of evil, and he is the ringmaster."

Ritz says, "Perhaps the FAANG does not exist as a separate organization. You borrowed the name C'thulhu from Lovecraft as a codename for the assassins. You called them the Legion of C'thulhu, as I recall, in other words, a League of Assassins."

She nods in agreement. "Yes, you're correct. T-K, The Accountant, and the rest of the Assbook luminaries are, primarily assassins, regardless of what other villainy they perpetrate. When we addressed non-murderous malicious activities, we credited their machinations as perpetrated by a different group, which we dubbed the FAANG. In addition to hacking, data theft, and sabotage, they encompass crime, fraud, deception, political corruption, human trafficking, and destructive illegal drug activities. Pretty much any organized destructive activity that is not direct, wholesale murder."

Twit chimes in, "So, prolly this Accountant fellow is Lovecraft's 'Great Old One,' C'thulhu himself, and all the rest are merely his lieutenants."

Ritz adds, "I think you're onto something, kid. To whatever extent the FAANG is a separate organization, they report back to the same evil master. But Lovecraft's evil was a fictional being. Effectively a God, ageless and immortal, a cosmic entity of tremendous power. Even so, this Accountant appears unremarkably human. Ascribing supernatural alien origins is a reach too far, I believe."

She asks, "So, you don't accept the idea that he might be extraterrestrial?"

Ritz shakes his head. "It's an extraordinary claim with insufficient evidence. I have seen many people claim that UFOs are real and claim to have seen grays, lizard people, little green men, and so on. But, for all I can see, those come from too much weed or Welsh rarebit-driven indigestion causing disrupted sleep. Lights in the sky always turn out to be optical illusions or satellites. So, I don't believe in UFOs. Prove me wrong."

She does not respond to his rejection of aliens. Instead, she grabs a slice of pizza, tousling Twit's hair as she does so. With a smile, she says, "I am too tired to debate it further, so I'm crashing here tonight. See you guys later." With that, and another slice, she heads for the stairs. She starts up the stairs, pauses, and turns back to Twit and Ritz apparently to say something, but Twit has turned away, working on sharing the last pizza slice with Nixie. Instead of speaking, Athena catches Ritz's eye and gives a slight head tilt and a sly wink. Ritz, unnoticed by Twit, smiles slightly and nods.

# Chapter Nineteen

---

# Extra Terrestrial

*The neurodivergent individual can often have
radically different and original views of the world.*

C ALMLY SHE INTONES, "As the Sherlockians are wont to
quote, '*When you have eliminated the impossible, whatever
remains, however improbable, must be the truth.*' Hence, the
conclusion; the C'thulhu are extraterrestrial!"

"I thought Bruce Wayne said that!" he says with a lopsided grin.
Then, soberly, face darkening, he continues, "Harrumph! They
are not 'grays' or insectoids—they are human—too fantastic, a
leap too far. Besides, Holmes's fictional claim is patently false.
There is no *necessity* for a conclusion based solely on the remains.
For one, establishing the elimination of all other explanations is,
itself, impossible. Occam's Razor is a much better tool for selecting
among competing explanations."

"Occam's Razor is not always sharp!" She sighs. "I did not say
they are not human. I said they are extraterrestrial in origin.

Their leadership, anyway. Humans, yes, to the proverbial nineteen decimal places, but humans from another world, humans not of this Earth."

"But. But tha—that's…" his voice trails off, face frozen.

"Impossible? Of course! At least it appears so if the idea of non-Earthly humans is untenable. We fail at logical reasoning when we discard possibilities because of our preconceived notions. Such human bias how science often fails." She shrugs.

Stare on full-blank—he says nothing—several times.

Her calm tone belies a rising irritation at his obstinance, but that tone soon gives way to a soft fuming and grinding of teeth as she fights for calm. She reminds herself that what she conveys is a tall hurdle for a hard-nosed, ones-and-zeros White Hat.

She realizes he is firmly entrapped in the phenomenon of a *mass formation psychosis*, virtually hypnotized to follow the mainstream leadership in believing an idea, filtering his views through the lens of confirmation bias. He believes there are no alien humans because society reinforces that belief. His belief has been firmly cemented in the realm of common sense; a truth considered so self-evident that it may not be questioned. He cannot easily accept contradicting information.

After a long, pregnant pause, she continues. "What if I tell you the presence of extraterrestrial humans is well-established? What if I tell you that there are many thousands of extraterrestrials? Fully human people, I mean—not some bug-eyed, non-human species—living on Earth at this moment. Whole communities of human refugees from another world with earth-born children and grandchildren? Aliens who interbred with Earth natives. Star children, unsuspecting dreamers, undocumented immigrants from another star, refugees from their home world's destruction."

She pauses her cynical soliloquy as though she has spotted steam spewing from his ears. Taking a deep breath, she continues before he gathers the will to interrupt. "If I tell you that, is it still unreasonable to believe the Legion of C'thulhu are not from Earth?"

He shakes his head in disbelief. "I don't believe it. How can you say that? Where's the evidence? Or as Sagan decreed, ECREE!"

She responds, "Sagan never defined the 'Extraordinary' in his aphorism. His acolytes often invoke ECREE to discredit research dealing with scientific anomalies. Claims that merely violate mainstream consensus do not rise to the level of truly extraordinary."

Flustered, he begins, "But the consensus of reputable scientists like...."

She takes his hand and peers into his eyes. "Are you aware of the 'disclosure project' and its movement?"

"Slightly. I have listened to late-night interviews of UFO true-believers who claim a government conspiracy keeps the 'truth' of UFOs from the public. I don't consider them credible."

She nods. "Quite correct, they are not credible. By design! The movement is a carefully orchestrated disinformation campaign designed to discredit the idea that extraterrestrials are on Earth. The principals behind the movement are believers, of course. They honestly believe their claims, except for those few in on the joke and working to keep it going. These faithful and their followers are honestly working to expose a supposed government conspiracy. There is no government conspiracy. The movement—so lacking in credibility—espouses such fantastical claims that society automatically discredits anyone who would express such ideas. This movement intentionally exploits well-understood psychological traits that foster a follow-the-leader trance-like behavior, wherein the masses employ vicious ad hominem attacks designed to enforce mass compliance. Words become weaponized. Words like 'UFO nut' and 'conspiracy theorist' become weapons to attack and disparage anyone who dares talk about aliens. Innocent terms are weaponized, declared derogatory, racist, or said to uphold some negative stereotype and thus may not be used. But when name-calling and public shaming fail, things can easily escalate into physical violence. When carried to extremes, such behavior is becoming recognized by the medical community as a form of mass psychosis."

"I don't understand. If there is no conspiracy, why the charade?"

"I did not say there is no conspiracy. I said there was no government conspiracy. The government is not hiding an alien presence. The government itself is unaware. The conspiracy is real but does not involve any government, not of any nation."

He pulls away and paces back and forth in frustration, almost anger, as he wrestles with the conflicting concepts. "You're talking nonsense. Aliens living on Earth for generations, and the government does not know! How can that be? Where did they come from?"

She sighs. "Wheels within wheels. Yes, there are aliens—extraterrestrials, I mean; humans from elsewhere—living on Earth. Tens of thousands of them. Some have been here for many generations."

She reclaims his hand. "Trust me; this is the truth. I cannot explain or prove it, and I shouldn't have brought it up. I ask you to believe me on simple faith."

"Yeah, I can see that engraved on my tombstone. 'He trusted Athena.' Poignant yet..." He raises his hand in frustration. "Alright," he sighs. "Suppose I believe you. If the government is unaware of these supposed extraterrestrials, how are you? The Director of the Agency is aware of a secret invasion, yet the government itself is not. You speak in non-sequiturs."

A pained expression darkens her face, and a soft groan escapes her lips. She leans into his chest, holding him close. He embraces her in silence, unnerved by her reaction. Stumped, as usual, by emotional cues, he is unable to fathom her distress. After a few seconds, he deduces she is wrestling with strong emotions. Long moments pass without words as he struggles indecisively, trying to decide how he should react. Unsure how to respond and unable to cope, he does nothing, which, paradoxically, appears to be the optimal reaction.

Finally, she pulls back. He kisses her and touches her cheek. Regaining her composure, she says, "The government, as an organization, does not know about them, has no projects concerning them, no investigation, and no secret files. However, many individual government officials do. These government officials know, and they keep the secret. Those aware of this are invariably extraterrestrials, descended from extraterrestrials, or connected in some way to the extraterrestrials. Some extraterrestrials hold high office, and descendants of aliens hold many positions. There is also a smattering of natives sympathetic to the alien cause."

"Fantastic," he whispers. "You are saying hostile extraterrestrials invaded and infiltrated the government without our knowledge, and except for a few human traitors, the government remains unaware? That is a plot straight out of a 1950s sci-fi tale. Invasion of the Body Snatchers? Heinlein's Puppet Masters? Is this infiltration limited to the US? Or is it a worldwide phenomenon?"

Anger flashes in eyes wetted with fierce emotion. "I have made a terrible mistake. I should not have mentioned it, but having done so, I realize I have botched it horribly. You think I am crazy, and I have given you a bizarre, wrong-headed, Hollywoodesque concept of things."

She takes a couple of deep breaths, forcing a willful calm, and then continues. "The extraterrestrials are not hostile. Neither are they invaders. They are refugees. They came here long before the country's founding—the earliest came to Earth in the times of the ancient Greeks, around 400 BC. Indeed, they ARE this country's founders and citizens in every sense, as much as any European settlers. In fact, it is no accident that America's founding fathers were so familiar with the ancient Greek philosophers and drew their inspiration about morals, ethics, and the sense of independence, all the fundamentals of a democratic society, from the ancient Greek civilization. Their influence is precisely why and how the US founding is so historically unique. These people brought a perspective to freedom and human rights that Earth's humans lacked."

Her irritation rises again, astounding and alarming Ritz with her passion. He struggles to keep his face calm as her ire flares with unwonted fury.

"Human chattel has been a hallmark of every civilization since the dawn of prehistory. All Earth's human populations have held, sold, and been chattel. It is the greatest stain on humanity, humanity's original sin. Even today, the practice flourishes unabated in some dark corners of the Earth. Yet, for all the historical battles, these aliens have fought the despicable practice everywhere they have established themselves. Wherever an abolitionist movement arose, there was an extraterrestrial behind it."

She draws a deep breath and again wills a measure of calm. She says, "They are citizens of the US, citizens of Earth, who merely chanced to have ancestors from another star, from a planet they call Ashera. They have not infiltrated anything. They have risen to power honestly and fairly and, as a group, have the best interests of society at heart. Our staunchest patriots are often of alien descent because they or their ancestors came here as refugees and understand the value of freedom and safety."

"I don't understand," he begins. "The C'thulhu are a penultimate evil."

"Yes, certainly. Evil exists in any group. I can't explain the C'thulhu, but they are a tiny few. We suspect they are a rogue splinter group, unconnected, unknown to the Asherans. These alien refugees are, on the whole, worthy people who arrived as refugees, not invaders, and they began arriving so long ago they have fully assimilated. Some continue arriving, but most have been here for generations, and Earth is their home. The C'thulhu are invaders—chaos and evil incarnate and wreaking immense damage. I cannot reconcile them."

He asks, "Are the C'thulhu from the same origin planet?"

Her eyebrows rise in astonishment. "Excellent question! You possess an intuition for eviscerating assumptions."

He shrugs. She continues.

"We have default assumed so since they are human. Humans of Earth and Ashera are genetically related. DNA argues for a common, if unknown, origin. That the C'thulhu could be a third, possibly unrelated human line that originated entirely elsewhere is a novel idea. Or are the C'thulhu merely rogue Asherans, as we assumed, and it is their hidden puppet masters, *The FAANG,* who are truly alien? We are not certain they are different groups, only that there appear to be multiple factions with different tactics and motivations."

"Ashera? Asheran?" He questions. His expression reflects stark astonishment at her attachment of a name to the aliens.

As though this was long-understood information, she nods. "Ashera began to die following a technological disaster and gradually became uninhabitable. It remains so. Ninety-nine percent of the population perished. Save for interplanetary migration, their entire race would have died. But instead, the Asherans spread to other planets, including Earth. At first, they arrived in small numbers. Over time, multitudes of Asherans sought sanctuary on Earth, though this was not their only refuge. There are other planets where Asheran outposts survive.

"Nevertheless, most have settled and invested in Earth as their forever home. That is why they seek positions of power in government. They are not invaders but vested citizens who have experienced the horror of watching their home-world die."

He shakes his head in disbelief. "Dear one, you nearly convince me yet have not offered a shred of proof. I work in the government's most secretive spying agency, doubtless the world's most adept. Yet I see nothing, not the faintest hint of such a secret population. How might you know this?"

She shakes her head and sighs. "I've said too much—what I have already told you is much too much. You cannot know this, and now I am likely in trouble for this conversation."

"You are Director of the Agency. Promote me. Raise my clearance."

She turns away, body language signaling an unwillingness to continue the discussion. "It's not so simple. Rank and clearance within the Agency are meaningless in this context."

Unwilling to accept rejection, he presses her. "You said there are humans, er, I mean native Earth people, who are aware of and sympathetic to the cause. How do I become one?"

She raises a hand as though pushing him away. Shaking her head slightly, she says, "The majority of Earth-born Asherans are unaware of their off-world ancestry, and disclosure to incognizant descendants of Ashera is rare. Even more so, disclosure to a non-Asheran is strikingly uncommon. Yes, there are a few, but a trusted sponsor must nominate any candidate. We are risk-averse and will not continence a vetting, much less disclosure, without cause."

He freezes! Eyebrows askew in astonishment, he falls silent. His face turns pensive for long moments, replaying her words in his mind, once, twice, and thrice in shocked disbelief. She studies his face, noting a reflection of his emotional turmoil as a panoply of emotions flies across his face. She is puzzled; she replays their conversation in her mind, uncertain what she said to trigger such a reaction.

He takes her hand and holds it as he thinks. She moves to pull away but doesn't struggle as he insists. Moments later, his face softens, his eyes brighten, and he lifts her hand and gives it a gentle kiss.

"I see the way forward."

She flies up a cross expression. She is vexed—she has somehow surrendered control and recognizes the fact, but how she slipped up eludes her. "You must have a sponsor to be considered. Absent a compelling motive, it will end there. Worse, the Asherans might perceive you as a threat. How do you envision overcoming such resistance?"

"I offer my unparalleled talents in service of stopping the C'thulhu as a disclosure incentive. I am betting that my cyber warrior skill set, practiced with my informed and willing cooperation, is exactly the compelling reason the Asherans need to endorse."

She refuses to meet his gaze. In an oddly lowered voice, "You might be right. The C'thulhu are a profound threat, and the Asherans would do well to recruit you. How would you find a sponsor?"

He does not respond quickly. Her face lifts toward him, and as their gaze meets, he smiles. "Here comes the easy part. I already know an Asheran, and a high-ranking one too, if I am not mistaken. So I am betting I already have a sponsor."

Surprise flashes: her eyes narrow suspiciously. "What do you mean?" she asks. "Who do you. ..." Her voice falters; her heart skips a beat, perhaps to acknowledge she has betrayed her hand.

He doesn't answer immediately. Instead, he draws Athena closer, nuzzles her softly, and sighs. Softly, he says, "Your angst over our seemingly minor age difference, magical seductiveness, athleticism. Many little things. ... But a moment ago, you said 'We' instead of 'They.' If I didn't already put it together, this is the blow-off. It fits. You are Asheran! Unless I miss my guess, you are also an ancient and high-ranking one, using Asheran technology to appear so young and attractive. Please, don't lie to me; trust me instead."

She leans her head back and closes her eyes. Steeling herself for an emotional rollercoaster ride, she breathes deeply, struggling for inner calm.

"Dear child, I would not lie to you, not if I could avoid it, but if necessary for your protection, I might deceive you by omission or misdirection. Lying is an unsavory tactic I try hard to avoid."

She sighs and draws him closer. They sit in silence for several moments; he begins to fear she won't continue.

"It was inevitable, I suppose. The moment I climbed into bed with you, the die was cast. I should have realized opening the door to intimacy would be my undoing. But, instead, I have placed you at risk for the basest of reasons."

She kisses him tenderly, another pause before continuing. "Yes, dear one, I was born long ago on Ashera—I resist telling you this because I do not wish you to see me as somehow less than human, which is also why I hide my age. My longevity is a fluke, a DNA research project that succeeded much too well."

With a lopsided wink, he responds, "Then you're my alien. Yes, it is a shock to realize it and have it confirmed, but, in truth, I already knew it beyond doubt. You have tells, dear one, little mannerisms and body language that I have learned to interpret. I find such things challenging, true, but I have mostly learned to cope. I do have questions, though. You claim to be human, yet you imply terrific age, far greater than the human lifespan. How can this be?"

"Asherans are human; we love as humans, and we feel the same highs, lows, pains, and joys as Earth's children. We are fully human, DNA indistinguishable, even to inter-fertility. True, I came to Earth long ago, and my age makes me an elder; it does not make me non-human. Even hyperdactyly is an entirely human mutation. I share this characteristic with the recent president of Mexico, for example, and he is not Asheran. Nevertheless, I helped found this country, and it, and Earth, is my adopted home, one I fight to defend."

He realizes she has side-stepped his question and raised another. How ancient is she, anyway? And why mention fertility? Is there something he should know?

She continues, "We have been at war with the C'thulhu for decades. We desperately need your unique talents. As Director, I contrived to recruit you to leverage your abilities without revealing the true mission. As my personal Paladin, devoted to me alone, I imagined using your talents without your fully informed understanding. Now, caught out, I agree that a fully informed and committed Hat is more trustworthy. Will you take up the cause and become my willing warrior in the coming battles?"

Silently, he wonders, "Will I do for love that which others may not do for money?"

# Chapter Twenty

# An Evil Maid

*Lateral thinking is a common hallmark. Research
shows a link between neurodiverse traits and unusual
& novel ideas, which occurs due to a strong ability to
think outside the box. The neurodiverse are far more
likely to generate creative ideas than neurotypicals.*

"**I**S THAT IT?" ALEX asks. "It's tiny. It appears innocuous, at least as much so as any ordinary thumb drive. So how does it work?"

"Yes," Ritz replies. "In cybersecurity, we often say: Once an attacker has physical access to your machine, they pwn it—they can do anything. It's called 'The Evil Maid' attack, an example—and not merely a theoretical one—of how an attacker can access an unattended device. It uses an exploit called ThunderSpy to break into computers and extract information. So an attacker who can get the briefest temporary physical access to a computer can read and copy all the data, even if your main storage is encrypted and your computer is locked or set to sleep."

"This can exfiltrate data from a computer otherwise considered secure?" Again, skepticism shows in Director's voice.

"Absolutely! When we travel, we frequently leave our valuable clamshells in hotel rooms, trusting they are safe. Usually, they are, but not if there was an "evil maid" working in the hotel—a cleaner (or someone disguised as a cleaner) who, in their duties, takes advantage of their physical access to compromise our device. We think because it's locked and encrypted, it's safe. But not from ThunderSpy. ThunderSpy is extreme stealth; it leaves no traces of the attack behind. It does not require the user's involvement, i.e., no phishing or malicious hardware that the attacker tricks you into using. ThunderSpy works even if the victim follows the best security practices. For example, locking or suspending their computer when leaving it—even if the system administrator has set up the device securely and enabled full disk encryption—is almost worthless. The ThunderSpy-equipped attacker merely needs mere minutes alone with the computer."

Twit adds, "This device, plugged into a USB port, unlocks the lock screen of any clamshell. The flaw is deeply rooted in the silicon and affects every machine based on this flawed silicon, which is all of them."

Director asks, "Whimsical name, or is there a hidden meaning? It looks like an ordinary flash drive."

Ritz shrugs. "Infosec products tend to have bland, descriptive names. Hak-X sincerely tries to inject humor and a whimsical spirit into the field. They also make the Wi-Fi Pineapple, for example. The Pineapple is a sign of hospitality. Since it was created to help infosec professionals and pentesters find vulnerabilities in the hospitable nature of open Wi-Fi, the name naturally follows—no hidden meanings. In this case, we exploit flaws in the silicon which a hypothetical hotel employee who gains physical access to an unattended computer might exploit—the 'Evil Maid' of the name—to undermine silicon-based security controls. It works on any computer."

An awkward silence descends. Seconds later, Twit picks up the discussion. His voice lowers, and he becomes somber. The slow-talker is in command. "Once unlocked, there are many ways to get files out of a target computer. Copying data to a removable device is simple unless the target is well-versed in security, and Sprocket is extremely well-versed. She is a security professional, not some unwary and trusting civilian; one cannot walk up to a secure system, plug in a thumb drive, and copy files. If you steal her password and override the firewall, she will know it happened. Any insecure storage attachment leaves tell-tell tracks which security watchdogs will flag."

The young man pauses. His companions eye him, impatiently waiting. Between his slow speech and dramatic pauses, they are growing impatient.

He resumes, "Not all exfiltration methods require copying to a storage device. There are several network protocols for moving files. FTP is ancient; SCP is a modern, more secure replacement. Any such exfiltration will raise flags if the computer is on a secure network. If it is not on a network, of course, such tools won't work anyway."

"We know a thing or two about computers and networks, you know," Director interrupts, her impatience showing.

Ritz touches her arm. Softly, he whispers, "Please, let him continue."

After another frustrating pause, the young man proceeds. "The trick then is to catch her clamshell unattended and not on a network. There is a protocol called SMB, used for sharing local network resources. Storage arrays use it, for example."

Ritz nods. Less technically versed than the others, Alex stands with crossed arms, with a bored expression on his face. Director is tapping her foot but otherwise showing restraint.

Twit holds up a second, much smaller device. "This is not a thumb drive. It is a specialized computer that mimics a LAN interface and a local SMB storage system. Copying files to removable drives is a security risk and a red flag to managed systems, but those same systems trust secure SMB LAN connections. We will abuse this trust. The device will emulate a trusted LAN-based storage system. The computer is deceived into believing it is writing files to a secure, trusted file system."

"Are you sure this is undetectable?"

Twit shrugs, and the slow-talker vanishes.

Ritz adds, "It does not report to anyone. Besides, it will not be on a network. It instead pretends to be a network unto itself, a connection to the target computer. It mimics an entire, secure LAN. The target computer itself will, of course, record the activity, but it will appear unremarkable. It will leave tracks but not trigger unusual alarms. No one is likely to examine it closely enough to uncover the deception. That's the easy part."

Director glances at him with raised eyebrows. Then, she asks, "What's the hard part?"

Alex clears his throat. "The human part—gaining access to her clamshell. Someone has to get close to her. It can't be Ritz; she knows him too well. She doesn't know me, so it appears I am elected; it may not be easy—this is her clamshell, not a stationary Agency workstation. It seldom leaves her possession unless she locks it away. If there is incriminating evidence, it will be there, not in her Agency workstation.

"This job calls for a raven. Someone has to get close enough to her to gain five minutes alone with her clamshell."

Twit asks, "What's a raven?"

Director responds, "You're young, Twit, but not so young that you do not understand how potent weaponized sex can be. Humans will do nearly anything for sex."

Twit giggles. "I know. Remember, I made your Athena avatar so super sexy. I'm not a child. I know about sex."

Director agrees, "You're certainly not. You have grown so much since we adopted each other. Then you will understand that espionage uses sex extensively. This is not well dealt with in fiction, with a few notable exceptions. It's not quite like 007 with a new conquest in every scene. Rather, it is an organized process with many variations. A woman may cozy up to a man and become his girlfriend to get inside his defenses, gain access to his home and wheedle information from him. Or she may entrap a married man into a compromising position and blackmail him. Similar entrapments are used against gays, particularly closeted ones who do not wish to be exposed. Thankfully, these techniques no longer work as they once did, as society has become more open and forgiving about such things. Wives are more likely to forgive, and if not, divorce is easier than being tried for treason. Gays are less likely to care about being outed, at least here in the West; some countries still persecute gays. There are various terms; a sparrow or a swallow is a woman who uses sex to obtain information from a mark; the distinction is one of technique. A honeypot is an entrapment for blackmail purposes. A raven is the male version of a sparrow."

"Why the trickery?" Twit asks. "You're the Director. Can't you cite security concerns and demand her computer?"

"Certainly, but that would tip our hand and if she's up to nefarious activities, she probably has failsafes. For example, if we merely ask her to open the clamshell, she might purge any incriminating data before we could capture it. Also, we will have a massive advantage if we can get into her machine without her knowledge."

Ritz chimes in, "Like, we can feed her false information or read her plans and anticipate actions, that sort of thing, right?"

Director adds, "Exactly, yes, much like knowing an opponent is reading your email, and you create false emails to mislead them, that sort of thing,"

# Chapter Twenty-One

# The Human Part

*Those strongly neurodiverse experience various degrees of difficulty with social interaction and communication. Other characteristics include atypical patterns of activities and behaviors, a focus on details, and unusual reactions to sensations.*

"I DO BEG YOUR pardon, Miss, so clumsy of me," Alex says apologetically. He has intentionally contrived to spill his drink on Sprocket's dress. That his drink is mere water and nary a drop touches the fabric is irrelevant. The third try at the faux accident he has worked so hard to engineer pays off as he makes a show of wrestling the sloshing drink to safety and dabbing the faux spillage with his handkerchief.

"I do hope you can forgive my awkwardness. I am Alex. May I offer to pay for your cleaning bill?"

She reaches out her hand, sloshing her beverage in the process. "My name is Spomenka, a namesake for my Bosnian grandmother, but my friends call me 'Sprocket.' I hope you will be my friend." She winces in embarrassment at how slutty that sounds. "I mean, don't call me Spomenka," she quickly adds. Then, "Oh Crikey..." as she realizes she has spilled her beverage too.

"It appears we are both in need of fresh supplies," he says. "Permit me to ply you with liquor as you recite your grandmother's amazing story. What are you drinking?"

"Why, bourbon, thank you," she replies as he notes a soft pink flush highlighting her dimples.

"Ah," he says, "bourbon. I should have guessed." He gracefully extends his left hand to collect her glass. "There is a vast difference between whisky and the divine elixir of bourbon. As vast a chasm as that between a mere spirit and whisky itself. It's a pleasure to meet a fellow connoisseur who understands such distinctions." With a slight bow, he proceeds to walk the vast distance, all three feet, to the bar.

She stares as Alex moves with a grace that turns her insides to jelly. How could a man merely walk and be so sexy? She loves the way he sounds—the deep timbre of his voice, his cultured phrasing, silky and yet so masculine, the personification of the expression 'bedroom voice.'

A man possessing such an overpoweringly sensual voice could be ugly as a frog and still be sexy as hell. Ugly? Not! Movie-star bearing. Trim and athletic with apparent education and charm. Plus that voice! Without understanding, she responds to his overpowering Asheran male pheromones. She fears her panties will fall of their own accord.

She notes but does not register Alex's unreadable expression as he returns with two snifters. He hands one to her. "Here, my dear Ms. Sprocket," he says.

Sprocket thanks him demurely and waits for him to initiate conversation. Not that she is capable of intelligent conversation at this instant. Alex's innate animal magnetism has hit her like a ton of bricks. "OMG, he puts me in heat," she thinks as a volcanic rush makes her insides quiver. She is ashamed and guilt-ridden for feeling this way.

What began as a defense mechanism when she was a pimply overweight kid is now a titanium shield against domination by her baser needs. When she falls short of the 'good girl' aspirations she espoused when younger, she deflects the blame; it is never her fault. But if Sprocket understood the subtle power of the genetically engineered Asheran pheromones he inherited from his mother, she would appreciate that tonight it truly isn't.

She embraces her shield's imminent failure.

The echoing slam of steel doors—the buzz of electronic locks. Unseen forces decide who moves freely and who stays put behind cold steel.

Throughout his century-long life, Alex has avoided jail. Until now! He wishes he had avoided it today. He is acutely embarrassed—at being caught. As a raven, his seductive skills, like his mother the sparrow, have never failed him. Never has a raven crashed so ignominiously.

Fortunately, his tenure inside is brief. Vouched-for by the Agency, he soon walks out—chastised but nevertheless released; his mother can indeed be persuasive.

The mission had started positively enough. The date with Sprocket had begun with promise. Alex contrived to meet her socially and charmed his way into her apartment. His youthful appearance and near-supernatural attractiveness did the rest.

His seductive powers had also been his undoing. He was wrestling the clamshell when she emerged, dripping from the bath, energized for another round. Both their plans derailed. Her anger flared hot and vicious; whether fueled more by his attempted theft or her own sexual frustration is debatable, but the Yankee Fist she seemingly pulled from nowhere stifled debate.

He might have physically overpowered her and run, save for the equalizer. The sight of a spectacularly endowed, totally naked, and ragingly furious woman, pointing a Glock 43 with the practiced ease and confidence of a trained marksman, will quail the strongest of men. Whether he was more surprised at her anger and sudden armament, or she at his naked deception is unclear. He still might have escaped, but his stunned shock and hesitation at the incredible sight was his undoing.

Sprocket's position at the Agency attuned her to Cyber espionage. His immediate arrest was predictable when he was caught with incriminating digital munitions, facing her unabashed, aggressive posture and intimidating weaponry. Caught naked and exposed, he managed to palm the storage device, but not the more cumbersome "Evil Maid." Although exposed, the exfiltration was successful. He escaped with the data, although later retrieving it presents a fresh nuance. He swallowed the device.

Sprocket is waiting at the Access Control Vestibule when Ritz arrives. "Good morning, Ritz," she says. She clutches a cup of Bux, with her mask untied and dangling from one ear for sipping.

"Good morning, Sprocket," he says. Instead of his usual dorky grin and nerdy greetings, he is darkly severe and quiet, eyes down, not meeting her gaze. She does a cartoon-worthy double-take as his manner grips her attention. His face is deadpan; even the aroma of her Bux fails to wrinkle his nose under his simple gray mask. He says nothing further, and she grows apprehensive as the moments slink by in strained silence.

It is her turn at the mantrap. She dismisses her mounting apprehension and glugs the Bux's dregs. Discarding the cup, she steps into the cage as two armed guards materialize at the interior exit. Startled, she presents her security badge, and the inside door opens immediately. One of the guards says, "Please come with us." She glances at Ritz. His face is stony, impassive, eyes down as though he hasn't noticed.

She usually takes an elevator to her twenty-seventh-floor workstation. Instead, they escort her to a holding room near the first-floor vestibule. The cell is stark, with a table and a couple of chairs. "Please have a seat," the guard says, "Special Agent Marco will be with you in a moment."

Skeptical of the 'in a moment' promise, already feeling bladder pressure from the Bux, she wonders what she will do for a bathroom if they make her wait long. Tossing aside her face mask, she barely takes a seat when a man in a tailored dark suit enters the room.

"You!" she says. The Special Agent before her is none other than Friday night's date-cum-computer thief.

Alex dons a wan smile. "Yes, me," he says. "Hello, Sprocket." The sensuality in his voice is muted, and his magnetic pheromones are merely operating in dazzle mode. He no longer intends to seduce her; she is no longer amenable to seduction. Nonetheless, she thinks, "Damn, he is sexy," even as she contemplates her situation's severity.

Laying out a tablet, he stands beside it, placing himself near but not overly close to her seated position.

He leans in and says, "I owe you a profound apology for Friday night. I should never have allowed you to catch me exfiltrating your computer. I meant to leave you with a pleasant evening's memory, not a feeling of anger and betrayal. So, again, I'm sorry, but I have a problem I must solve, and I believe you hold the key."

She stares at him, uncomprehending. Finally, she asks, "Am I under arrest?"

"Let's not talk about unpleasant things, such as arrest. That is a dark path I'd rather not go down just yet. So let us first explore other pathways. As I said, I have a problem. Perhaps you have a solution. Let's find out together, shall we?"

"What is the problem? What solution do you think I have?

He lays out for her the compromising documents and messages they uncovered. "There is a leak in the organization, a mole inside who is spilling secrets to some dangerous people."

"That's what Nehemiah said," she responds. "He recruited me to help him find the mole." Then, at Alex's questioning expression, she adds, "Agent Scudder. He recruited me to help him find the mole. I have been working with him for months."

Alex's expression deepens. "Who is Agent Scudder?"

Slightly exasperated, she replies, "From the thirty-first floor. *Technology Management Department.* I met him right here, inside the office."

His eyebrows fly up in surprise; he picks up the tablet and begins pecking furiously. Finally, after several long seconds, he glances up. "Give me his name again, please."

"N-e-h-e-m-i-a-h S-c-u-d-d-e-r," she spells slowly. He pecks some more, and several long seconds pass in silence punctuated by additional pecking. Finally, he lays the tablet aside.

"That's what I thought you said—a few problems, though. First, no one by that name or a similar name works here, has ever worked here, or has visited as a contractor or guest. Second, we do not have thirty-one floors. The top floor is the twenty-ninth. Third, there is no such department as the *Technology Management Department*."

She turns pale. "But that's impossible! He came to my cubical here in this building and introduced himself. He showed me his badge and took me to his office."

"How did you go to his office? The elevators do not go to the thirty-first floor. There is no thirty-first floor to go to."

"The public elevators don't. But the executive elevator does."

"Executive elevator?" His eyebrow displays his shock. "There is no executive elevator."

She smiles. "Nemo says, 'you can't get there from here; you have to go someplace else and start.' I have ridden it multiple times. You have to go to the fifteenth floor and take it from there. It only goes between the fifteenth floor and the thirty-first."

He asks, "What about the thirtieth?"

Her puzzled expression suggests she never considered it. "Well, I guess it probably stops there too; I assume as much."

Then she adds, "Is there a restroom nearby?"

# Chapter Twenty-Two

# Assessment

*Most have average or high intelligence—they learn quickly yet have difficulty applying their knowledge in ordinary situations and adjusting to social demands.*

THE FAINT, SHIMMERING HAZE flickers unnoticed in the darkened alley. The shimmer, manifesting at the edge of perception, is imperceptible to all but the most acute senses. The shimmer indicates an unimpressive doorway. Unimpressive in appearance, that is, to one lacking the sophisticated instruments of a fourth-level Portal Physicist. Nonetheless, it is the Earth-bound terminus of a quantum flux stream of exceptional density, a stable Bifrost bridge to another realm.

The portal brightens, clouds and dims, and a shape shimmers within the haze. A sudden gust disturbs the trash in the alley as, with a soft 'plop,' a figure steps forth. Lean, pale, ashen gray, small-boned, pristine suit, blue shirt, bow-tie, thick plastic-rimmed glasses—Nehemiah Scudder, a.k.a. the Accountant, has returned.

Six blocks away, a distinctive ding disrupts the concentration of one Air Chair occupant and disturbs the sleep of the other. Eyebrows elevate—Twit flies up an app, decodes the message, and releases a soft whistle. The gray feline jumps to the floor and retreats from the desk. Tail twitching, pupils dilated, he stares nervously as the agitated human grabs a mobile and pecks at its screen for several moments.

"Come on," he mutters as he waits for the encrypted handshake and the secure communications icon to turn green. Finally, he establishes a private channel into the Crypto Cavern. A few more clicks and, "Professor, can you talk?" he whispers. A moment's pause. "Good," he continues in a firmer voice. "Soft Cell has raised a four-star alert. One of our luminaries has reappeared and is texting."

"Yes, him—Yes—That's the point... not only has he reappeared on our radar, but it is—No! Not him! YOU! He placed a bounty on YOUR head. He mentioned YOU by name! Right! Thirty-minutes!"

With that cryptic exchange, he rings off but does not close the encrypted channel. Instead, pale and nervous, with shaking hands, he places a rapid-fire succession of calls interspersed with several texts. The Dojo is soon to become crowded.

He delivers several more messages in rapid succession via encrypted communications. Then scooping up the feline, Twit coos, "Professor wants private time with her secret friends. Come on, Nixie, we are not wanted." He lovingly tucks the compliant animal into a soft-padded carrier, muttering, "Secrets, always secrets, all this time, and she still doesn't trust me. I've about had enough of this crayolia."

_ell_

"Unbelievable!" bellows Director, slamming the desk with her hand for emphasis. "How could they operate so freely right under our noses? They have diverted the Agency's Cloud to their cyber efforts."

Alex tosses the suspect sketches on her desk. Director glances at them and then at Alex. He says, "They were, and undoubtedly still are, inside our building!" His voice is soft, but his agitation is evident. Not wishing to be overheard, they closed the door and spoke softly, but his angry alarm was no less vociferous for the soft tones.

Director Novak asks, "My God, how can this be?"

Alex shrugs. "They have taken control of the local Cloud Stack in this building, it is true, but our primary data centers remain untouched, especially the Cybersecurity Initiative Data Center. This penetration is bad, but we can recover. Only the systems used locally by the Toolmakers and other programmers are infiltrated and thus compromised. Although our in-house data center operates as a FedRAMP-certified data center, it only serves in-house needs. In addition to supporting our local firewalls, it supports various security infrastructures, the personnel database, card keys, credentials, and the like. So we know how Scudder got his fake credentials and created his fake _Technology Management Department_."

Director Novak waves her hands in frustration. "Is that all?"

Alex nods. "All the Agency's real data is in the CIDC. In addition to penetrating our systems, they added a massive installation to our data center, taking advantage of the power and cooling. I asked IT to analyze our past power usage in hopes of spotting when this array came online. The penetration seems limited to the security infrastructure and, of course, spying on our activities. There's no

malware, nothing destructive that we could find, but we don't
know what the added equipment is or its purpose. I have plans
with Ritz to have him examine it this afternoon."

Director says, "Yes, Ritz assures me CIDC remains untouched.
I asked him to dig in and monitor what they are doing here
but not to disrupt them just yet. As long as we know of their
presence, and they don't know we know it, we can turn it into
a strategic advantage. But let's discretely move our activities over
to servers in the CIDC and set up a Potemkin village of faux
activity. However, don't tell the users, especially Sprocket. I don't
think she's compromised, but let's not take any chances. She was
deceived but honestly thought she was working for the Agency, so
I don't plan to prosecute her."

Director then asks, "Do you have enough trustworthy people to
get it done? Loyal Asherans, I mean. Will you need to bring in
outside resources?"

"Yes, I have Asheran IT staff members I can trust. I will bring Red
Team members from other offices if I must."

"Good," she says. "How quickly can you switch things up?"

"I will begin immediately. I'll let you know more when I have an
assessment."

Director asks, "Did you investigate the supposed elevator to the
mythical thirty-first floor?"

Alex nods. "I took Sprocket to show me the location. There
is a defunct elevator left over from the 1970s when computers
were gargantuan and required a high priesthood to manage them,
but we decommissioned it decades ago. It served the data center,
allowing easy movement between the floors without exiting the
secure data center area. Sprocket insists it was a perfectly ordinary,
functioning elevator and says she rode it twice, first when recruited
six months ago and again about a month later. She says she visited
Scudder's offices and met his executive assistant."

"How did she even get to the fifteenth floor? Our in-house data center is strictly off-limits."

Alex nods. "Yes, the twelfth through the seventeenth floors originally comprised the primary Agency data center back in the mainframe days. Our data center is now at the CIDC, but those same floors currently support a small in-house data center. Six floors and those are but sparsely populated with servers and such. We were planning to turn four of them into office spaces and consolidate the servers we house here into two floors, and even that would have been lightly filled. Or were before Scudder put in his machinery. Now it's packed. Except for routine maintenance and other occasional services, no one goes in there. That's no doubt how they could add such a massive structure to the data center and not be caught. Security is extremely tight. It is what the IT folks call a 'lights-out' facility, meaning unattended machines. It requires specific credentials to get through the doors. Even I, at my clearance level, can't usually get in there without IT supervisor approval, which I now have. As Director, your authority does not extend to this realm either. So, most of the time, it is deserted, and they took advantage of that to walk in and take it over. Probably used the same faux elevator to get in. Once they had physical access to the systems, they could do anything they wanted without detection. When this is over, I think I will recommend video surveillance of all unmanned centers."

She responds, "Most already have it as standard practice. Ours was too small and insignificant—an oversight in light of this. All the staff and users are right here in this building, so it was overlooked. It exists between a local on-site center and a remote FedRAMP cloud, neither truly one nor the other. The only reason we still have it at all is bureaucratic inertia. It's a playground for our in-house teams; apparently for extraterrestrial invaders too."

Alex shrugs. "Decades ago, people worked in the data center, but technology has changed. The fifteenth-floor vestibule was where mere mortals could submit 'jobs' to the computer staff and then return to pick up the results. When we went 'Cloud' and moved out the people, we decommissioned the elevator; we no longer needed it, and elevators are a maintenance, security, and liability headache. So, the car is locked on the 15th floor, and its power is disconnected. It hasn't moved in decades.

"High-Security credentials are necessary to get in. Sprocket says Scudder took her there, that he had the proper credentials. They walked through the fifteenth-floor security door, got into the elevator, and rode to the thirty-first, perfectly ordinary. I had Lucas from the engineering department inspect it. He assures me that the elevator has not been used in decades and could not be used now under any circumstances, not without significant work and mandatory inspections."

Director asks, "How do you explain her assertion that she rode the elevator?"

"I don't. At least not yet, but I intend to have a portal physicist examine it. But, of course, it will require clearances to get them and their equipment into the building."

"You think there was a portal? How could that be? I highly doubt a portal would locate itself so conveniently. It is as though there's a law of portal physics that requires they always appear in the most inconvenient spot possible. Besides, I presume she didn't mention getting naked for this elevator ride. Transiting a portal while clothed is, of course, unlikely. The portals we know do not well tolerate non-living matter."

"I don't think anything; I am seeking data. There are but few ways one can enter and leave this building. A portal is, in theory, one possibility. I doubt she would be too shy to get naked for a portal, but, right, she would have certainly mentioned such a thing. We don't know all there is to know about portals. Our enemy may know more."

Alex continued, "I have asked Sprocket to continue doing as Scudder asks but to notify me directly, and only me, of his every move, every request. I intend to use her as a double agent as long as I can. I also placed surveillance on her workstation. I think she's an innocent, but I am taking no chances that Scudder will use her as a conduit for misinformation."

Director stares at the sketches for several seconds. One is an artist-rendering; a man, lean, small-boned, pristine suit, blue shirt, bow-tie, thick plastic-rimmed glasses. The other depicts an Asian woman with long black hair in a business suit. "It would appear that we now have a name for *The Accountant*. What about T-K? Did Sprocket have a name for Scudder's assistant?"

"He introduced her as Mary, the same as she gave Rufus at the Hashtag, but she doesn't remember mention of a surname. The name 'Mary' is far too common to be useful, and besides, we don't know that Scudder's name is real either. Still, it is uncommon enough to be a useful handle."

Alex adds, "They have penetrated the Agency, but so far have not realized that Asherans control the organization. We feared the worst when we learned they compromised one of your identities. Fortunately, 'Director Novak' appears safe enough for the moment. Hazel Stone, not so much."

"Hazel is the identity I used to adopt Twit. If that is compromised, then he is at risk. They will certainly go after him if they connect him to an Asheran. Rufus has moved him away from immediate danger, but we must sever all ties between Twit and Hazel. I think perhaps it is time for an Operation Lazarus event."

"Maybe," Alex agrees. "The 'gift of Methuselah' does have its hardships. It's a shame to orphan him once again. First, his mother, now you."

She sits and, head in her hands, sighs. A tone of futility and depression enters her voice. "It is frustrating to walk away from years of work and a carefully nurtured identity to start anew. How many times have I done this? How many more lost and abandoned children must I bear?"

His voice turns soft and child-like, Alex places his hand on her shoulder. "Mom, don't go down that path. It's a path of darkness."

She places her hand on his. "My child, you've only lived a single century. You're still my baby. You scarcely grasp the burden of which I grow so weary. In moments of weakness, I envy those who escaped my fate. Volunteering as a lab rat in my foolish youth was romantic; pushing the limits of aging and death was a worthy quest. But unfortunately, we succeeded far too well; going on and on while watching those around you fall is not a blessing. However, you also must bear the burden I have unwittingly bequeathed to my progeny."

# Chapter Twenty-Three

# Alien Congress

*ASD now includes conditions previously considered separate—autism, Asperger's syndrome, childhood disintegrative disorder, and an unspecified form of pervasive developmental disorder. Some people still use the obsolete term "Asperger's syndrome" for those at the mild end of the autism spectrum.*

"Uh, hiya Boss," says Ritz, removing his mask. His unclothed face betrays naked astonishment. "Wh-Why are you here?" Expecting Twit, finding the youngster is uncharacteristically absent—the Dojo empty save the unexpected visitor—Ritz is unsettled and nervous.

"Hello, Ritz," answers Rufus amiably without looking up. *Pointy-Haired Boss* is not driving today; his mien is intense and focused. More surprising, not only is the man unaccountably present in the crypto cavern, but he is also seated at Ritz's workstation, intently engaged—the first time Ritz has seen the man touch a computer.

Rufus raises a finger to say "stand by" in response to the question as he continues pounding the keyboard. Ritz gapes in open-mouth astonishment at the man's flying fingers.

Finishing in a furious prestissimo of keystrokes, terminated with a forceful slam on the return, Rufus pushes away from the desk and turns to face Ritz.

"I assume she is not with you?" Ritz, flummoxed and bewildered, merely shakes his head.

Waving a hand in dismissal, Rufus adds, "Nah, she wouldn't be. She went to settle the kid in another Dojo. I am sure he's not happy. He's gonna be a lot less happy soon. He's about to be orphaned again. But right now, we need this big old house for a serious confab. About you, young man, about you!"

"Wha...?" he begins.

Eyes twinkling, *Pointy-Haired Boss* pops his head up for a brief moment. "Yes, young fellow, it's strikingly unprecedented," he says. "You have no idea the honor you are about to receive! We are voting tonight to bring you into the fold, spill our innermost secrets, and make you one of us. You are nominated to become an honorary Asheran."

"Wha?" Ritz repeats. Then, he adds, "Who?"

"Why, the Asheran Elders, of course!"

"You?" Ritz, awash in information overload, is verging on a freeze. Shaking, he sits down—a bit too quickly—and closes his eyes.

"Yes, me too," he intones sardonically. Then he laughs. "Yes, Director Novak admitted she divulged our secrets during pillow talk. We wish she hadn't done that, but she believes your Hat skills are the game-changer we need in our war against the C'thulhu.

Carelessness, rank irresponsibility, but I follow her logic. It's a reach, but she may prove to be correct."

"War?" Ritz asks.

"No less than a war for civilization itself." He waves away Ritz's attempts to interject. "There has been organized opposition to our presence as long as we have been on Earth. In the early 1800s, there was even a political party that targeted us. We're an elitist secret society, they claimed. Ha! We have always been able to turn their paranoia to our advantage. But this foe, this organization we call the C'thulhu, or FAANG, are a most worrisome threat."

He sighs as though weary of cleaning up other people's messes. "She has endangered many people's lives, including mine, to save you. Not the first time either. Her rash actions have often skirted the edge. Now we must meet and decide what to do."

"Boss, I ..."

"Son, it's not that we don't trust you. Quite the opposite. One does not earn a White Hat by being unreliable; the Agency does not elevate fools. This meeting is not only about you. It is mostly about HER, her actions, and decisions she made without consulting others."

Rufus notes the stress on the Hat's face and realizes he is challenging the younger man's ability to cope. However, despite the bumbling persona he wears in public, Rufus is astute enough to recognize that the Hat's extraordinary skills come with a price.

Rufus steps closer and places his hand on Ritz's shoulder. "Asherans have lived on Earth for a long time. We are numerous, tens of thousands, but a tiny fraction of Earth's humanity. Asherans have been here for centuries, living with the indigenous population, guiding and helping human society. We possessed high technology when Europe was at the height of medieval times. Our people explored Earth long before our home planet died, and afterward, well, Earth became a refuge for the last of our kind.

"Whenever we revealed our presence to other humans, things have gone disastrously awry. So, we stay low-key, organize, communicate via secret societies, and try to stay out of public consciousness. I pray this does not prove to be the terrible disaster the Morgan affair was."

Ritz, speechless, struggles to assimilate this information. "Uh..." His mouth opens and closes, but the words falter. "Buh..." The most he can manage is a few incoherent monosyllables.

His hands fly up and cover his eyes. He sits for long moments in silence. Shocked, Rufus—taken aback—his face is a study of fascination. Finally, after a few seconds, Ritz drops his hands to his lap as he regains his equilibrium, his face a forced mask of blank expression as he stares at Rufus.

Then, taking a deep breath, the Hat returns. Firmly in control now, he says, "Yes, she admitted the Asheran existence. She convinced me that my talents were crucial to the fight against the invaders, and I volunteered to become a cyber warrior against them. The only thing I ask is to be informed and to understand who I am fighting for and who the enemy is. I do not wish to be an ignorant hired gun, a paladin kept ignorant and fighting walls of secrecy. Of course, I can drive the Air Chair and fight cyber-attacks and other point skirmishes. However, I can do much more if I am engaged in strategic planning."

"Exactly!" Rufus exclaims. "Our original plan was to use your cyber skills without your knowledge or consent. Surgically and tactically, use your abilities, treat you like a mushroom, and feed you BS stories about the various tasks' origins and purposes. Insofar as we intended you to be aware, these jobs would be just another highly compartmentalized Agency initiative aimed at the international APT groups."

Ritz shrugs. "Why did that change? I presume it was related to that mysterious folder she placed on my desktop?"

Rufus nods. "Indirectly, yes. That folder contained a link to the C'thulhu organization. We knew it was hot, that it was dangerous. But no one imagined a simple forensic probe would bring such dramatic retaliation. So, we planned to have you complete an investigation, off books, and unrelated to any Agency case."

The Hat nods in agreement. "Unfortunately, the Ph3DoRA was already on their radar. The Hashtag meteor."

Rufus' face turns dark and grim. "Until they impacted the Hashtag, we were unaware of their space-based assets. Until we arrested Sprocket, we were unaware of how deeply they had penetrated the Agency. We underestimated their capabilities and aggressiveness. When the FAANG linked the Ph3DoRA to your investigation and sent their three top C'thulhu assassins after you, she decided the risk you faced was too high. She decided to bring you into the fold for your protection. She decided! Without consulting with the other Elders, she took it upon herself to reveal the reality of the FAANG, the C'thulhu, and especially, we Asherans, risking all our lives in the process. She may be the senior Elder, but no single Elder, even one as ancient as her, can make such decisions alone."

The Hat states, "They were bigger and better organized than you imagined! Do you think they will resort to meteor shots again?"

Rufus shrugs. "I doubt it, but it's hard to be certain. Repeating the meteor strike would draw excessive attention. One can be explained, but an arterial barrage would give the game away. So, I suspect they won't play that card again unless they become exceedingly desperate."

Ritz nods. "It's extreme, but they are extremists."

Rufus nods in agreement. "The fact that we underestimated them so badly is why we are having this emergency gathering of the Congress of Elders. This evening you will meet the top of the pyramid, the Elders of every Asheran organization."

Ritz asked, "What about all the secrecy, the cell structure, the compartmentalization?"

*Pointy-haired boss* again returns for just a moment as Rufus laughs cartoonishly. Then, sobering, he says, "Compartmentalization is for the plebeians, the operatives in the field. We're introducing you at the top, which shows how important she believes you are. But although you will meet them, they won't be giving you their phone numbers or even their real names. You have been deemed trustworthy, but even so, you won't learn enough to expose the organization to many risks. But you're on the inside, or soon will be. We are about to go to war, and the Elders want to have their say about it. But, despite her near-supernaturally vast age and unparalleled experience, our Senior Elder does not get to decide this alone."

In an oddly softened voice, Ritz says, "Senior Elder, vast age, ... supernatural, huh? Well, she did admit she was older than I would believe."

Boss shakes his head as *Pointy-hair* peeks out thru a twinkle in his eye. "You have no idea, son. You have no idea."

The gavel slams home with a resounding crack! Then two more follow in rapid succession, each louder than the last. Finally, the room falls shockingly silent, stunned as a fourth, sharper crack is followed by additional clatter accompanying the unintentional disassembly of the gavel itself.

Members arriving over several hours have been socializing and partaking in catered food and beverage. Finally, all invited officials are present. The extraordinary meeting of Elders is about to begin.

The instrument's wielder glances at the broken pieces in momentary bewilderment before tossing the shattered remains aside.

"Is there anyone present senior to me who cares to challenge my wielding of the gavel?" she asks. The group murmurs momentarily, then quiets.

"Does anyone present outrank me?" The question is rhetorical. She is the Elder by a wide margin. Not all Asherans share the curse of Methuselah. Only a few of the Elders, those who are her progeny, have an inkling of her actual age. Even many of her descendants only know she is ancient but not how long she has lived.

Redundantly, she asks again, "Does anyone desire to wield the gavel in my stead?" She glances at the damaged instrument. A voice from the crowd calls out, "Go ahead, Phryne, this is your shindig." Minor laughter ripples through the room. She ignores the outburst and pretends not to have heard.

"Hearing no opposition, I hereby call this meeting to order. But before we begin, is the lodge tiled? Look around. Is there anyone here who is not of us?" Her words exclude Ritz sitting behind her on the dais.

"Here!" Someone shouts, pointing to an older gentleman wearing a waiter's vest and carrying a serving tray. The crowd turns to him. The Chair addresses the waitperson, "Please, sir, we appreciate your service and thank you, but we must now ask you to leave." Then, pointing to the tall, athletic-looking man with movie-star handsomeness standing near the door, she adds, "Warden, please escort our friend to his car, see that he is paid, then take a turn around the outside and ensure we are indeed private? Probably best to run a quick scan for electronic surveillance too."

Moments pass in silence as privacy is assured. The mansion is packed. Many organizations and orders comprise the widespread

Asheran fraternity. The top official of each regional directorate is present, along with a smattering of lesser officials.

Meetings of the Congress of Elders are extraordinarily irregular. Gatherings that also include senior officials of various ranks are unheard of. This singular meeting hosts the highest number of senior Asherans ever to gather under one roof. Except for Ritz, all those present are high-ranking Asherans. Every senior Asheran on Earth and a few who traveled to Earth for this meeting are present.

Alex returns and nods at the speaker. "All clear, Worshipful Master," he announces.

"That will be quite enough of that 'Worshipful' nonsense, son." The crowd laughs softly. Her dislike of the classical hallmarks of her senior rank and title within the fraternity is well-known. Fifty years earlier, such titles seemed important. However, the formality has receded in recent times.

Alex tweaks her publicly when opportunities arise. She perhaps called him 'son' for the simple reason that he is her youngest son. Nonetheless, her tone carries a gentle rebuke for his calling her Worshipful Master. He almost answers, "Yes, Mom," but bites down on the words. The situation is too grave for banter.

The Chair claps her hands and says, "Let us begin. I hereby call to order this extraordinary meeting of the Congress of Elders. Firstly, let the record note the Congress last met some five-plus years ago."

From the floor, "Seventeen years, mom!"

A ripple of laughter begins and dies away in an instant. "The chair stands corrected and asks our secretary to please confirm and enter the precise date and time of the previous meeting." Then, with a wink, she adds, "Will you see to it, son?" A few titters ripple and fade.

Stepping from behind the lectern as though to impart a less formal tone, the Elder faces her audience. "I come before you tonight as the most senior member of this most senior clan to consider two matters. Both are highly important; one threatens our very existence, the other may bring our salvation."

She pauses to let her words settle. She scans the audience and makes eye contact with each member, gazing deep into the souls of a critical few. Then after several moments, she continues, "First, I wish to introduce a new member candidate. He is not of Asheran blood. You know how rare it is to invite one who is not of us to join our order. We are voting not merely to invite him to join us but to go further. I am asking to make him an honorary Asheran, fully one of us, something we have never in all our history done. But we face an extraordinary threat, and he must play a critical role in the challenges ahead. We cannot afford anything less than his full commitment and involvement in the battles ahead. I ask you to interview him tonight and vote on his admission to our ranks."

She turns to Ritz. "Ritz, please join me."

She turns to the audience as he stands and steps in front of the rostrum. "Ladies and Gentlemen, I present *Rithwick Jahi Pringle*."

Ritz bows slightly. The audience greets him with total silence.

"Ritz is a martial artist. Not Jujitsu, Kung Fu, not of a physical discipline, but an artist in the arcane ways of the cyber. He is a White Hat of near-supernatural capability."

His cape swells and flutters.

A voice from the rear interrupts, "Worshipful Master, we have many talented people among our ranks. In fact, our scientists invented most of Earth's current cyber technology. So why bring in an outsider?"

She reaches for inner calm; the question is valid. Asheran influence has been a major factor in Earth's technological advancement. "Alex, you are correct, but we lack Hats at his level and face a dreadful enemy. Therefore, we need every possible asset on our team. Ritz is more than merely a talented White Hat; Ritz's hyper-focused memory and his deductive ability for the cyber far exceed anyone I have ever met. I said his talent borders on the supernatural, and I was not exaggerating. Beyond his cyber skills, he possesses the intellectual perspective and insight we desperately need. Our enemy has demonstrated near-supernatural ability as well. I believe that without Ritz on our side, that enemy may well triumph. We need his perspective and unique skills.

"Ritz has already deduced far too much of our history to ignore. We are at a crossroads, facing a crucial threshold. We must decide whether or not we accept him. But you must understand that if we fail to embrace his contribution, we will likely all die. So we must welcome him into the fold and accept him; else, take drastic steps to protect ourselves and our secrets."

She does not elaborate on what sorts of steps. His cape wraps itself protectively around his body.

"On that table are the traditional three bowls," she points toward the rear wall. "One bowl holds black marbles—the second, white. The third contains blue marbles. There is a cloth bag on this scale. Each directorate head present must interview this young man. You may take as much time, ask as many questions as you like, and confer with your teammates. We will not adjourn until everyone has voted. Be thorough, but don't waste time. No one may leave this house before the vote is complete. After interviewing him, each is to choose one ball and place it in the bag.

"When the scale tells us everyone has voted, we will open the bag. We seek a unanimous vote. If everyone agrees, we will bring Ritz fully into our directorate. A single non-white marble, and..." She lets her voice trail away.

A woman down front asks, "If you believe we need his abilities, I agree that this Congress needs to consider adding him to our roster. But, Phryne, I protest! This meeting should have been held before inviting him in. We should have voted whether to reveal our existence, much less invite him as an adopted Asheran citizen. This is most irregular! Does he understand the meaning of the colors?

Does he understand the consequences should he receive a black marble?"

The group begins muttering. The Chair glances around, searching for the gavel. Failing to find it, she then claps her hands loudly. "That won't happen! I won't allow it! No further discussion! Interview him. Decide. Vote! Vote as though all our lives depend on it! Because, trust me, they do!"

The crowd chatters. His cape curls and shrinks, intimidated by the prospect of a black marble vote. But what of the blue?

Her irritation is rising. She claps again. "Silence! No more chatter! Interview him, ask your questions, and vote. Debate is closed!"

Alex steps forward, offering a new gavel. She accepts with a nod, steps to the lectern, and proceeds to bang the gavel. Alex winces at the force of her strike, although the new instrument survives, by what margin he is unsure.

The Chair continues, "The second, the perhaps more dire circumstance is the return of a notorious assassin. An Assbook luminary, yes, one of, if not the worst, very likely the leader, the top man in their organization. This causes ut to rethink the code names we have used for what we considered two organizations. It appears there is only one, and he is the head. The Accountant, or as we now know his name, or at least the name he is using, Nehemiah Scudder. Worse, someone has possibly betrayed us. We've been doxed! He has the IRL names of several members, including myself, and intends to 'balance' our accounts. He has never failed at such an intent, with one noteworthy exception." She indicates Ritz. "Despite two attempts, he has missed Ritz. We believe he intends to correct the oversight. Ritz needs our protection as much as we need his help."

# Chapter Twenty-Four

# Time for War!

*The neurodiverse develop coping mechanisms to cover up the intrinsic difficulties they experience. Still, these strategies take a lot of work and can lead to exhaustion, withdrawal, anxiety, selective mutism, and depression.*

A GAIN, THE GAVEL STRIKES, calling the group to order. The Chair begins, "I understand that some have questioned my leadership, have considered my actions ill-advised. That may be. I have certainly taken risks in what I consider a good cause. But I am weary of armchair second-guessing. If you don't trust my leadership, now is the time to change it. Anyone who wishes to assume my position may do so with my blessing and support. If anyone wishes to wield the gavel in my stead, now is the time. Please step forward and say so."

The crowd murmurs, but no one steps forth. The debate over her leadership reflects a growing fear of the enemy instead of a desire for power by an opposing faction.

"Anyone?" she exhorts. Murmurs echo throughout the large room, but no one steps forth.

The group is on the second day of the meeting—the debate over her leadership has raged without resolution, although they voted to accept Ritz. She was not surprised. Despite her opponents' skepticism, as Elder, her recommendations still carry immense weight. She can be persuasive, even among those who thoroughly understand her powers. Ritz's acceptance into the secretive order was never in doubt.

As the moments pass in silence, no one steps forward to receive the gavel. Finally, she bangs again and continues. "Whether or not I remain the leader, we are at war! You can vote to replace me, challenge me, or follow me. What you cannot do is ignore me or ignore those intending to kill us all."

She steps from behind the lectern. "In 1940, having assumed office after the defeat of Chamberlain, the British Bulldog gave his first official address. That speech was a rallying cry to the citizens to unite against a brutal and implacable foe. His alarm has gone down in history as perhaps the greatest call to arms ever. I should know; I helped him write it."

A tinkling of laughter ruffles through the audience.

"You laugh, but I am telling the truth, and you know it. You do recall Winnie was one of us, right? He knew and valued my long years and many lives. No matter. Dispute my authorship if you must. I could borrow his words, for they apply as thoroughly to us today as they did to that besieged country."

She squares her shoulders and lowers her voice to a gravelly timbre, almost as though to channel the roaring lion himself. "Instead, I will remind you of the seemingly hopeless odds the British faced against the Nazi war machine and their utter resolve to prevail. I tell you now, we must muster equal resolve, for today, we face an equally implacable foe. Where the British met a superior force intent on dismantling their country, we face a technologically superior force actively undermining the foundations of civil society."

The room has fallen silent as her words captivate the audience. She pauses and gazes around the room, staring down those who would doubt her assessment. "An enemy we scarcely acknowledge has set their sights upon civilization itself and infiltrated our institutions. A genuinely alien force from neither Earth nor Ashera: they attack our infrastructure. Villainy, which we do not understand and have no desire to fight, but one that brings the fight to us. We are forced against our will into a fight for survival itself."

She unfolds a sheet of ancient, yellowed paper with scrawled handwriting and studies it momentarily, then lifts it above her head, holding it out to the audience. "I hold that original speech, penned in 1940, in my own hand, from my own scrapbook. Whether you doubt or trust the authenticity of this mere piece of paper, you cannot question the validity of the message. It is a message as crucial for us today as it was on that fateful May day in 1940. As he laid forth that day a policy of war, so we must today. We must wage war, with all our might, with all the strength that God can give us; to wage war against monstrous, alien villainy."

Spreading the ancient writing paper with both hands and again assuming an oddly gravelly timber, she reads, *"And you ask, what is our aim? I can answer in one word: It is victory, victory at all costs, victory despite all terror, victory, however long and hard the road may be, for, without victory, there is no survival."*

Mic drop—the house is stone quiet.

Alex begins slow clapping, and a couple of others join him. For a brief moment, the audience sits frozen, unsure how to react; then, the house explodes. Her use of the historical speech as a call to action has worked. Doubt in her leadership has evaporated in recognition of the otherworldly threat. Although no one quite understands yet what it means, the Asherans have declared unrestrained war on the C'thulhu/FAANG.

Ritz sighs in frustration as the Elders debate. It is one thing to declare war and yet quite another to fight. The Asherans have been fighting the C'thulhu for a long time yet are politically unprepared for a real battle. Unlike a nation-state where war is often necessary and an entire populace can be mobilized against a common foe, the Asherans on Earth are a clandestine, secretive group focused on blending in, keeping a low profile, and protecting their secret existence. Unlike Athena, Alex, Rufus, and the rest of the Agency Red Team, the Congress of Elders approaches the threat of extinction as any risk-averse political group. Left to their instincts, they will debate and argue but never accomplish anything practical in preparing to defeat the enemy. They apparently believe that if they address the C'thulhu in a businesslike manner, they can negotiate a peace deal. Even though the group acknowledges that Scudder is the head of an implacable alien force intent on destruction, the favored approach focuses on competition and negotiation, not unrestricted, balls-out warfare. They lack the stomach for a real fight.

He takes Athena aside. He whispers, "These people are politicians, not fighters. How will we kill Scudder if all they do is sit around and endlessly debate?"

She nods. "Yes, the battle will ultimately fall to our Red Team. Should they oust me as their leader, we will still lead the fight, for we have no choice. There is no one else who is able. But their support means money and resources we must have. Some of them have real fighting experience, and we can count on them to help. War and politics!"

"What was that name they called you? Sounded like Fry me. Is that another of your secret identities?"

She rolls her eyes. "Yes, a few elder members remember a name I used long ago—they knew me then as Phryne. It's from an ancient Greek word that literally means 'toad.' I suppose it was a charming nickname then, and I am still Toad to some. Close family uses it too, though not in the same way. Not exactly a name I care to embrace today; I have some unpleasant memories from that life; I nearly died. My indiscretions always haunt me. But, I like Athena better; I think I shall reinvent myself as Athena."

Ritz smiles. "Well, you are Athena! But I have a new name to call you in private, should I become vexed. I will call you Toad when you vex me." He leans in to kiss her, but she avoids his advance.

"Not here," she says. "I don't want it to appear we are intimate in front of these people. Also, it might undermine my authority in the war."

"We are alone, but I understand. Still, I get the impression that it would not surprise anyone. Am I wrong?"

She sighs. "I suppose you're not wrong. But unfortunately, my reputation is well earned, although I have lived long enough to no longer care about such things. A man is respected for his conquests and considered manly for them. A woman, not so much—even among Asherans. So, let's not rub their faces in it; it might become a distraction. We want their focus on the war, not my libido and sexual peccadilloes."

He winks. "So, am I one of your conquests? Or are you one of mine? I find this all so confusing. Am I respected for seducing the magnificent Toad, or is she to be judged weak for succumbing to my masculine wiles?"

She laughs. "Both, dear one, and trust me, this would not be the first time your Toad has faced judgment for her errant, unbridled sexual needs. But enough love talk; I am becoming distracted myself, and I must not. Instead, I must persuade this herd of cats to follow us into battle lest this caucus degenerates into a bacchanalia without our desperately needed commitments. Unfortunately, I am not alone among Asherans in my worship of the ways of Dionysus. Trust me, Dear, there will be many conquests before this Congress adjourns. Let me get back in there and see if I can move their debate into productive channels before the wine flows and the panties begin to fall."

She turns to leave. Then impulsively turns back, discretely scans the room for observers, and with sudden seriousness, embraces and quickly kisses him. Then, darkly, she says, "Promise me, my bae, that you will look after and mentor Twit. I shan't be able to after this." With that, she squeezes his hand, pulls away, and, leaving him stunned, returns to the meeting. Her gavel bangs loudly for attention as he stumbles into the crypto cavern and falls into the Air Chair, placing his head in his hands. His cape shrivels and flicks back and forth in frustration.

He sits in silence, contemplating. Athena's last words unnerved him. He remembered Rufus' earlier remark about how Twit is "about to be orphaned again" in light of what just happened. She also said she was going to "reinvent herself as Athena." Then she called him her bae! She is not one usually given to juvenile slang or terms of endearment. Dropping bae on him as she did was incongruous and a bit frightening. He is doing the math and not liking the numbers. She asked him to look after Twit; He suspects Twit is not the only one soon to need looking after.

Rousing himself, he logs into the workstation and flies up his tools. He has work to do.

# Chapter Twenty-Five

---

# Hat Unchained

*Estimates are that 10% of the neurodiverse have a degree of extraordinary abilities.*

A FTER FIVE DAYS OF haranguing over details, much having little to do with the actual war with the C'thulhu, the Elder's Congress agrees to give Athena and her Red Team unlimited resources to fight their enemies and absolute discretion in the deployment and use of those assets. Each regional directorate committed all its IT and Cyber resources to support the Red Team. Then, with their meeting adjourned, the Asherans decamp, leaving the ancient mansion empty and unguarded. Not even Twit is in residence.

During the night, a small fire smolders in the basement. The fire spreads slowly at first, but soon the 110-year-old mansion is engulfed. Fire apparatus from five stations rush to the scene, but the firemen are powerless to stem the disaster. Nothing is salvageable from the ruins. The magnificent 12,000 square foot, 35-room Stone Mansion is no more. They attributed the fire to the spontaneous combustion of rags carelessly left in the basement near the furnace. Despite being unoccupied, the fire marshal lists—and the news duly reports one fatality: the elderly nonagenarian owner and sole resident, Hazel M. Stone.

When they tallied the combined resources, Ritz was stunned to discover how thoroughly the Asherans dominated Earth's technology sector. They number thousands of programmers, IT Support personnel, cyber warriors, and dozens of Hats among their ranks. Further, each Asheran brings dozens of potential paladins they control and can count on to assist without fully knowing the nature of the threat. Ritz worried about too thinly spreading his solitary talents to fight the invaders, and his relief at realizing that he has a cyber army at his command is palpable. Certainly, they need a vast body of resources, and thanks to Athena's wrangling and cat-herding, they have them.

He faces the monumental task of categorizing the talents joining his team, particularly the White Hats, assigning their credentials to access his encrypted communications channels, and divvying up the various jobs to those best able to handle them. Fortunately, Alex came to his rescue. Although not deeply technical, Alex is the finest planner and manager Ritz has ever met. Of course, Rufus, Ritz, and Athena provided input, but the plan was all Alex's. Alex created a massive command and control hierarchical matrix organization; the likes of which Ritz had never before seen. Ritz merely had to mention something that needed doing, and Alex ran with it, assigned a resource, and got it done. Ritz's every wish and whim came to life with a suddenness that he found almost scary.

The most complex task was to relocate every application and service on the infested local Agency servers. First, each must be moved to trusted FedRAMP Cloud services. Then, they must replace each relocated service with a similar faux service lest the invaders spot the offloading. Of course, all the activity must take place without tipping off the invaders. It was a massive, complicated, and finicky job, but Alex and his team pulled it off in less than a week. Normal bureaucratic channels would have required many months, and no doubt would have bungled such a complicated undertaking.

Another monumental task involved acquiring explosives and engineering their placement and concealment such that the explosion would destroy the invader's equipment with the least possible damage to the legitimate equipment and building. It would not do to collapse the skyscraper.

These tasks are all straightforward IT and Engineering processes needing little oversight by the Hat, especially a Hat of Ritz's capability. He merely needs to outline the jobs to Alex and get out of the way.

Ritz must focus on the alien equipment grafted into the data center. Before destroying it, they must understand it, which means bringing in a giant brain, an alien brain belonging to an aging Asheran physicist called Max. Still unfamiliar with portals, Ritz marveled at how quickly Max arrived from another planet once they decided they needed his talents. He appeared the same afternoon.

Max and Ritz then deep dove into the alien system, unraveling its secrets. Along the way, he learns about portals, and his mind boggles at the concept. He exclaims, "Portals violate every law of physics! Impossible!"

Two weeks later, Ritz presents their findings to an assembly of Asheran leadership, including Rufus, Director Novak, and Alex.

"Here is how it works," Ritz says while drawing incomprehensible diagrams on the whiteboard. His explanations have left his audience bewildered.

Director Novak has learned that full-on Ritz unchained mode is scary to behold. Disheveled, hair askew with several days' unshaven stubble and highly frenetic—Ritz is in nerd-ecstasy, with a gigantic whiteboard, a large bag of new markers of every conceivable color, and a captive, attentive audience, plus an unlimited supply of Modafinil with a mocha-Java chaser.

He is sufficiently caffeinated; Director Novak, Alex, and Rufus are struggling to follow and slightly afraid to interrupt and ask questions.

"It requires immense compute capability to manipulate the quantum flux with such precision. A bazillion computes! Max could describe the process, although we cannot replicate it. We can't do it! It's impossible!"

Director Novak arches her eyebrows in question. "The portals are a natural phenomenon. Asherans have been using them for interplanetary travel for centuries. The C'thulhu have merely learned how to control them."

"Ah! That is precisely the point! There is nothing 'mere' about what the installation downstairs does. Yes! Yes! It applies structure and control to what is otherwise a natural phenomenon, which is an oversimplified description of a complicated, impossible thing. It is akin to reproducing the impact and power of nature's lightning in a hand-held device, with the precision aim of long-range artillery, and doing so on a galactic scale. Portals naturally occur between planets, but when and where they do so is not under our control. The energy comes from the quantum flux of the Universe itself, not some gigantic stack of 'AA' batteries! This installation not only exerts precision influence over natural portals but can create portals on-demand with unimaginable precision, stability, and control."

"If Max understands how it works, why can't we replicate it?"

"Two reasons," replies Ritz, struggling to rein in his enthusiasm. "First, it is much more than mere CPU resources. The math involved is spectacularly resource-intensive. Just as graphics processors break down complex scenes into tiny elements and assign the computational tasks to multiple GPU processor cores working in parallel, so must the quantum elements be processed by many qubits. Instead of tiny graphic elements, the computational process operates at the atomic level."

"I see," she says, "instead of hundreds or thousands of graphics cores for a GPU, we need billions, maybe trillions of qubits."

"Yes, yes! More! More! Many, many more!" Ritz gushes animatedly, his excitement again rising. He can barely restrain his frenetic animation as he writes '5E25' on the board in red letters. "About 50 trillion of trillions. A cubic meter of air has about 5, followed by 25 zeroes of atoms. It's an incredible computational scale. They could not manage it using all the conventional computers on Earth, plus those of millions of other Earths combined. They have replaced and augmented our cloud stack with a quantum computing stack unbelievably far beyond Earth and Asheran technology. It doesn't exist! It CAN'T exist! It's unimaginable, impossible, and yet, there it is! Six floors of our building are virtually devoted to the most massive, most complicated quantum computer ever imagined! Like having a blockchain with fifty-trillion-trillion miners all plugging away. More so because it's quantum-level processing, not classical Von Neumann processing. Unimaginable scale! Incomprehensible scale! Galactic scale!

"Max is impressed!"

He pauses for breath and pushes his wild hair from his face. His caffeine and Modafinil-fueled deep dive into portal physics and quantum computing has unwound his OCD-driven reserve and pomade to expose a side of Ritz that Director Novak has never imagined, much less seen. Although not himself a physicist, Ritz possesses the intellect and basic science and engineering understanding to grasp and explain the theory behind the portals, once broken-down Barney-style by the aging Asheran portal physicist.

"But second," he continues, "and more daunting, are the energy requirements. The energy necessary to open and maintain a transwarp conduit between worlds exceeds all the energy available to humanity by at least three orders of magnitude. Even that may wildly under-estimate the requirement. We don't know how they obtain such energy! I would insist it is flatly impossible, except that we have proof it happened. Happens, in fact, so regularly that it is almost mundane."

"So," asks Alex, "that's how they Macgyver a portal over the elevator doors to produce the illusion of an unremarkable elevator ride while transporting the unwary Ms. Sprocket to the non-existent 31st floor?"

"Precisely. The required control and synchronization are incredible. It is stunning and terrifying that Scudder and the C'thulhu would use such unearthly technological resources on such a pedestrian illusion. In this case, the portal may only reach across town to another building. Still, this same installation also manages various Portal nexuses within a hundred miles of here, with the remote end in another solar system. The quantum installation occupying the 12th to the 17th floors is an interplanetary transporter, much as the Great Bird of the Galaxy, Roddenberry himself imagined!"

Director says, "We know the C'thulhu agents, the Accountant, and others, secretly access our facility via a portal on the 15th floor. They have unfettered access to our offices but do not know we have discovered this. They do not know that we have discovered Sprocket is their agent and that we have turned her to our cause."

Alex replies, "Yes, we have two options. Dismantle their installation and block future access or exploit their ignorance. The explosives we have planted give us the first capability, but how can we manage the latter?"

While Ritz and Max unravel the mysteries of the massive quantum array in the Agency's local IT center, Alex pursues other, more militant activities. He heads a task force dedicated to tracking down and killing or capturing every Assbook entry. Killing them was the first intent. Most of them are considered far too dangerous to be allowed to live. As invading aliens from another realm, Alex insisted that they did not know what abilities or technology they may have. Allowing them the potential to warn others is not an option. Hence, except for a small number deemed worth interrogating or useful as bait, the explicit orders were to kill on sight, and without warning, without exception. Even the fear of an identity mix-up leading to an unfortunate innocent death is not a reason to hesitate. Given the stakes, they must be treated as vermin to be exterminated. Asherans are not squeamish in dealing with assassins and terrorists. Backed by the resources pledged by the Elders, Alex intends to decisively end their machinations at any cost.

Accordingly, Alex dispatches nearly one hundred Asheran military teams brought from another planet for this purpose. Each has a complete dossier on its target, including all available intel on their last known location, associations, and so forth. Over the following month, the teams track and kill some eighty-four adversaries. Those who remain appear to have gone into hiding, having deduced they were hunted.

Nehemiah Scudder, now believed to be the mastermind, the capital 'C' in C'thulhu, is at the top of the team's kill list. He is suspected of being based on another planet and using artificially created and controlled portals to travel at will. Therefore, the team needs bait to draw him out, to draw him to Earth where they can engage.

The assassin we call T-K, who calls herself Mary, is thought to have a special relationship with Scudder. She is one prize assassin that did not escape, nor was she summarily killed. Instead, the team plans a sting operation to scare her, hoping she will call Scudder for help.

After a lengthy search, they discover T-K has a small apartment on the lower east side where she lives alone, without even a cat.

Ritz asks, "Is this the building?"

"Yes," replies Rufus. "Remember, we don't want her to know we found her. We want her to merely fear we are closing in and close to finding her. Catching her is not the goal. We could have arrested her long before now; it's Scudder we want. We hope this 'near hit' will prompt her to call Scudder, and we will trap him."

"Got it. T-K doesn't know you. You watch the street and signal me when she approaches the building. I will step out of the nearby alley and let her see me, but I will be headed away from her and won't spot her. She will see me and, hopefully, call Scudder. Max and his team monitor the quantum array for activity and scan the local space-time continuum for signs of portal formation. Once they spot his entry point, we will meet him with deadly force."

Athena says, "Remember, we are only supposed to draw Scudder to Earth. After that, Rufus and I will scramble teams to intercept him. No doubt Rufus and Alex will lead that action, although I am desperate to kill him. We will deal with T-K after we have killed Scudder."

Ritz jumps up. "I want in on that action too. I want to see Scudder ended."

"Better stay away from the action. You're not a fighter and are too valuable to risk."

"Maybe, but you're more valuable than I. Besides, Scudder wants me; he's already tried to kill me multiple times, so I think my value as a lure could be useful too."

"There is that, I agree. You're right. Scudder may not know me from my brief appearance as Trixie or the Hazel Stone identity. If we dangle you as a lure, it may draw him out, but it's risky."

"I know it's risky, but the whole purpose of our mission is to kill Scudder and eliminate the C'thulhu threat. He will kill us all anyway if we fail to trap him. So, get into position now; she routinely arrives home soon. Let's hope she follows her usual schedule."

Accordingly, Rufus takes a position across the street, and Athena stations herself down the block. Ritz settles in the alley where he can appear at the right moment for her to see him. They wait, Bluetooth earbuds in place, and secure BPP voice channel open.

After nearly thirty minutes, they are becoming restless. They are tightly keyed for their mark's arrival. Finally, Athena whispers, "She just stepped off the train. She's headed your way. Be ready."

Rufus, lounging across the street, apparently reading a newspaper, whispers. "I got her. Ritz, get ready, step out on my mark." Rufus begins a slow countdown as the mark makes her way toward the front door. The countdown reaches zero. "Now!" whispers Rufus. In that instant, Ritz steps out of the alley and turns left without noticing the tall, attractive, professionally-dressed Asian woman with long black hair. She looks at him but does not react. Neither does the woman enter her building. Instead, she continues walking as though she had all the while been heading elsewhere. She casually raises her phone, speaks into it briefly, and then tucks it away.

A curious drama unfolds like a scene in a movie. A comedy. A well-known (in clandestine circles) White Hat calmly strolls the city street, nonchalant, whistling tunelessly, seemingly unaware of his surroundings. Behind him, a notorious female assassin ambles as though merely out for a Sunday walk. Behind her, an older, slightly rotund, and shabbily dressed gentleman with a folded newspaper tucked under his arm, steps along smartly as though attempting to catch up to the woman. Finally, a half block behind, another Asian-appearing woman with her equally long black hair streaming behind her is overtaking the older man.

"Pick up the pace, Ritz. She's gaining on you. We don't want her to get within knife range."

The four of them walk this way for several blocks; the assassin is challenged to match Ritz's stride and overtake him without breaking into a run, while her followers, with no such hesitancy, are closing the gap and soon, unbeknownst to the killer, are near to accosting her.

The Asheran physicist Max joins the call to relate the nascent portal's location, which is forming approximately a block ahead. Scudder will soon join the party. With this confirmation, Rufus reaches out and takes the woman's elbow. "Mary, My Dear," he says. "How wonderful to see you again." Before she can pull her knives, his Fitz Special introduces itself as well. "Please, step over here; we must have a brief chat. I have a proposition for you that I am sure you will find most interesting." Just as he takes her aside, Alex steps up and flashes his badge, disarms her, removes her phone, and places her in handcuffs. He tells Rufus, "Go ahead and help Ritz and Athena. I've got her."

At his signal, two uniformed officers appear, and together, they move the surprised assassin toward a waiting car.

Rufus breaks into a run to catch up with Ritz and Athena as they approach the opening portal. Despite his unathletic appearance, he moves with startling alacrity.

Ritz and Athena pause at the portal as it brightens, clouds and dims, and a shape shimmers within the haze. A sudden wind gust sweeps Athena's long black hair as, with a soft 'plop,' a figure steps forth. Lean, pale, ashen gray, small-boned, pristine suit, blue shirt, bow-tie, thick plastic-rimmed glasses—Nehemiah Scudder meets them face-to-face, an expression of surprise as he realizes he has neatly stepped into a trap.

# Chapter Twenty-Six

# Battle

*Frequently they are the loners who never quite know how to greet others or the aloof who aren't sure they want to greet anyone. Some are collectors who know everyone at the flea market by name and date of birth, the non-conformists who cover their cars in bumper stickers, and a few are those oddball professors everyone has in college.*

A QUIET CLICK PUNCTUATES the stillness. Director's hand, empty a moment before, holds an impressive though dingy, olive drab firearm.

Mask drooping, Ritz's naked face bespeaks stunned surprise, only to repeat itself a half-second later when Rufus' snub-nosed .38 Fitz Special joins the party.

Ritz takes a slow, careful step back. His cape wraps itself protectively around his body.

Scudder halts mid-step and tilts his head slightly to peer over his plastic-rimmed glasses. Like a cloud of microscopic fireflies, a speckly shimmer adheres to his form, crinkling the surrounding air.

Not reacting as one staring down the barrel of .45 caliber doom, a sinister smile plays across his face as he turns toward them. Ignoring Ritz and Rufus, the assassin focuses on their leader. With slow, precise movements, he removes his glasses, polishes the lenses with his silk pocket square, tucks them gently into an inner jacket pocket, and meticulously returns the hanky to its proper home.

Athena speaks. "Hello. Scudder, is it? I've been looking for you! I would like to be able to address you by name. In the past, we've only called you C'thulhu and FAANG, codenames we used as we studied and unraveled your organization. We are so gratified to meet you in person. What name would you have us use?"

Squaring his shoulders and adjusting his jacket, he says, "C'thulhu? FAANG? Bah, how little you know—meaningless syllables. Noises to name gods who you scarcely imagine. Know that I am Eichworen, and we have honorably served the Council of Eddore for millennia. Be glad you face me, Nehemiah Scudder, a mere servant of that august body, and not the gods themselves. I am far more merciful than they."

Waving the M1911 for emphasis, she asks, "Why are you here? What do you want?"

He shrugs. "When the forest grows too wild, a purging fire is inevitable. I am that fire."

Assuming a thin, raspy voice, with emotive 'B' movie bulging eyes, Rufus steps forward and pokes the Fitz Special squarely at Scudder's chest. "Hehe, I love fire. Hehe. My friends love it too. Hehehe. When I set them on fire, they run around and scream. Will you be my friend?"

Scudder ignores him. Eying Ritz as though speaking directly to him, he adds, "Some 12,800 years ago, Enkig, Third of Eddore, razed this planet with an asteroid sent by his own hand! With one brutal swipe, he ended your civilization."

Ritz interjects, "Huh? Civilization? Why kill a few primitive hunter-gatherers?"

"Hah! How little you know! Your legends of Atlantis and Lemuria are but faint echoes of a past long swept away. Enkig sterilized this planet with fire and ice, and the Council, confident that humans merited no further attention, turned to more urgent matters."

Cocking an eyebrow, Athena says, "And yet, here we are. Sloppy workmanship, I'd say. Tsk tsk. Gods with giant egos can be such bunglers."

Rufus adds, "My kind of god; clumsy, bungling, and conceited."

Scudder's smile turns to steel, and his eyes narrow as he shifts his gaze from Ritz. He drills into Athena as though attempting telepathic mind control. "The Council had other concerns; other worlds that required their attention. Do you imagine you were so important to Eddore? You were a virus, a bug to be squashed, nothing more. Driven to near extinction, yet like a fungus, you surge back as the Council tends other matters."

"Inconsiderate of us. I must look him up and apologize." As she speaks, her features soften, and her manner warms. She now has his full attention as an invisible battle for control begins. Her voice, previously mocking, turns sensual, and wave after wave of her pheromones fill the space between them. Rufus, recognizing her shift in tactics, shuts up. Ritz, too, opts for silence. Both men know her powers.

Under her influence, Scudder's voice turns gentle, almost intimate. "Ah, but your resiliency piqued Enkig's curiosity. Like an unusual fungus or a strange-looking insect. When you grew back, he gave you over to the Eich as playthings, lab animals for experimentation.

He gave us a free hand, so long as you did not escape your petri dish, your planet.

"I culled your numbers at Gobekli Tepe and again at Catalhoyuk. By the time of Ggantija, you were once again ripe, and I culled the herd again.

"Since the Ice Age, for over ten thousand years, the Eich have intervened to limit, shape, control, and prune, like shaping an exquisite Bonsai. I cut and trim an earthquake here, a pestilence there. I keep things balanced just so.

"Hamangia, Sumer, Skara Brae, Sodom, Gomorrah, Ancient Egypt, China, Greece. Like a surgeon, I pared away at each one. Caesar did not burn the library at Alexandria; I did. The Roman civilization did not pass peacefully into the night—I was its assassin."

She says, "The fall of Rome prompted what some have considered a time of ignorance, barbarism, and superstition. Your doing?"

"Not at all," he replies, his manner warming. "After the Roman fire, I went elsewhere. But, I had spent far too much time fiddling around." Amusement tugs at the corner of his mouth.

"I bet you and Nero played a fine duet."

"Ha-ha." He fairly cackles. "Yes, Nero and I left for a while and took a delightful little vacation. Between the fall of Rome and the mid-1800s, the troubles of that era were all on humanity's head. Humanity and the Church, or rather the corruption within the Church, especially after *Alfonzo di Borgia* became Cardinal. Your specie thrives on strife! Despite the corruption, warfare, terror, murder, and bloodshed under the House of Borgia, they produced Michelangelo, Leonardo da Vinci, and the Renaissance. They had brotherly love, five hundred years of democracy, and peace in Switzerland. And what did that produce? The cuckoo clock!

"Bah! Popes playing at kingship, a licentious priesthood, and institutionalized moral hypocrisy. Frankly, I expected your species to die, and you nearly did. The Plague of Justinian, the Black Death, and the Bubonic Plague's resurgence in Italy, London, and China killed millions. Not my doing, though I would be proud to claim the credit. No, that blame lies in your own hand; you did that to yourselves."

She says, "Then the Enlightenment drew you back? We were getting uppity again, so you founded the Golden Circle, the Red Men, the Fenian Brotherhood, the KKK, murderous secret societies worldwide, am I right?"

He smiles and nods. "Let's not forget the Black Hand."

"Ah," she says. "One of your agents assassinated Ferdinand then? I've often suspected C'thulhu, excuse me, Eichworen activity in such history-altering events."

"Ah, yes, the Black Hand was my hand in Sarajevo that day," he replies. He smiles in wan amusement as he nods acknowledgment. "I thought it an inspired bit of manipulation. I established vectors for strife, class struggles, and racial tensions. Between the race-baiting communists and the secret supremacist societies, I expected enough wars and turmoil to occupy your attention for another millennium."

Her tone waxes sensual. Even this demigod responds to her pheromones, visibly relaxing his guard under her smile. "I am guessing that young Adolph fell into your influence as well ...."

"Oh no, he was not my agent. The man born with what would become the most infamous name in history was but an ignorant and lazy peasant, too stupid to graduate High School. He fancied himself an artist but couldn't pass a simple art school entrance exam. Did you know the Academy of Fine Arts Vienna rejected him twice? He could barely eke out a living as a common laborer while he played at being an artist by making bad watercolors that no one would buy. When I found him, he lived in a homeless shelter, an insignificant pimple on humanity's ass."

She lowers her weapon ever so slightly to encourage him to talk. "So how did he become the most infamous man of the 20<sup>th</sup> century?"

"Ha! There's the splendid irony! He didn't. I killed him on his 20th birthday."

She nods and smiles, lowering her voice and turning up the pheromone onslaught another notch. "So ... That was you!"

He bows slightly, taking credit. Under her magical influence, he is becoming proud, cocky even. "I consider it my best performance—A little over the top, I suppose. But yes, I eliminated one insignificant and worthless human, took his place, and gave him the most infamous C.V. in human history."

"Impressive. So, you faked his suicide in that bunker. Whose corpse did they find?"

He fairly cackles. "Ha, that was the greatest comedy of errors I ever saw. I prepared an elaborate death scene, and the Russians destroyed it. The bones credited as his are, in fact, those of a young woman. Ah, those crazy Russians."

"You've been busy during the Cold War, too."

"Eh, not exactly. I gave a young, arrogant politician a nudge with a fictional "Missile Gap" report, and he did the rest. What is it with your politicians? Such arrogant self-righteousness. Anyway, I took another vacation; I skipped nearly a decade."

"So, that wasn't you in Dealey Plaza?" Her voice projects raw animal magnetism as her influence engulfs him. He relaxes visibly under her beam.

"No, I missed the fireworks that joyous day. That was all your politicians, though I would have been proud to claim it. One brutal bully kills another and blames it on a patsy. Who cares? The strife and turmoil I have inflicted over the last few decades scarcely differ from what you inflict on yourselves. I take a few years' hiatus and return to find things just as chaotic as I left them. And yet, despite pandemics and riots, you've unlocked nuclear energy, rudimentary spaceflight, exploded computing and communications, and have discovered the elemental Portals. I cannot allow this last. You may play with spaceflight, but cannot escape your planet."

"Our people have been busy," she says, almost as though taking personal credit for humanity's progress. Her eyes practically glow with hypnotic energy.

His voice lowers a notch and softens. "Ah, but you speak of the past when it is your future that should concern you the most. Your species cannot abide stagnation; it is change itself that drives you, strife that propels you—the drive to evolve and grow. But evolve into what? That is the question—a truism, perhaps, but applicable all the same. You will go no further. You will not be allowed to escape your planet to threaten other worlds. Enkig would be most vexed."

Shifting his stance, his voice rises; he gesticulates to emphasize his words. Without warning, he has thrown off her seductive influence and remembered his intent. "It is time to return your kind to the Stone Age, to wipe your works from the face of the Earth. Indeed, I am the fire that destroys all."

A deafening **BOOM** punctuates his remark. "Good thing I brought my fire extinguisher," she says as the .45 slug strikes his shoulder.

The concussive blast from the massive .45's first shot unnerves Ritz. He covers his ears, watching as Scudder, nearly felled by the first round, regains his footing and instantly conjures a flickering, though almost invisible shield. The first few rounds from the .45 leave their mark despite his armor before he engaged the shield.

Overconfident, stunned, and caught off guard under her hypnotic influence, he has overestimated his armor and underestimated the power of the M1911. Scudder staggers backward, nearly falling under the impact. He grabs his shoulder, visibly wounded, his face contorted in shock and rage. Then comes another and another, round after massive .45 round. Almost genteel pops from the smaller .38 intersperse the ear-shattering reports of the .45. Both fire and fire again until exhausted.

Scudder, expression dumbfounded, shocked, and angry, stands as though facing a roaring gale, holding his shoulder as a massive green stain spreads down his side. He is badly hurt but still on his feet and able to fight. His shock morphs into a smirk as subsequent bullets strike the new shield and vanish in a flash of light, mere inches from his body. Their ammunition exhausted, he laughs weakly and without his customary disdain. Then, steeling himself in obvious pain, he raises a hand. "You have sealed your fate."

Then, with a toss of his hand, he unleashes a blast of telekinetic force and waves away the three warriors like so much confetti before a storm. They fly bodily down the alley, slamming into an unyielding wall.

Bruised and scuffed, the three collect themselves and turn to their assailant, only to discover they are alone. Nehemiah Scudder has vanished.

"That went—not so much," she says as she picks herself up. "I think I need a bigger gun."

Rufus groans and shakes his head. With visible effort, he hauls himself to his feet, standing unsteadily. "I think I broke some ribs."

Ritz is the last to stand; he's the most rattled, scared, and unsettled by the confrontation with their nemesis. He mutters, "I think I had a childish accident."

"He could have killed us but didn't," she says. "He was bleeding."

Rufus channels his cinephilic Austrian accent. "If he bleeds, we can kill him," he misquotes. Then, dropping the pretend accent, he adds, "Your first shot badly hurt him. You surprised him, had him off guard and disoriented. He probably would have killed us otherwise."

"I was aiming for his head—he moved as I fired."

"That's why I always say to aim for center mass. But more importantly, you seriously hurt him. His body armor took the brunt of your first slug, but it still nailed him. He was bleeding badly. That shot almost rang the bell. Too bad he managed to raise a force shield. You might have deeply penetrated his personal armor with a little more firepower."

Ritz asks, "Wha-What's with that shield? And how did he fling us like that?"

"Uh." Rufus shrugs. "I don't know how he conjured that body armor, and as for the shield, well, shield is the wrong word. It looked like a portal. He wasn't deflecting the bullets, like his armor, but sending them elsewhere. I wonder what was on the other end.... But as to his apparent mastery of telekinesis, I have no clue. I've never seen anything like that, except in science fiction movies. Maybe he's a Jedi."

Ritz says, "Jedi! Right! Ha! Sith maybe." Then he raises his voice in sudden inspiration. "The quantum array! It allows the creation on demand and fine manipulation of portals. Who says a portal is only for transportation? That's how he did it—created a portal on demand; sent the bullets somewhere else. Though I don't see how that would enable telekinesis. That's something else."

Athena says, "A few weeks ago, I would have said 'impossible.' Manipulating Portals with such precision is far beyond our ability, but the C'thulhu, or perhaps I should say, the Eich appear to have mastered portal science. Sadly, you and Max have shown us just how much we must learn. We can't hope to match his science."

Rufus huskily says, "We're gonna need a new plan." Then he adds, "We can't conjure portals, or telekinesis, but we can level the playing field. We can destroy that Eichworen quantum computer and prevent them from doing so either."

"No!" She says, "They are unaware we found their machinery. We must not squander the advantage. If we merely destroy it, they will vanish only to return better prepared. We must play this hand strategically. He spoke only of Earth history and never mentioned Asheran influence. Perhaps there's a strategic advantage, too; he may not know about our presence and how we control the Agency. He may not know Asherans are in the game."

Silence, thick and gloomy, reigns as the three ponder strategy. Ritz scratches at his mask. Then, finally, he says, "How bout dis; we hide explosives in the machine and then lure him into another confrontation. Just as we open fire, we can detonate. Catch him by surprise."

She says, "A good strategy, assuming we get another chance at him. We already have the explosives. Alex has been working on that for weeks; it's nearly done. But there's a rule about shooting at gods and kings..."

"Don't miss!"

"Right! Assuming we get another shot at him, we need an undetectable control method."

Ritz says, "We have secure comms. Fortunately, our encrypted Black Phones have gone unnoticed by the C'thulhu, probably because we didn't rely on them much."

"Are you sure they can't break the encryption with the quantum machine?"

His eyes droop. "My encryption is the best in the world, but that quantum array is out of this world—not a cliche, I mean it literally. It is so far beyond any possible science we know that it can only be alien in origin. We've stayed secure, if we have, only because they haven't yet noticed our hidden channel. Against that machine, any encryption is like putting a screen door on a submarine. I knew our comm was useless the instant I understood that monster machine's capabilities. We need a new class of mathematics."

Rufus says, "Won't work anyway. We can't stick a phone, especially an encrypted one, in the machine to trigger the bomb. He would detect any cell phone. Planting explosives without detection was challenging enough. A cell phone would be a dead giveaway."

"Won't use a phone!" Ritz rips off his mask in rising excitement, his animated response causing his companions to peer sharply at him.

Rufus begins, "How...."

Interrupting, Ritz plows ahead. "We use simple radio! A passive receiver. No two-way, no transmitter, no cellular connections to detect. Push a button, a relay closes, and KABOOM!" He waves his hands expansively.

Rufus says, "Sure, but plain radio has limited range. Without tapping into a cellular network or some other kind of signal repeater, we couldn't detonate from more than about a mile away. Probably less in the city; radio needs line of sight."

"Not all wavelengths need strict line-of-sight, and there are plenty of repeaters we can freely use to extend the range. Amateur radio repeaters are free and open. Only need a receiver tuned to a local repeater output channel. Send an activation code through the repeater, the receiver picks it up, and Scudder gets a rude surprise as his quantum array disintegrates into so much junk."

"Without a transmitter, how do we prevent false activation? How will we know it worked? Without two-way handshake communications, won't it be unreliable?"

He shrugs. "Open-loop control, definitely, but we can mitigate the risk. We'll use a rolling high-security code like in a keyless entry system to prevent false activation and send it many times for redundancy. We'll know it works when Scudder doesn't kill us."

Director and Rufus arch eyebrows at one another, at Ritz, then again at each other. Then, turning to Ritz, Director asks, "Won't this require engineering to create the receiver, the trigger, and such?"

"All the items we need are available from stores in the city. Hams have been controlling things remotely for a hundred years. Easy peasy. I can get the materials and put something together quickly. You and Rufus get with Alex on the explosives and make sure they are ready. I'll get with Twit, and we will supply the trigger."

Director says, "Do you need Twit? I want to keep him out of this."

Ritz shrugs. "He has talents we need. I can keep him unaware of the Asheran aspects. Just let him assemble the hardware."

She shakes her head. "Keep him unaware. Maybe he can wield a soldering iron, but he must not learn anything about the larger mission. If he gets exposed, Scudder will go after him. I can't have that. I must protect him at any cost."

Fear crosses his face for a moment. He wonders why she is so protective of the kid. He wishes someone would protect him like that—he would stay out of it too, if he could, but after a moment, Ritz says, "Agreed. I will recruit him to build the gear, but he won't know specifics about its purpose."

Then, almost as an afterthought, he adds, "And I want a gun! A big one!"

# Chapter Twenty-Seven

# Weapons

*Everyone is somewhere on the scale between
neurodiverse and neurotypical. We must all
learn never to apologize for our imperfections or
idiosyncrasies, but to take them as a challenge,
something to learn to leverage rather than overcome.*

I T IS FRIDAY, AND the week has spilled all over itself as usual.

Bang! Bang! Bang! Gunshots echo hollowly in the deserted indoor gun range. The shooter, a tall, athletic woman with long black hair, lowers her weapon.

Under the careful tutelage of Athena and Rufus, Ritz has begun learning the art of marksmanship. Guns are profoundly against his nature, but so is defenselessness. Therefore, he was surprised to learn that firearms and marksman training in the city is readily available to the Asheran contingent, contrary to popular perception.

"See Ritz," Director says, holding up the gun, "The M1911 is called a Forty-Five because of the ammunition it uses." She picks up a cartridge to emphasize her words. "It oozes authority and gravitas. The .45 ACP is the One True King. Various ammunition formulations are available, with up to a staggering 1100 Joules of impact, about the same as dropping 250 pounds one full meter—don't drop it on your foot! It has a massive recoil and makes huge holes in the target."

Presenting the gun, she explains, "This is what is known as a semi-automatic. It is also called 'single-action.' That means you must cock it before the first shot, but semi-auto means it automatically loads and cocks itself again after each shot, ready for the next. The 'semi' means you must release and pull the trigger for each shot. Unlike a fully automatic, it will not fire again until you release and pull the trigger."

Retrieving her target, Ritz notes she has put three holes in the center. Any tighter, and she could have used the same hole for all three. "You make that look easy! Let me try!"

She shakes her head, "Not yet. School first. One thing to remember about the M1911 is that after firing, it leaves the hammer cocked, ready to fire again, with a live round in the chamber. So always, and I mean ALWAYS, ALWAYS, ALWAYS engage the thumb-safety."

Ritz's expression reflects doubt. "Safety or not, that doesn't seem safe."

"First, It's a gun. It is NOT! Ever! Safe! Not ever. Second, if the chamber is hot, it is cocked and loaded. ALWAYS. You should always engage the safety, but it is no more—or less—safe one way or the other. It's a FUCKING GUN! It is intended not to be safe."

Ritz is appropriately impressed. "H-How do I un-cock it?"

"Glad you asked. That's the next lesson. One sure way is to fire it until it runs out of bullets. But if that is not your intent, then first, remove the magazine." She demonstrates.

"Second, pull the slide back to eject the live round, then do it again and visually confirm that there is no cartridge in the chamber." Again, she suits actions to words. "Then do it again and stick your pinkie finger in the chamber." She does so. "Then, after you are absolutely, totally, completely positive there is no round in the chamber, point the firearm in a safe direction, disengage the thumb safety, and stick your thumb between the hammer and the frame. POINT THE FIREARM IN A SAFE DIRECTION and tug the trigger, using your thumb to gently lower the hammer." She does so. "When the gun is in this state, we call it *Condition Four*, de-cocked with magazine well and chamber confirmed empty."

"Wow," he says. "Couldn't I just use my thumb to lower the hammer like that without ejecting the round?"

She sighs. "I don't recommend it, especially for a rookie. If there is a live round in the chamber, never de-cock and carry it hammer-down. Doing so is a prescription for an accidental discharge. Cocked and loaded, with thumb-safety on, which we call '*Condition One*,' is less risky than hammer-down on a live round, believe it or not. But always remember, it's a FUCKING GUN!" She slams the table for emphasis.

Ritz jumps and recoils, though whether at the table-slam or her language is unclear. "When we faced Scudder, I heard you cock it, and obviously, there was a live round in the chamber. Am I wrong?"

She smiles the sort of smile a parent uses when caught out by a precocious child. "You're observant, and not wrong. Chalk this one up to 'do as I say, not as I do.' The M1911 wasn't meant to be de-cocked, though some who should know better sometimes do so, myself included. We call that '*Condition Two*.' It's dangerous and not recommended. Also, if the hammer gets away from you, the slide will likely break your thumb. Not to mention the damage an accidental discharge can do. So don't! I mean it. DON'T! Don't follow my example."

Handing the empty weapon to Ritz, she says, "Here. Now show me how to properly de-cock."

When handling a handgun for the first time, people are always surprised by how heavy they are.

He nearly drops it.

He de-cocks the weapon. She says, "Now you are hammer down on an empty chamber. We call that *Condition Three.*"

She calls out '*Condition One*,' '*Condition Three*' and '*Condition Four*,' to have him place the weapon in each state. After several cycles stepping through the motions, cocking, and de-cocking the unloaded weapon, she is satisfied. Ritz is a quick study, but she makes him repeat the exercise several times even after she is convinced he has mastered it, because even brilliant students can fall victim to muscle memory or simple carelessness. Finally, she hands him the loaded magazine.

"Show me how to load and unload the weapon. Be careful! These are live rounds. Show me *Condition Two.*"

He does so, then he repeats the process, dropping the magazine, racking the slide, ejecting the round, and then de-cocking as she demonstrated. Then he repeats it, stepping through each condition several more times, emptying the magazine.

"Excellent! Now you get to shoot it. Here's a fresh mag. But before you do, let me introduce you to the grip safety. The M1911 has TWO safety mechanisms—there is also a third one, which I will get to. The thumb safety prevents the gun from firing when activated. The grip safety is different. It was designed to prevent a drop fire if the gun fell out of its holster while on horseback. The grip safety allows fire only when it is gripped properly. If you have small hands or a weak grip, the gun may not fire. It requires a firm grip." She demonstrates. Despite her femininity, she has the requisite strength and grip.

She says, "I mentioned a third safety. That means the safety between the shooter's ears. There is simply no substitute for training and practice. Before I allow you to carry this weapon, you must prove you are qualified, and that means practice."

Ritz and Director are alone in a vast indoor concrete shooting range. Before loading the magazine, he struggles to get his ear protectors in place with one hand while holding the weapon with the other. He has learned the value of suitable protection. His ears rang for hours after their encounter with Scudder.

He is surprised at how difficult the weapon is to shoot. Learning the basics is easy, but hitting the target is hard, and getting good, preternaturally good, takes years. Getting to Director's level takes lifetimes!

After emptying the first clip without hitting the paper, he exclaims, "Damn, that's hard; how'd ja do that?"

"More years of practice than you'd believe!"

The team has been busy in Scudder's absence: Explosives planted, radio components engineered and tested. Nonetheless, as the days pass without Scudder appearing, the team grows apprehensive, worried that he plans an ambush that will catch them unprepared. They strive daily to improve their game in anticipation of their next encounter with the Eich. Regular weapons practice became a daily habit, not only for Ritz but for everyone.

One morning, Ritz has just entered the gun range where he, Director, and Rufus have been training. Distance blurs the line between a "boom" and a "bang." However, he is close enough to be sure this was a bang. This gunfire is markedly different than either the M1911 Director favors or the .38 Fitz Special Rufus carries. Athena had stated her intention of acquiring more potent firearms. Thanks to the Agency's status as a branch of Law Enforcement, they can legally obtain weaponry nominally off-limits to civilians.

Noticing Ritz, Rufus asks, "Like my new toy?"

Ritz eyes the unfamiliar weapon with suspicion. This is not a handgun, but at about 20" long, it's not a long gun either—he thinks it resembles a science-fiction movie prop.

"What is it?"

"This is a PS90—full auto, 900 rounds per minute, with each round having much greater velocity than the M1911. But, more importantly, it's designed to penetrate kevlar vests. And force fields. The M1911's fat, relatively slow bullet is effective against soft tissue, but the P90 is more effective against armored targets."

Director holds up a pistol; Ritz momentarily mistakes it for the M1911. She says, "This FN five-seven uses the same ammunition and has almost as much penetrating power. Only it's a semi-auto, like the .45, and holds up to 30 rounds."

He holds up a cartridge. "These babies are military grade. The skinnier hard-cast bullets strike at nearly twice the velocity and are effective against armor. The .45 is heavier and hits with more total energy, but the P90 is faster, penetrates better, and throws way more bullets. If she was able to wound Scudder through his armor with the .45, this one should nail his ass. My Fitz Special is worthless in battle, but this baby brings a whole new game."

Lapsing into his cinephilic persona, he intones, "*Say hello to my new friend....*"

# Chapter Twenty-Eight

# Codename Overlord

*Human relationships can be especially challenging and tiring. They worry about what they just said and what someone else just said, and how or if that all fits together, what they will say next and what the other will say then, and do they owe them something or is it their turn to owe me, and why do the rules change depending.*

T HE FOUR STARE AT the widget, breath held tight until a quiet click punctuates the silence. "Hah," says Ritz. "Toldja."

Director asks, "How long did it take?"

Rufus, examining a display, responds, "That last time was 96 milliseconds, but that's misleading. Two repeaters were already active. We know from past trials it can take 500 milliseconds or more for the repeaters to detect the incoming signal and engage. We can't control that."

Before them is a sloppy breadboard of electronics modules, a gadget comprised of receivers tuned to the output channels of three nearby Ham repeaters. The contraption responds to a coded control sequence, closing a relay when it receives the same signal from two of the three repeaters within a ten-second window.

"The worst-case test clicked the relay in just under one second. That is rather long in a firefight. We need to improve that."

They will wire the relay to several small placements of explosives hidden within the massive quantum computer filling the 12th through 17th floors of the Agency building. Placing—and hiding—the explosives was a challenging task, carried out by Rufus, Alex, and Director while Ritz and Twit were building the electronics.

The young wizard formerly known as Twit, interjects, "Our trigger squawks on three channels. The receivers listen on three matching repeater outputs, but we can easily add three more."

The others turn to him. Finally, Director asks, "What would be the point of adding more repeaters? Improving the odds that two will be available?"

"Not three more repeaters. Add the input channels of the three we already use. That way, if we're close enough, we bypass the repeaters entirely. They don't care if they hear the repeater output or our signal direct. The receivers are voting on the output. Any two agree, and blooey!" Fitz *né* Twit waves his hands.

"Interesting," says Rufus. "We do not know where we will confront Scudder. We will have a nearly instantaneous response if we can draw him close. It could require an additional half-second or more if we are further away, but we are covered anywhere in the city. Neat trick, I like it."

Fitz interjects. "We should have a fail-safe, a backup. Just in case the radio fails."

Ritz nods, and Rufus clasps his hands together and rubs them. Deadpan, Rufus says, "So, you're saying there's no redundancy?"

Weeks pass after the confrontation wherein they wounded Nehemiah Scudder, and the lack of alien retaliation is starting to wear. They seriously injured him but expected a rapid return; his fierce promise to kill them keeps the team on edge. They expect assassins around every corner and worry over the possibility of meteor strikes.

Although the threat of a surprise assassination still exists, that threat has diminished considerably. Alex's assault against the Assbook entrants has borne fruit. A few high-value targets like T-K were captured and interrogated, but they killed those of lesser strategic value on sight. The Asherans evidenced no remorse at summarily executing professional killers. It's a hazard one accepts when picking up the assassin's mantle. A vanishingly few escapees remain in hiding, demoralized, powerless, and hunted.

Pinpoint meteor strikes, too, are a worrisome possibility, although the Asheran scientists opined that further space-based weaponry usage was unlikely. However, Ritz is not so sure.

The Asheran physicist contingent, led by the aging Max, maintains a 24-hour watch on the interdimensional flux, tracking the natural portals as they form and dissipate. They are especially alert for Scudder's artificial formations.

Maintaining an intense 24/7 vigil for weeks on end is demanding. Still, thankfully, the Asherans can rally a massive army of agents, scientists, and engineers to keep the lookout sharp. Ritz, Rufus, and Athena take turns at the early-warning station while continuing to shoulder their regular duties. The effort also involves many non-Asheran Hats and tech adepts. Although not fully aware of the scope of the mission, trained paladins man various routine monitoring posts. The Asheran scientists handle the actual portal monitoring, but non-Asherans man the far-flung communications network that tracks the portal movements. The secret of the portals is closely guarded. Even Ritz is largely out of the loop, with but slight knowledge of portal-related matters.

Determined to protect him from harm, Athena has become a fiercely protective mother bear protecting her child, guarding Twit as though he were her own blood. Finally, Ritz intercedes on the kid's behalf to assign him a minor monitoring station; she insists on keeping him ignorant of the mission's true scope, especially the extraterrestrial factor. She insists he must not learn of Ashera or any other alien aspect, portals, or especially her origins and age.

That, in itself, is not particularly striking; the Asheran secret is closely held. The Asherans wall of secrecy makes the Manhattan Project appear like an open-source effort. Nonetheless, Ritz has difficulty comprehending her reluctance to share her secrets with her adopted son. Ritz reflects on the revolving mother figures in his and the kid's lives.

There is a difference between privacy and secrecy, he decides. Ritz is not a naturally secretive person. Parents keep secrets, he muses, and marvels that he was allowed to discover the Ashran secret; he still does not know Athena's actual age.

Finally, the alarm sounds. An artificial portal is forming nearby. Ritz spots the alarm first. Then, as he launches himself out the door, he shouts, "It's Scudder! Tell the team. Arm the deadman trigger. Tell Alex to get into position, too."

"Scudder!" he thunders, feeling the painful intensity of his shout deep in his vocal cords.

The Accountant freezes. Turning to face Ritz, he smiles. "Ah, Mr. Pringle. Good day to you. Sorry to say this shall be your last." He raises a hand to strike.

Ritz draws the M1911 from his jacket, pointing it squarely at the villain. "Maybe. But unlike the last time we met, I am not defenseless."

Laughing, Scudder can barely be understood as he chortles, "He-Ha-he, so you're not, ha-ha, you think. That small but noisy steel phallus won't help you." The fireflies around Scudder's body grow brighter as he speaks. "You remember how ineffective the lady-gun was against my shield last time. Why do you think this time will be different?"

"I saw it penetrate your armor, saw it wound you, saw you bleed, shield or no... This close, I won't hit your shoulder. Center mass is easy from here. And I ain't no lady!"

Just then, another joins in. "But I am, or so I've been told. And I have a new lady gun." She waves the Five-seveN.

Scudder's fireflies grow denser and brighter, virtually forming a solid shimmer around his body. "It doesn't matter," he smirks with disdain. "Do your worst. My newly augmented shield can stop a Mark 8 shell."

Rufus steps into view and raises the P90. "I don't have a Mark 8, but the 50 rounds in this 'lady-gun' still pack a wallop. I bet it'll make you wince."

Conjuring a shield/portal, he obviously does not wish to test his personal armor's strength against their new armament. As the portal materializes, Ritz subtly pushes a button in his pocket. Nothing happens. He coughs.

Recognizing his cough/signal, Director and Rufus both press the buttons on their respective transmitters. Nothing happens—again.

Scudder's smile turns rancid. "Don't you hate when you go all-out to prepare a surprise party for someone, and they refuse to be surprised? Indeed, I deduced your plans and disabled your receivers. As soon as I have eliminated the three of you, I shall dismantle your explosives. I grant you that it was a valiant effort, you nearly succeeded. I congratulate you on a game well-played, but the game is over; now you die." As he speaks, he again raises his hands as though to strike.

Director raises her voice. "Alex? Now would be excellent." She holds up her phone with an active call.

Scudder's face shows surprise. Focused on the radio, he had overlooked the open call. They stand frozen as though cast in amber. One second, two seconds... Before the count reaches three seconds, Scudder's shield/portal disappears. His expression turns to one of shock.

Ritz fires. At such close range, the impact of the massive .45 is painfully visible as Scudder reels under the blow. Ritz fires and fires again until his clip is empty, his last shell spent.

Scudder is shaken but standing. The .45 has made itself felt, but his force shield remains intact. No green stains besmirch the villain's impeccable suit.

As Ritz's weapon exhausts itself, Director's Five-seveN speaks up. Spots of green now decorate her target's clothing, but they reflect little more than mosquito bites. Her penetrant shells, too, find their power spent against his shield, unable to more than scratch the target behind it.

Rufus' P90 joins in, expending its entire magazine in one extended full-auto burp. The 16-inch barrel of the bullpup design and the superior power of the black-tipped shells, at last, make their point. Even mosquito bites can be deadly if numerous enough.

Screaming in pain and rage, Scudder drops his jacket and glasses as he launches into a wild run, discarding clothing items as he retreats.

They glance at each other in surprise—surprised that their foe is not still merely standing after that assault but able to run. "Where?" Ritz begins.

Rufus shouts, "The Bowery! The portal nexus in the Bowery. He must not reach it."

Launching after Scudder, Director shouts into the phone, "Alex, meet us at the Bowery portal!"

Dropping her phone, bag, and weapon, she begins unbuttoning and unzipping. Half a block into her pursuit, she flings the partly unbuttoned dress over her head, kicks off her shoes, and accelerates, pursuing her quarry clad only in a near-transparent chemise.

Rufus chases after her but lacks her speed. He also lacks her ecdysial grace as he fumbles to unzip, unbutton, release, and drop various items while running.

Ritz, surprised by their unexpected disrobing, hesitates. Then, as they disappear around a corner, he rallies, slams a fully loaded magazine into the pistol, and chases after them.

Unsure where they have headed, Ritz does his best to follow. Instinctively tracking their trail of disruption and pandamonium, he makes several turns before becoming lost in a confusing yet strangely familiar maze.

He would have lost them if not for their shouts and the startled bystanders in their wake. As it is, he is uncertain into which alleyway they chased the quarry. Then, just as he is about to start picking at random, he spots Alex.

"This way," shouts Alex. "They're headed for the Bowery Nexus." Ritz has no idea what a nexus is or where he might find one, but the puzzle slips to the back of his brain as he spots the weapon in Alex's hand. Alex is carrying the biggest handgun Ritz has ever seen. Not a gun enthusiast at heart, Ritz does not recognize the S&W 500 and does not know it has almost five times the stopping ability of the FN—All he can say is it's damn big!

He follows Alex, discombobulated, flummoxed, and somewhat off-balance. Three blocks later, they charge into a familiar dead-end alley. Overcome with an odd sense of déjà vu; Ritz realizes this is the same dead-end alley where he and Director had eluded Scudder and T-K months before. He begins to suspect this dead-end alley might be home to one of the portals the Asherans had mentioned.

Director, Rufus, and Scudder face off in the alley, all utterly naked. Ritz wonders if he will ever be able to unsee that which no man should view.

Scudder, leaking green ooze from many punctures, holds them as though bound in place by some unseen power of the mind. The three, posed as though in a strange diorama, are frozen as though trapped in amber. Rufus and Director press their foe, attempting to grab him, held at bay by his invisible telekinetic force, as unarmed as they are unclothed.

Ritz boggles at the power their foe wields. He had assumed Scudder's control relied solely upon the quantum array, but even with its destruction, he still possesses powers of—what? Telekinesis? His force shield still sparkles. Utterly naked and without support from the quantum array, the villain remains unvanquished.

While Ritz is busily boggling, a faint, shimmering haze flickers into existence inches from the alley's far wall. A larger version of the shield Scudder had displayed in their first encounter appears spontaneously.

Ritz goggles dumbstruck as the portal brightens and stabilizes. Then, with a start, he realizes why the Accountant and T-K had abandoned that first chase so many weeks ago. They assumed he and Director had escaped via this natural portal. That they had merely climbed the fire ladder to another floor had not entered their minds.

As Scudder moves toward the portal, Director screams, "Stop! Alex, don't let him get away!"

Rufus shouts, "Shoot him, stop him."

Alex tries to aim his massive weapon, but Rufus and Director are too close to his line of fire. He scrambles toward Ritz, and as he does so, Ritz remembers that he still holds the M1911.

Ritz raises his handgun. Unfortunately, this shot is not so easy. Unlike the minutes-earlier confrontation, the distance makes this a challenging target for a marksman of Ritz's limited experience. Closing one eye and squinting, he fires.

He misses—then misses and misses again. Ricochets echo the alley, endangering everyone but Scudder.

Finally, his fifth attempt elicits a flash of impact from the demigod's shield. Scarcely staggered, Scudder has reached the portal, and Alex has reached Ritz's side. The massive S&W barks, striking center-mass. Scudder falls. The giant fifty-caliber bullet penetrates the flickering shield sufficiently to inflict a wound far beyond those caused by the smaller weapons. Green blood sprays dramatically, soaking Rufus and Director. Apparently mortally wounded yet still fighting, Scudder waves a hand at his assailants, and a forceful wave of telekinetic force knocks Alex and Ritz asunder.

Alex's S&W fires again as they fall, missing the intended target and grazing Ritz in the leg. Lacking a personal shield, Ritz is down, taken out of action by friendly fire. Ritz's shocked brain wonders what the hell was so friendly about it. At this caliber, even a slight graze is severe. His leg shows a massive scratch and a quickly oozing red stain.

Pain explodes as Ritz realizes he has been hit. He grasps his leg, trying to stem the crimson flow as he writhes in pain.

Scudder, wounded but still moving, drags himself painfully erect and staggers toward the flickering portal. On reaching it, he falls into the insubstantial void as though collapsing in surrender to his injuries.

Crying "Noooo!" in chorus, Director and Rufus dive for the portal, entering mere milliseconds after Scudder. Ritz, regaining his feet despite his injury, hobbles toward the event horizon. Although he has recently accepted the existence of portals, he has yet to grasp the nuances of the natural ones such as the one his friends just fell into. As a result, he does not truly understand they got naked because natural portals do not readily transport non-living matter. Hence, he attempts to follow, fully dressed with gun in hand.

Alex shouts, "Stop!" but Ritz ignores him.

When the tip of his gun touches the field's surface, the portal emits a soft plop and vanishes. Ritz sprawls ignominiously.

Stuffing the S&W into his waistband, Alex runs to Ritz, stripping his belt for use as a tourniquet. Moments later, bleeding somewhat staunched, Alex helps him to his feet.

"Can you run?" Alex asks Ritz.

"I don't know. Hobble, maybe..."

"Then let's hobble out of here. Cops usually stay away from this part of town, but we've made a lot of noise we do not need to explain. Let's go."

Leaning on Alex and holding his unbelted pants while trying to hang on to and hide the pistol, they clumsily scram.

A van cuts in front of them two blocks from the scene, and a door opens. The kid commands, "Get in!"

The two pile into the van, and between the stress, shock, blood loss, and anxiety, Ritz passes out.

# Chapter Twenty-Nine

# Bittersweet

*Many never receive a diagnosis and live with other labels: they are the creative eccentrics, the inventors, the space cadets, the math geniuses, the great musicians, writers, and artists who astound us and animate our lives.*

A WARENESS DAWNS SLOWLY. FIRST, clatter: people talking, televisions playing in the distance, things barely heard. Then, as noise intrudes on his consciousness, next comes the smell—antiseptics, cleaners, medicine-like flavors. Then with a rush, he remembers being shot, a hasty tourniquet using his belt, and a fast hobble from the scene.

His gun! What happened to his weapon?

Awareness slams him in the gut, and he sits up! Or intended to—that was a bad idea, but unfortunately, he is weak. His muscles don't respond. He must be drugged; he realizes he is in a hospital.

At his movement, he senses someone next to the bed. Focusing, he realizes it is Fitz.

"Hey, Kid. What happened?" He can barely get the question out, struggling not to slur his words.

"You got shot—sprung a leak. Leaked out most of your red juice. Alex and I brought you here; they plugged the leak and refilled you. So you'll return to the Air Chair in a couple of days. Got an ugly scar on your leg."

"I remember the firefight. Alex shot me! With a fucking monster gun, the biggest fucking gun I ever saw! Where are Athena and Rufus? Did they stop Scudder?"

Fitz shrugs. "You mean Professor—I don't know about Scudder. Alex called and told me to bring the van to the Bowery. Me, with only a learner's permit! But he insisted. When the cops stopped us, I discovered it was loaded with ammunition and firearms. Surprise!" The kid waves his hands expansively.

"So, what happened?"

"Lucky, I skated. Alex was with us, so my nominally illegal driving was legal. Legal enough, anyway, except for the big chase scene and running from the cops. Chased me right to the hospital emergency room. Since you were unconscious and bleeding, they overlooked my rule-breaking. Alex flashed his badge at them, but they arrested him anyway; something about illegal firearms. He said they were his, and I was blameless. I hate to think what woulda happened if they'd stopped me before I picked you two up. Anyway, we got you to the hospital. A bit of argument, but I stayed here and waited till you woke up. The End. Oh! Except some cops want to talk to you when you wake up."

Ritz asked, "Where's Alex?"

"The cops took him. The van too, and the guns. Where's Professor?"

"Clueless! Last time I saw them, she and Rufus were chasing Scudder. There was gunfire and fighting, and they all three disappeared." Ritz decides to skip over the portals, force fields, or nudity—Fitz would think him crazy; he didn't half believe it himself, and besides, Athena had wanted the kid kept ignorant of such things.

Ritz lies quietly for several moments, then softly says, "Kid, I'm not sure she's coming back. She asked me to look out for you...."

Fitz sits woodenly, frozen, unresponsive.

After several seconds, Ritz begins, "Fitz..."

"I heard you!" He could hear the pain in the kid's voice.

Minutes pass in silence. Then, finally, the kid says, "I saw the fire on the news."

"What fire?"

"The dojo. Burned to the ground. Nothing left. The news said Hazel Stone died in the fire. It's not true, is it? That's the name Professor used. One of them. But the news said Hazel Stone was ninety years old. Professor wasn't that old! She didn't die in the fire, did she?"

The Hat is taken aback—his face displays shock and horror. Although he has not heard about the fire, he instantly connects the comments about the kid being orphaned again and reinventing herself as Athena. She does not want the kid learning about secret identities, Asherans, or other extraterrestrials. Finally, he shakes his head. "I don't know, Kid, I just don't know. I don't know anything about a fire, but...I think she expected to die."

Ritz's soft whistle falters and fades as his destination looms; his rideshare pulls up to the red curb in front of the familiar dark, gray, featureless monolith. He struggles briefly with his crutch as he climbs out of the vehicle to stand in line at the sally-port.

A wan grumble leaks through tight lips, his face turns pale, and his heartbeat quickens with stifled dread. He used to love his work and White Hat status but hated the tightly controlled environment. Oppressive security measures approaching needless harassment were a necessity he could once accept, albeit with a coarse internal dialog. Now he cannot imagine why he did. True, it's an excellent job with respect, high pay, and status, but he believes someone with his skills can earn bank anywhere. He intends to test that theory.

With Director gone, he no longer has a reason to continue as a Hat. Without Director adding spice to his days, without fundamentally enjoying his work, and with the oppressive burden of extreme security, it just isn't fun anymore. It took a gunshot wound to make him appreciate life. So, when Athena vanished through that portal to another realm, he decided he must reclaim his life. Today is his first day back from his injury. He has his resignation letter in hand, and they owe him many weeks of unused vacation; he intends today to be his last day. With no personal effects in his cubicle to clear out, he hopes this visit will be brief.

As he enters the 29th floor, Ritz ponders briefly to whom he should tender his resignation. Boss is gone with Athena—wherever that is. Instead, a new, unfamiliar face occupies the Director's office, a man he has never met. Ritz briefly wonders if the new Director is Asheran. He considers how he might inquire without tipping his hand. But unfortunately, he can't exactly knock on the door and ask, "Excuse me, sir, but are you an extraterrestrial?"

Ritz decides it doesn't matter, that he doesn't wish to know. He wants to be done with the Agency and the Hats, secret societies, extraterrestrials, and everything else. Especially Athena and her merry band of manipulative, pheromone-wielding Asherans. He has no wish to be a pawn in the games of people who can manipulate his psyche, bypass his judgment centers, and cause him to agree to anything, no matter how ridiculous. He believes he now understands why Athena did not want Fitz to understand her more deeply. That's fine with him; he wants nothing more than to forget that these people exist. It will be a favor to the kid if he can also distract Fitz from thinking about his time with Athena as his ersatz mother.

The kid must live with him now. No problem, as they get along terrifically, but his tiny apartment won't do, and finding a nearby replacement won't be easy. Finding apartments in the city is challenging, so he and Fitz discussed it and decided a clean break would be best. No more regimented cyber security jobs. They agreed to move to California and launch a new kind of Crypto startup. He has ideas around the novel application of Crypto technology to manage the identity, name, image, and likeness of athletes and actors. Partners, founders of a Silicon Valley startup. He likes the sound of that.

Besides, he has responsibilities now. He has a teenager to raise, a promising young cybersecurity padawan who needs his guidance; he promised Athena he would care for the kid. And Nixie will look after them both.

**THANK YOU, DEAR READER!**

Thank you so much for reading **Undercover Alien**. I hope you enjoyed reading the story as much as I enjoyed writing it. Positive reviews from awesome customers like you help other readers to feel confident about choosing **Undercover Alien** from among the competition.

Could you please take 60 seconds to go to https://www.amazon.com/review/create-review?&asin= B09YNG2JD3 and share your happy experience?

We will be forever grateful. Thank you in advance for helping us out!

Click the link or snap the QR Code to go directly to the Amazon.com **Undercover Alien** Reviews Page.

Please visit the Undercover Alien Reviews Page and leave a nice review.

https://www.amazon.com/review/create-review?&asin= B09YNG2JD3

# The Story Continues...

**Opening chapter of the next, although as yet untitled story in the Undercover Alien series**

Consciousness encircles Lex even as he fights to keep it at bay. With a start, he awakes and instantly wishes he hadn't. Phantom fingers of blue-grey smoke curl around his face, and the stench assaults his nostrils. Yet it is not disagreeable compared to the acidic reek of urine and putrid fetor of feces. He opens his eyes and instantly regrets it.

He is lying in a fetal position against a wall, back toward the sidewalk, hiding his face from the passersby, no more desirous of seeing them than they are of seeing him. The cardboard box that had served as his bed was soaked in fresh urine.

His urine.

Today is not his first morning baptism, not his first day to begin with a dampish blush in his crotch. Many were the mornings his mother had cussed, berated, and beaten him for wetting the bed.

Mother!

Why must she intrude on the warm gray fog of awakening? Morning begins with a small cloud of existential confusion; those few seconds spent sorting the context of life—what day it is, what happened yesterday, and which horrific events were merely dream figments—those moments should be his alone.

It was the leap from the cozy womb of motherly love to the harsh reality of a flawed Mother's Code. The Mothers code, hardwired into the kernel of men's brains, creates an expectation of unconditional love. When manic-depressive bipolar illness warps and distorts that mother's love, the pain of abuse and rejection becomes unbearable.

He resents her intrusion, even though it is only memories of his troubled past haunting his more troubled present. He dropped out of school and left home to escape her wild mood swings, vile temper, and incessant rages, but he can't escape the pain and guilt.

He climbs the wall, dragging himself erect. Then, collecting the fragments of his mind, he turns and surveys the city. Thankfully, he realizes the feces is not his, but another's, deposited nearby while he slept. Perhaps the defecator had contributed to the baptismal flood as well. He did not doubt the wetness of his crotch was his own, but the quantity soaking the cardboard was far greater than he could have voided. Plus, his meager stash of pot and cash is gone. He feels nauseous and overamped, wishing for a hit to settle his nerves. Presumably, his anonymous visitor had rifled his pockets while he slept.

Standing, he unsuccessfully suppresses the urge to retch. Then, steadying himself with one hand on the wall, he gingerly steps away from the mess and begins stagger-walking. He has nowhere to go, but he heads there anyway. He scans the street looking for a shower truck—it is early; the generous tourists might buy lunch if his stink doesn't shoo them away.

**Join my mailing list to be notified when the next story becomes available:** ***https://NathanGregoryAuthor.com***

# About the Author

Nathan Gregory writes books, which shouldn't surprise you since you are reading one. Nathan insists there is nothing inherently wrong with writing, as long as you do it in private and wash your hands after.

Before he succumbed to the nasty habit, he was a respected engineer, contributing significantly to the practice of networking and the commercial Internet we know today. Moreover, previously he was a highly sought-after electronics technician in the days when electrons were aggressive, vicious little beasts that often required wielding a hot soldering iron and holding raw, leaded solder in one's teeth to subdue them.

When not chasing rogue electrons, he often played a mean game of billiards, made awesome **Pool Hall Chili**, and cooked incredible, mouth-watering hamburgers.

Nathan's journey with Science Fiction predates even the rogue electrons, spicy chili, or scrumptious hamburgers; you see, he came of age during the Space Race!

When, on September 12, 1962, JFK said, "We choose to go to the moon," Nathan had already launched a rocket to the moon with **Rick Brant** in John Blaine's "*The Rocket's Shadow.*" He went to Mars with Heinlein's "*Red Planet*" and "*Podkayne of Mars,*" became a "*Space Cadet,*" trekked across the moon with Kip and the Mother Thing in *"Have Space Suit, Will Travel,"* and trod the *"Glory Road."*

Edgar Rice Burroughs' Mars/Barzoom Epics with **John Carter** and the *"Princess of Mars"* were inspirational classics. A Keto devotee, he fully intends to live long enough to, like Heinlein's *"The Man Who Sold the Moon,"* **Delos D. Harriman**, die on the moon.

**Note to Elon:** You two really should talk!

By the time "Star Wars" captured the public imagination in 1977, Nathan had already dreamed it a million times. So naturally, it should be no surprise that he should eventually degenerate into a Science Fiction writer.

Check out my author's website for FREE short stories, family tales, and my FREE BLOG! Subscribe for regular news and updates.

https://www.nathangregoryauthor.com/

Please check out the Nathan Gregory Amazon **Author Central** page.

https://amazon.com/Nathan-Gregory /e/B00QZHIIBK

Please check out my YouTube channel. I have many good videos you might enjoy.

https://youtube.com/channel/ UCD4vPm_YoJvInuWhF2IICJQ

Please follow me on Twitter.
I rarely tweet, but when I do, it's a keeper. You won't want to miss a single one.

https://twitter.com/nathan_gregory

Please check out my Pinterest pages. Tons of interesting stuff there, including my infamous recipe for **Pool Hall Chili**.

https://www.pinterest.com/wa4otj/

Please visit my LinkedIn page for a peak into the fascinating world of my cybersecurity and crypto-token day job.

https://www.linkedin.com/in/nathantgregory/

Please visit my Bookbub Author's Page.

https://bookbub.com/profile/nathan-gregory

Please visit my Facebook page for various odd posts, old family photos and more.

https://www.facebook.com/nathan.gregory.923

Please visit my Instagram page.
You never know what interesting and eclectic,
wild and crazy things you might find there.

https://instagram.com/nathan.gregory.923

Please check out my Goodreads public page.

https://www.goodreads.com/author/show/
8578172.Nathan_Gregory

# The Writings of Nathan Gregory

### Science Fiction

In 2014, I wrote a wild story purely as self-therapy and escape, with no intention of publishing it. It was unabashed male-fantasy, written as stress relief. During the process, a distaff buddy asked to read it. I was terrified! I just knew she would hate it and feared she might never speak to me again.

It took some time, but she eventually wore me down and I gave her the manuscript. She loved it! Not only that, but she shared it with her friends who also loved it and encouraged me to publish it. Eventually, I gave in; it went on sale in February of 2015. That story began what has become my Chromosome Adventures series.

Please visit the **Chromosome Adventures** Amazon Series page.

https://amazon.com/gp/product/B0753GBNNX

Please visit the **Chromosome Quest: Love, Dinosaurs, and the Clockwork Apocalypse** Amazon page. Now available in eBook, paperback, and audiobook.

https://amazon.com/dp/B00R8NXS56

**Chromosome Quest** is the opening story in the **Chromosome Adventures Series**, introducing the protagonist 'Fitz,' the Mentor 'Petchy,' the Goddess 'Teena,' and the stone-age world he dubbed 'Planet Oz' and its fur-bearing human inhabitants. Their epic fight was to shut down the runaway AI on Teena and Petchy's home planet and retrieve the genetic database at the heart of the fertility plague. The story is an unabashed male-fantasy, fun-loving romp through a variety of Science Fiction tropes, not intended for the sensitive, easily offended souls.

Please visit the **Chromosome Conspiracy: The Aliens, The Agency, and the Dark Lensmen** Amazon page. Now available in eBook, paperback, and audiobook.

https://amazon.com/dp/B00ZM3RTP4

**Chromosome Conspiracy** brings the stone-age 'Fur girls' to Earth looking for Fitz's help with a new problem. The adventure begins as he seeks to protect the fur-bearing alien women from the machinations of Alex Marco and the 'Men in Black,' that is until Fitz's girlfriend and several others are killed, and MiB Agent Jill Smith is badly wounded at the hands of a new super-villain. Facing a common foe, Fitz joins the Men in Black to fight the evil Gharlane. A bit tamer, and more of an adventure, I suspect the easily offended might still find something to take offense at.

Please visit the **Chromosome Warrior: PSI, Dark Energy, and the Alien Ragnarök** Amazon page. Now available in eBook, paperback, and audiobook.

https://amazon.com/dp/B01N984GDH

**Chromosome Warrior** sees the fate of all human civilization hanging in the balance as Fitz, Jill, Petchy, Teena, Alex, and the Fur girls ally with a strange other-worldly energy-being against the evil Gharlane. With a lesbian heroine, this one is a tiny bit kinder to sensitive souls, but still certain to offend someone.

Although a prequel to these three, Undercover Alien begins a whole new series.

Please visit the **Undercover Alien: The Hat, The Agency, and the Quantum War** Amazon page. Now available in eBook, and soon in paperback, and audiobook.

https://www.amazon.com/dp/B09YNG2JD3

### Non-Fiction

My non-fiction features a pair of documentaries that tell the untold origin backstory of today's commercial Internet. The creation and funding of the ARPANET and the technologies we use today are well-told, but there is another side to the story that academia has failed to adequately explore, that of commercial networking before the Internet assumed the role.

From its cold-war beginnings until its commercialization beginning in 1992, the Internet forbade any form of commerce. Yet, globe-spanning commercial networks existed for more than two decades before the Internet legitimized online eCommerce.

The story of the creation of the concept of remote computing we call 'Cloud Computing' today began in the 1960s, with the first globe-spanning commercial cloud coming online in 1972. From February 1972 until well beyond the end of 1992, these commercial networks carried the world's e-Commerce traffic while ARPANET and its cousins remained the private playground of academics and politicians.

**The Tym Before...** tells the story of creating these first commercial networks and the remote cloud services they powered.

Please visit **The Tym Before.... The Untold Origins of Cloud Computing** Amazon page. Now available in eBook, paperback, and Hardcover.

https://www.amazon.com/dp/B07BCJHJHQ

**Securing the Network** tells the story of the subsequent commercialization of the Internet, beginning with the first commercial peering point, MAE-East, for which the initial order was placed on September 29, 1992. By mid-1993, the MAE was in place, and by 1994 it was carrying 90% of the world's commercial Internet traffic.

Please visit the **Securing the Network: F. Scott Yeager and the Rise of the Commercial Internet** Amazon page. Now available in eBook, paperback, and Hardcover.

https://www.amazon.com/dp/B01N4CQX1F

## Kindle Vella Episodic Fiction

With the advent of Kindle Vella, I have begun writing serials for publication in the episodic format.

**A Walk in the Woods** is a one-of-a-kind first-contact romance, and is my first story in this format.

Please visit the Kindle Vella page and enjoy **A Walk in the Woods** a one-of-a-kind first contact story. Now available in exclusively on Kindle Vella.

https://amazon.com/dp/B098GGH4BK

**Tommie Powers and the Time Machine** stands at four completed episodes as this is written. This story is a juvenile that is perhaps closer to a Tom Swift or Rick Brant story, and it relates the backstory of young Twit in Junior High School. Its fate depends on feedback from you, dear reader, but I hope to soon return to it and add several new chapters. A second Tommie Powers story, "*Tommie Powers and the Invisible Spaceship*" is in the concept phase, and I hope to begin writing it soon.

Please visit the Kindle Vella page and enjoy **Tommie Powers and the Time Machine,** a juvenile Science Fiction Adventure story. Now available in exclusively on Kindle Vella.

https://amazon.com/dp/B099Q8FHLY

# (R)ed (T)eam (F)ield (M)anual

**R**ED **T**EAM GUIDE TO slang and leetspeak. Some items, such as crayolia, are wholly invented for the story, but most are 100% real and actually employed in gaming and hacking. In particular, the HAT terminology is a play on actual hacker slang. The terms are real, although we may tweak their real-world usage and definitions slightly.

## HAT LEXICON

White Hat, Black Hat, Red Hat, Green Hat, Grey Hat, and Blue Hat. No, these are not haberdashery, and not fictional. A Hat is the Cyber Warrior equivalent of an advanced degree. One earns a Hat by demonstrating near-supernatural cyber skills. Different colors of hats denote different skill levels and associations, with a 'White Hat' as the ultimate skill level and who sees their job as a high and noble calling.

**Black Hat:** Black Hats are criminals and nation-state-sponsored cyber warriors that use their technical skills to destroy, defraud, and blackmail. They are classical villains who possess strong expertise and knowledge to exploit security vulnerabilities and bypass security protocols, to break into systems, primarily to make money, or, when employed by governments, to simply disable and destroy critical infrastructure.

**Blue Hat:** A rogue hat out to take personal revenge for a real — or perceived — sleight from a person, employer, institution, or government. Blue hats deploy cyber attacks on their enemies purely to cause harm. They often engage in doxxing and post the personal and confidential data of their nemeses in public channels to expose and damage their reputations. Blue Hats are very close to Black Hats in most cases, distinguished by motivations. There are two types of Blue Hats, and we invented the term Indigo Hat to separate them and denote the other, more socially acceptable type.

**Couch Potato:** An open-source video management system for capturing network-based video streams.

**Grey Hat:** A rogue whose intentions are often good but who doesn't take the ethical path. They may penetrate a system to expose vulnerabilities without the owner's consent but typically don't look to cause harm. Instead, they draw the owner's attention to the vulnerabilities and often offer to fix them for a fee. They often release information about vulnerabilities to the public once they are patched to gain recognition in the cyber community. If a company doesn't respond or act quickly enough, they may disclose the info publicly even if the vulnerability hasn't been fixed in order to force the owner to act.

**Green Hat:** A Hat trainee who is learning Cyber skills. Green Hats exhibit a desire to learn about Cyber warfare and listen to and learn from more experienced Warriors. Slightly advanced above a Script Kiddie.

**Hat:** Generically, one who uses Cyber skills, usually in some form of Cyber-Espionage. Seldom used alone, usually modified with a color. Various colors of Hat denote skill levels as well as motivations. Within our story, we treat a Hat as the equivalent of an advanced degree. The word is always capitalized unless referring to a physical item of clothing.

**Indigo Hat:** A variant of Blue Hat that has not gone rogue. A Paladin with better than average skills and who works outside of an organization. Often an outside "security consultant" hired to independently test the new systems and find security vulnerabilities before they are deployed.

**Mudblood:** One completely lacking in cyber skills. Someone who considers simple texting or email daunting, intimidating, and confounding.

**Paladin:** A Hat who has been recruited into a cause but does not care beyond getting paid. A "Gun for Hire" who is intensely loyal to his employer's paycheck. He is not devoted to the cause but rather to the employer. TWIT is an Indigo Paladin who Director uses without fully informing him. He is intensely loyal to her, even though she keeps him largely in the dark, especially about her secret lives.

**Pirate:** A Cyber Skilled thief strictly in the game to steal for personal enrichment. The Pirate is purely a thief.

**Red Hat:** An offensive Cyber Warrior whose typical pursuit is to attack and stop black hats. They're known to launch full-scale cyber attacks to bring down the bad guys' servers and decimate their resources. In nation-state cyber warfare, they invade the cyber systems of foreign governments and organized crime syndicates with the intent of disabling or crippling them.

**SCIF: S**ensitive **C**ompartmented **I**nformation **F**acility — A secure room protected against eavesdropping by physical and electronic countermeasures. A real Department of Defense term for a real facility used to protect sensitive information.

**Skiddie:** a.k.a Script Kiddie. The lowest expression of Cyber skills. No Hat, but someone who can, with luck and patience, use simple scripts and tools and perform basic Cyber activities. Usually a juvenile, a Script Kiddie or Skiddie (Always capitalized) is the first rung on the ladder to Cyber skills, immature and lacking social skills. While a Skiddie can be any unskilled Cyber vandal, within the trade, a Script Kiddie is a raw recruit and is expected to soon graduate to a Green Hat.

**ThunderSpy:** A very real tool for breaking into locked computers. It exploits silicon-based vulnerabilities and facilitates the type of attack known as "The Evil Maid." All very real.

**Toolscraps:** a.k.a. Tool Scraps. Bits of hacked together code, often created by a Hat in proof of concept of some cyber exploit. Typically, such bits are then handed to a Toolmaker who turns them into generally useful tools.

**White Hat:** The polar opposite of their black hat counterparts. They use their technical skills to protect the world from evil hackers. Companies and government agencies employ white hats as information security analysts, cybersecurity researchers, security specialists, penetration testers, etc. They may work as employees, independent consultants, or freelancers and employ the same hacking techniques as black hats but do so with the system owner's permission, and their intentions are noble. A skilled White Hat is a high and honorable calling.

**YetiKey:** A hardware authentication device used to protect access to computers, networks, and online services that supports one-time passwords (OTP), public-key cryptography, and authentication, and the Universal 2nd Factor (U2F) and FIDO2 protocols. It allows users to securely log into their accounts with one-time passwords or using a FIDO-based public/private key pair generated by the device. YetiKey also allows for storing static passwords for applications that do not support one-time passwords. A fictionalized version of real devices that provide these functions.

### CHARACTERS NAMES AND CHARACTERISTICS

**Director:** The "Goddess" figure in the hero's journey motif. She is introduced as **Athena** in *Chromosome Quest*, which then morphs to the nickname, **Teena.** In *Chromosome Warrior*, she is Minerva/Min and Dr. Mathes before she is revealed as Teena. In *Undercover Alien*, she is Director, Professor, Director Novak, Gwen Novak, Hazel Stone, Trixie, and Phryne. She is gradually revealed to be very old, over 2000 years, having come to Earth from Ashera before 300 BC. Her longevity results from a runaway genetic experiment on her home planet. In addition to near immortality and multiple identities, she speaks many languages, has extraordinary powers of sexual persuasion, and thus can bend almost anyone to her will. She is libidinous and licentious and has borne many children due to her long lifespan. Many living Asherans are her descendants. She is also an illusionist, able to easily alter her appearance, and skilled with sleight-of-hand.

**Boss:** a.k.a. Rufus, Athena's grandson. He is very old himself, and has sired many children. In the *Chromosome Adventures* stories he is known by the nickname **Petchy**.

**Alex Marco:** Athena's youngest son. He is her "baby" at only about a century in age, and likewise has carelessly scattered his seed about.

**Ritz**: *Rithwick Jahi Pringle*, a.k.a. Ritz Pringle. The story's main protagonist. Purely Earth human, no Asheran blood, but autistic and an extraordinarily capable White Hat.

**Nehemiah Scudder:** The villain. A non-human alien from Jarnevon with powerful telekinetic powers and access to highly advanced technology. He is a member of the Eich, who serve the Council of Eddore. His responsibilities include keeping Earth humans under control and not allowing them to attain space travel lest they escape Earth. The Eddorans fear humans will develop powers sufficient to challenge their rule of the galaxy.

**TWIT:** The leet handle of *Milner Fitzroy Smith*. He is in high school, just attained his learner's permit and is learning to drive. A young cyber-skilled Indigo Hat who assists Director in her activities, but he does not know about her secret lives. Or that she is his great grandmother, which is the actual reason she adopted him.

**Sprocket:** A nickname for '*Spomenka.*' She was named for her Bosnian grandmother. She is an ex-lover and current co-worker of Ritz. She plays only a small part in Undercover Alien, but hope we will see her again in stories to come. We don't know her surname, or history.

## Nerdy Slang

**Air Chair:** An expensive iconic desk chair favored by programmers and others who spend long hours at the computer. A real product, properly, the Aeron Chair by HermanMiller.

**Assassin's Codex** a.k.a. **Assbook:** A printed (or digital) book containing pictures of and information on known professional assassins and the occasional world-class cyber criminal.

**BAE: B**efore **A**nyone **E**lse — An urban slang term of endearment.

**Bashed:** Angered. Throwing things angry. Apt to unleash profanity.

**Bis:** Slang for cannabis, pot, marijuana.

**Bold as Brass:** Without shame. Usually suggestive of a prostitute (a brass nail), or sometimes gay men. Also tied to money, as in doing something for the brass, or boldly asking for money.

**Brass Nail:** A prostitute, male or female, gay or straight. Nail rhymes with tail, brass means money, hence a brass nail is paid tail.

**BSOD:** Blue Screen of Death. From the iconic Windows bright blue crash screen, meaning to freeze up, dumbfounded.

**Candy:** Performance enhancing drugs, generally classified as nootropics, used to stay alert for long periods when necessary. Most often Modafinil, although Adderall, Ritalin, Focalin, and alcohol are also common stimulants. Caffeine pills and nicotine gum or patches serve similar purpose. Other, harder drugs such as cocaine, meth and amphetamines may be used in extreme situations, although the use of such drugs is unsanctioned and seriously frowned upon. The harder drugs are usually called **Hard Candy**.

**Catphishing:** A type of deceptive activity involving a person initiating a social relationship for nefarious purposes. Typically a romance scam. Sometimes used by law enforcement to lure criminals.

**Clamshell:** A laptop computer, as opposed to a desktop (Workstation), tablet or smartphone.

**Couch-Potato:** A real software tool for monitoring security cameras.

**Crayolia:** Our story's version of 'Crap' or 'Crapola,' as in "That Crayolia is for posers." A form of non-offensive swearing. Pronounced kray-ol-leeya

**C'thulhu:** is a fictional cosmic entity created by writer H. P. Lovecraft. It was first introduced in his short story "The Call of Cthulhu," published by the American pulp magazine Weird Tales in 1928. Used in this story as the codename exterrestrial element of the bad-guy aliens, which we later learn call themselves Eichworen.

**Cyber Skilled:** Soft praise for one who possesses above average, though non-specific Cyber talents. A talented computist with a good understanding of underlying principles and practical day-to-day applications. Usually a compliment. i.e., "For a non-professional, she's quite Cyber Skilled."

**Cyber Warrior:** One who is highly skilled and who engages in cyber-warfare or espionage. A Ninja of the Cyber realm.

**Crypto-Cavern:** A highly secure virtual environment behind walls of cryptography. An encrypted server that is in a highly secure location. A cyber dojo encastled behind walls of impenetrable encryption.

**Didn't Hear the Chopper:** Also didn't hear the helicopter and other variants. When someone doesn't notice something that is blatantly obvious, usually from being focused on one's palm.

**DIVI:** A real-world type of crypto currency designed for anonymity, and for ease of small transactions. At this writing, a DIVI coin is worth about two cents, and can be traded anonymously in small untraceable transactions.

**Dogecoin:** A cryptocurrency that began as a joke and a meme coin originally intended to poke fun at the wild speculation in cryptocurrencies. Despite the satirical nature, it has gained traction and a practical degree of market capitalization.

**Dojo a.k.a. Cyber Dojo:** Similar in principle to a place where martial arts training occurs, a Dojo in this context is a sort of safe-house equipped for secure, clandestine Cyber activity. It can also function as a school, secure hiding place when one is in danger, and temporary sleep-over home for groups engaged in Cyber Warfare.

**doxxing:** The act of publicly revealing sensitive and personal information about an individual or organization with the intent of harming the individual.

**ECREE:** The Sagan standard, "**E**xtraordinary **C**laims **R**equire **E**xtraordinary **E**vidence." It is named after Carl Sagan who used the exact phrase on his television program Cosmos. However, the general sentiment was also expressed by Thomas Jefferson, in 1808, and no doubt was not new even then.

**Eichworen** a.k.a Eich: Underlings and servants of the Eddorans. These are characters from the Lensmen universe. Doc Smith, over the course of some seven books, constantly invented new bad guys, unraveling the layers of an onion, with the god-like Eddorans at the core. We meet an Eddoran, Gharlane by name, in the Chromosome Adventures series. Unlike the Eddorans, the Eich are organic beings and, although though effectively immortal due to their association with the Eddorans, their powers are limited. They are henchmen who do the bidding of the Eddorans. The Lensmen names and characters are used with permission of the rights holder.

**Extroverted Geek:** an oxymoron.

**FAANG:** Originally an acronym for Facebook, Amazon, Apple, Netflix, and Google. Used in our story as a code-name for the cyber-warfare contingent of the bad-guy aliens.

**Forced encryption key renegotiation:** A type of attack on encryption communications whereby an attacker injects commands into an encrypted session intended to cause the forced downgrade to a lesser form of encryption, or even cleartext communications. This is the mechanism the BEAST exploit used successfully on TLS 1.0, for example.

**GRU a.k.a. The Main Intelligence Directorate:** The Russian Intelligence organization. The directorate is reputedly Russia's largest foreign-intelligence agency, and is noted for its eagerness to execute risky, complicated, high stakes operations.

**Hak-X:** A fictional company that caters to the Cyber Elite. Actually a fictionalized version of the very real company Hak5, who bravely encouraged and supported writing this book by answering emails and graciously granting permission to reference their products in the context of this story. e.g., the WiFi Pineapple is a very real product they sell.

**Handle:** a name or alias.

**Hard Candy:** See candy.

**Hell:** A notorious Dark-web forum used for underground cyber communications. Where the 31337 meet to 3A7.

**HTC:** Modeled on the NSA training centers, the Warrington Training Center and the Interagency Training Center at Fort Washington. Not specifically identified as these locations, instead simply used as slang to indicate a Cyber Warrior training facility where Cyber Warriors earn their Hats.

**IRL:** Leet shorthand for "In Real Life" as opposed to cyberspace.

**Kali:** A highly specialized Linux distribution designed for digital forensics and penetration testing. It is maintained and funded by Offensive Security. Kali Linux's popularity grew when it was featured in multiple episodes of the TV series *Mr. Robot*. The tools highlighted in the show, and this story, are very real and provided by Kali Linux.

**LE:** Law Enforcement. Used to designate a handle thought to be working for the cops.

**Leet Handle:** The Leetspeak name someone uses to foster an illusion of anonymity in cyberspace.

**Lil'Friday:** Slang for Thursday, the day after Hump Day.

**Milk Road:** A darknet online black market operated as a Tor hidden service by the "Smoking Pirate." Obviously, this is a thinly veiled reference to the real-world "Silk Road." https://en.wikipedia.org/wiki/Silk_Road_(marketplace). What may not be obvious however is the Smoking Pirate, in addition to referencing the "Dread Pirate" of Silk Road fame, also tips the hat to the "Cuckoo's Egg," in which the perpetrator was identified by the brand of cigarettes he smoked.(https://en.wikipedia.org/wiki/The_Cuckoo%27s_Egg_(book))

**Modafinil:** A real nootropic drug used to promote wakefulness. A favorite drug in Silicon Valley, also one used by the military for long missions.

**Nerd Sniping:** Presenting an obsessive-compulsive person with a difficult or impossible problem, meant to absorb their attention to the exclusion of all else, to the point of risking embarrassment or even harm.

**NIFOC**: **N**aked **I**n **F**ront **O**f **C**omputer. An ancient Internet trope from the early days of Usenet. It was significant because before the advent of personal computers in the 1970s, computers were universally in places where being naked was impractical.

Then suddenly, the "personal" part happened, and there was no dress code. In today's world, everyone has computers at home, including in private spaces such as the bedroom and bathroom. Thus, today being casually unclothed while online is unremarkable. But for a while, home computers were somewhat rare and NIFOC was a real nerd thing.

**Non-Offensive Swear:** Swearing with the intent not to blaspheme. Like non-alcoholic beer or decaffeinated coffee. Pointless. What is the point of swearing if you're not willing to piss off someone, especially a deity?

**Open a Golden Parachute:** Slang for retiring. Often the next step for those who have reached their peter pinnacle.

**Petchy:** A slang term which like Heinlein's 'grok' can mean many things. Fundamentally it means a mood or attitude that falls somewhere between pessimistic and cranky. It is also the real-world nickname of a dear friend who is known far and wide as "Petchy." He was the inspiration for the character Petchy in *Chromosome Quest*, who is, coincidently, also "Boss," or Rufus in this tale.

**Peter Pinnacle:** From the "Peter Principle," slang for one who has been promoted to the level of their incompetence.

**Pineapple:** Also WiFi Pineapple. A very real wireless auditing and surveillance platform, designed to function as a man-in-the-middle device. Can also terminate highly secure VPN tunnels, and provide strong security in an environment where security might otherwise be questionable.

**PFM:** Protective Face Mask. In the post-pandemic and heavily surveilled world, we posit masks, often colorful and logo-bearing, have become commonplace fashion accessories, both as a protectant against health threats, and against unwanted surveillance. Metaphorically, masks signify identity. Changing masks is, in the life of a Hat, frequently associated with a change of identity. i.e., when leaving the HastTag in chapter one, he swaps his "Hak-X face-covering and Dark Web identity for a generic white mask and more innocent visage." There is both a physical and metaphorical mask being swapped.

**Pointy-Haired Boss:** Caricature of clueless middle management as depicted in the Dilbert comics.

**Polishing the Brass Rail:** The use of sex to obtain a promotion in the workplace, particularly executive level promotions.

**Poser:** Fake or show-off. Exhibitionist.

**Prolly:** Slang shortcut for probably. Used primarily by kids, not by leet or hats.

**pwn:** Usually pronounced as 'own' with a silent 'p', though renditions vary, and 'pone' is increasingly common, especially among the newbies. Means to defeat, dominate or humiliate another. e.g., "She's pwned us both." means she dominates the speaker. Originated from an ancient typo, it basically means to 'own' someone thru deception.

**Shellshocked:** Surprised and stunned, to the point of forgetting to snap a picture or otherwise respond to an unusual situation. Usually a result of not hearing the chopper.

**Smoking Pirate:** A tip of the hat to "The Cuckoos Egg" by Clifford Stoll, a famous true-life cyber espionage incident in which I was peripherally involved wherein the villain was identified with a particular brand of cigarette.

**SWAT:** An acronym for Strategic Weapons And Tactics, a police tactical unit that uses military-style weapons and tactics. In Cyber, the acronym becomes a verb meaning to call in a false threat report causing the police to raid an opponent, disrupting their play. Unfortunately, this has resulted in deaths when police burst into a home expecting a threat where there is none.

**Uncle Spook:** Slang for The Agency. A play on Federal employees common use of "Uncle Sugar" for their employer, the US

Government, which, of course, is itself a play on "Uncle Sam," for the US.

**VPN:** Virtual Private Network. An encrypted tunnel within which clandestine traffic may be carried without detection.

**Zero-Days:** A zero-day is a software vulnerability previously unknown to those who should be interested in its mitigation, like the vendor of the target software. Until the vulnerability is mitigated, hackers can exploit it to adversely affect programs, data, additional computers, or a network. An exploit taking advantage of a zero-day is called a zero-day exploit, or zero-day attack.

## LEETSPEAK

Derived from the word 'elite,' leetspeak, or often just leet, is a system of tweaked and intentional misspellings that originated in the early text-based online world. It uses character replacements in ways that play on their glyph shapes via reflection or other resemblance. Additionally, it modifies certain words based on a system of suffixes and alternate meanings and often uses oddball capitalization. Leet is used as an adjective to describe skill or accomplishment, especially in the fields of online gaming and computer hacking. The leet lexicon includes spelling of the word leet itself as '1337.' Leet enjoys a looser grammar than standard English, but the words are usually pronounced as they would be with a standard spelling. e.g., Ph3DoRA is pronounced the same as Fedora. Oddball letters are often silent, or pronounced as the original, e.g., as 'pwn' is pronounced 'own.' Attempting to pronounce leet the way it is spelled usually betrays newbies. i.e., attempting to pronounce the 'p' in 'pwn' marks a n00b {newbie}.

**1337:** Pronounced 'Leet' derived from the word elite.

**31337:** Pronounced 'Eleet' and means the same as 1337.

**7w17:** Pronounced 'Twit,' the leet handle of Director's Apprentice, an acronym for *'Tech Wizard in Training,'* or *'Tech Wizard in Town.'*

**kr4k3n:** Pronounced 'Kraken'

**f17z:** Pronounced 'Fitz.'

**47h3n4:** Pronounced Athena, the handle Twit gives to the spectacular avatar he creates to catphish kr4k3n. Director later adopts Athena/Teena as her new identity and transforms herself into Twit's juvenile fantasy.

**80w132:** Bowler — A style of hat, and a handle of Ritz.

**p02kp13:** Pork Pie — A style of hat, and a villain.

**Ph3DoRA:** Fedora — A style of hat, and the dark web handle of Ritz.

**h0M8uR9:** Homburg — A style of hat, an alter-ego of Ph3DoRA

**7R1l8y:** Trilby – A style of hat, and a handle of one of the villains.

Made in the USA
Las Vegas, NV
29 October 2023

79901115R00166